TRACE

Copyright © Casey Hill 2014

The right of Casey Hill to be identified as the Author of the Work has been asserted by her in accordance with the Copyright, Designs and Patents Act 1988.

All rights reserved. No part of this publication may be reproduced, stored in a retrieval system, or transmitted, in any form or by any means without the prior written permission of the author. You must not circulate this book in any format.

All characters in this publication are fictitious and any resemblance to real persons, living or dead is purely coincidental.

ISBN: 1514654024
ISBN 13: 9781514654026

TRACE

CSI REILLY STEEL

CASEY HILL

ALSO BY CASEY HILL

CSI Reilly Steel Series
CRIME SCENE
TABOO
INFERNO
HIDDEN
THE WATCHED
TRACE

1

MOST PEOPLE WOULD SAY THAT scent comes to them as a kind of wafting.

An invisible breeze that seeks them out, worms into their nostrils, covers their clothes, cobwebs in their hair. Reilly Steel will tell you differently.

Smell comes like pieces of a puzzle, she will tell you, if you know how to break it down. Take something simple, like a cake rising in the oven. Your mind will simply tell you: "cake", but someone with a skilled nose will notice cinnamon and nutmeg float in the air, and that the cake is moistened with buttermilk. For Reilly, it is no use simply being able to smell something. She needs to know what goes into the scent, the story behind it almost.

Right now, she can smell the sharp woody scent of Detective Chris Delaney's aftershave. She knows it's not an off the shelf high street brand, but something more expensive and luxurious. There are none of the harsh tones of alcohol that come with cheap aftershave, which she usually finds unpleasant. As she meticulously dusts for fingerprints, she watches as her colleague surveys the room with his typically serious expression. Reilly knows that beneath the calm of his exterior, his mind is going over everything at the crime scene, looking for the thing that is sticking out, the thing that may give the investigative team that essential head start.

Her olfactory senses also pick up stale coffee, emanating from the plastic takeaway cup being held by Pete Kennedy. Kennedy and Chris are partners, two of Dublin's finest homicide detectives. And as different as chalk and cheese.

'You're messing with my receptors, Kennedy,' she calls across the room and he holds up his hands in mock surrender.

'Gee, we sure did miss you when you were in the US of A,' he says, affecting a (woeful) American accent, 'but I've gotta tell you, things were nicely relaxed around here while you were gone. I guess now you're going to work me to the bone, until I'm a skinny 'oul fella.'

Reilly smiled. Not much chance of that. Pete Kennedy was your typical doughnut cop - overweight, and liked to tease Reilly about her own slim physique while he ate fat-laden lunches. He could usually get a smile from her where everyone else hits a wall. For all his bluster, she knew he was a great detective and always thought of him like one of those stingrays that lie dormant on the ocean floor, disguised as a rock, and then "bam" strikes exactly when the time is right.

What else is she picking up at this crime scene? The meal on the table. Set for two, both plates barely touched.

This is where the investigation is centered right now, after this morning's incident.

Reilly sighed, unable to believe that this has happened again. Only six weeks before, after always telling her staff not to get sloppy, to always take the necessary precautions, she forgot to take her own advice. That day, while at a crime scene uncomfortably similar to this one, Reilly had failed to wear a face mask while taking samples and collapsed on the job, having inhaled something she shouldn't have.

Early indications were that she would be fine, but it took her off the job just when all hands were needed on deck. Budget cuts wouldn't allow for the GFU to get someone else in, her boss had made that clear. 'Mend and make do,' Inspector O'Brien had told the forensic department, irritatingly Irish.

So Reilly had suffered an enforced period of leave that she wouldn't exactly describe as restful, some of which she'd spent in Florida. Now, while she wasn't going to jump to conclusions until they got it back in the lab, it seemed the substance that had caused her recent absence had materialized again.

To be sure, the white powder looked innocuous enough. It was sprinkled liberally on a plate, presumably meant to be dusted over a dessert. Reilly could see where someone had dragged their finger through it. She could picture it in her head, the woman bringing her finger to her mouth, perhaps in an attempt to be provocative or coy. It made Reilly wince, to think of the harmlessness of that action and its devastating consequences. It always got to her, how innocent people were of the things that would eventually kill them.

She stood in the center of the room and let everything soak in. All here would be meticulously recreated back in the lab, so they could go over it again and again, but there was nothing like being at the crime scene itself. Reilly believed that sometimes you could feel the vibrations of the things that happened in the room; that clues that might otherwise be missed were often ripe for the picking in the first few hours of an investigation. It was as though the victims themselves were urging them to see something. A fancy that Pete Kennedy might scorn at, but at this point Reilly had too impressive a track record to laugh too hard.

There was a knife on the counter, lying at a threatening looking angle, but that was not what had killed the victim. There was no visible blood anywhere, though her team would go over the place with luminol later. Reilly had a feeling they wouldn't find anything. This crime scene didn't smell like a vicious death. There had been no struggle here. The girl looked like she had fallen into a sweet sleep, as if waiting for a lover to come and wake her with a kiss.

Last of all, she looked at the victim. She always saved this for last. To look too soon might sway her emotionally as she surveyed the rest of the scene.

The woman was about Reilly's age. They already had a tentative ID: Jennifer Armstrong. According to the business cards in her purse, she worked in PR and Communications. The contents of her flat pointed to her having a busy life. Her fridge was stocked with single serve, low-fat meals, and there was a desk set up in the living room where she obviously worked a lot from home.

Her nails had already been scraped for residue, her hands plastic bagged. She appeared to be healthy, her muscles long and sculpted. She was wearing a low cut black dress and a pair of heels dangled from her flaccid feet. She had been dressed for romance. Reilly sighed. How neat it was, a death like this. Barely three hours after she had been discovered, and her team were already taking the necessary photos and samples.

Soon they would find out if the body itself held any secrets.

Gary and Lucy, the younger members of the GFU team, were slowly examining every aspect of Jennifer Armstrong's house.

No one told you when you started working in forensics that you would spend hours bent over the cheap fibers of someone else's carpet, shining a light on their bed sheets to reveal their most intimate secrets or running cotton buds over their kitchen surfaces. A lot of the time you couldn't believe that anything so mundane could yield the information you wanted, but people left evidence of themselves everywhere, especially when they weren't aware of it.

'Good to have the boss back isn't it?' Gary commented idly.

Lucy nodded, her head completely encased in the white hood attached to their protective suits. Gary could only see the pale skin around her goggles. They were taking huge precautions after what happened to Reilly last month.

'I'm relieved to be honest. Now at least we might have some chance with Grace's case. I still don't have any faith in that new task force. It's already been a couple of months and still nothing.'

Not long before Reilly's accident had forced her off the job, the GFU team had found a necklace in a house in Whitestown, a poorer part of the city, that had belonged to Lucy's sister, who'd gone missing seventeen years previous. Just remembering the creepy house where they had found the necklace made Gary shiver. A real freak show: mannequins and wigs everywhere. Against the odds, he wanted it to be a coincidence. He didn't even want to imagine how it felt to know that your sister might have ended up in a place like that.

The missing person case had been reopened, but everyone knew it was a tentative open. Resources were tight and there weren't many to spare, even for a case involving the daughter of a prominent member of the Irish police force.

Mostly he and Lucy had avoided the subject of the house and the mannequins and stacks of wigs found there. Gary felt as though it could only upset her. He knew she was strong, but this was her sister they were talking about. He didn't think he could be near an investigation that had anything to do with his own family. But now that Reilly was back, he guessed that it would once again be at the forefront of everyone's minds.

He and Lucy worked in silence for a while, concentrating on tweezing hairs from the carpet. They even bagged the ones that were long and dark and obviously belonged to the victim. Everything was a process of elimination. Under the microscope, you could sometimes see flakes of skin or a silvery half-moon of nail. It was amazing, he thought, how people were constantly shedding, leaving themselves everywhere. Humans were constantly regenerating. It was a process that had entranced him when he first began his studies. We could make astounding repairs upon ourselves. The body always had an imperative to heal itself. But yet, it was so fragile. Bend it the wrong way, apply too much pressure, too much heat or cold, pierce its outer sacking, and you no longer had a person. Just something that resembled a person in the way that a slaughtered animal resembled a cow.

Lucy Gorman had seen bodies rendered lifeless on the examination table of Dr Thompson. She too, knew how final death looked, how it played no tricks and lent no illusions.

It was hard for her to imagine that her sister had ended up like this woman. Grace had been undeniably alive the last time she saw her. Her vivid, perpetually annoyed big sister. Lucy thought hard. When was the last time she had actually seen Grace? Shouldn't that be something she remembered again and again over the years? Gone over and polished to a high shine like treasure? How could something like that have been forgotten?

She knew her mother clearly remembered watching Grace trudge down the road from the kitchen window, thinking that she would be back after school, after she had finished seeing her friends. Lucy could only remember some hard words, the slamming of a door. She pushed it out of her mind. She didn't want to remember her sister like that. They had been close, up until Grace was 13 or so. It was normal for an older sister to need space from the younger she knew, but they had never been allowed to get over it, to meet on level ground when they were both older because Grace had gone missing barely a year later.

'Luce?' Gary's call broke her reverie. Her mind shouldn't be wandering, anyway. She knew she was only thinking about this because Reilly was back. When the necklace was found and the case reopened her boss had promised Lucy she would do everything she could to help out with the new task force. But that was before she'd been poisoned on the job and placed on enforced leave.

While she was away nothing had happened. But now that Reilly was back Lucy was hopeful that things might finally progress. Her boss had promised to help and in truth Reilly was the only one Lucy trusted on this, and her last hope of finding some kind of closure with Grace's situation.

'Lucy? Come here, I want to show you something.' She followed Gary's voice into the bedroom. 'Look,' he said, indicating the bed, 'What do you see here?'

'I do believe it's a bed, Gary.'

'Enough with the sarcasm. Look at it. Someone's had a lie down.'

'So what? That's what beds are for.'

'Yeah, but I don't think it was the victim. The pattern of disruption goes from the pillows right to the end of the bed, as though whoever it was is a tall person. And heavier. The indentation in the bedspread is deeper than you would expect for someone of 60-something kgs.'

Lucy looked again. He was right. It seemed like whoever had lain there hadn't just stayed still, as though resting, but had rolled around a little in the bed. One of the pillows was crumpled as if it had been held, or crushed.

'I'm going to go over it,' said Gary.

'I'll help you.' She enjoyed working with him, even if his approach was a little full-on sometimes. He had been doing this longer than she had and she could certainly learn a thing or two from how observant he was. It was hard to fight the impulse to pull the bedcovers straight and plump the pillows. The victim had obviously liked things to be kept neat and tidy.

'Do you think it's possible that maybe they lay here together?' she asked.

'Maybe. But there was no sexual activity, although that doesn't rule out other stuff. But I have a feeling the guy came in here for personal reasons, or maybe to wait for her to die. It's hard to say.'

They took photos of the bedspread, zooming in on any ridges made by the movement of the body. It wouldn't give them much hard evidence, but it was interesting. It would be combed for trace, of course, which could be more useful.

After taking the shots, they started to examine the bedcovers and sheets. Lucy drew the curtains and Gary set up the lights. The bed glowed purple. There were no stains from semen or blood, but there were some spots of a heavier substance.

'What's that?' he asked.

Lucy got closer and looked at the marks under a magnifier. 'Something thick,' she said. 'Viscous. Maybe massage oil?'

They clipped the samples and bagged them. They would test them back at the lab. There seemed to be a reasonable amount.

'At least we don't have to go back to Reilly completely empty handed,' said Gary. 'She seems a little on edge since she got back.'

'I think she's got a lot on her mind. Lots to catch up on, I'd imagine.'

'Do you think her and Delaney will ever…you know?'

Lucy shot him a stern look. 'If Reilly even suspected you were speculating about that she would tear you apart.'

'With one look, I know. But half the force has a pool going. Two beautiful people like that, married to their jobs…it seems like a no brainer. They both carry this weird air of tragedy around with them.'

'Well, we know why that is in Reilly's case. But Delaney? I think he's just serious.'

'No, I heard someone talking about it. Bad romance or something. Plus the guy's got that fifty yard stare. I mean, you can imagine being terrified if he was cuffing you. Plus he never goes out with the rest of us.'

She shook her head. 'No wonder you're not in profiling. You're a gossip, not a professional.'

Gary was slightly hurt. Whenever he tried to get closer to Lucy, or have a little fun with her, she rebuffed him. He knew that she was keeping him firmly in the work colleague zone.

Still, he couldn't help trying.

2

'SO, WHAT DO YOU THINK?' Kennedy asked when the detectives had finished at the crime scene. He, Reilly and Chris had gone to a nearby pub in order to debrief and get some food. Kennedy always ordered cheesy lasagne and chips or a burger, while Reilly and Chris usually suffered any less than enticing salads on offer.

Reilly was glad of this return to tradition, but her recent sojourn to the US had her missing some of the more varied healthier offerings there.

'It's hard to say until the autopsy conclusions,' she said, 'but it looks as though that white powder may have been the culprit again.'

'It seems pretty lethal,' said Chris. 'You only had a whiff of it and it was enough to knock you out cold.'

'It never ceases to surprise me, the different ways people come up with to kill others,' said Kennedy. 'Just when you think you've seen it all.' He dragged a thick chunky chip through his sauce and popped it in his mouth, chewing meditatively. His wife Josie was always nagging him about his weight and his heart, but at the same time she also liked to cook him all his favorite foods. Reilly often heard him on the phone to her, requesting shepherd's pie or roast beef and Yorkshire puddings for his dinner.

'I think this guy is organized,' said Chris. 'I think he takes pride in the fact that he doesn't leave a mess. He's in control and he doesn't get nervous. He's smart. Smart enough not to leave a decent fingerprint in the place, anyway.'

'Here we go,' said Kennedy. 'The great philosopher begins to analyze every last little piece of information.'

Chris was notorious for his musings after they had been at a crime scene. He would surmise at length, often guessing at traits about the unsub that would later turn out to be true. Kennedy didn't give him any credit for it though. He was a traditionalist: hard evidence only.

'We don't even know that it is a he,' Reilly pointed out. 'That could have been a dinner between friends last night, or two sisters. How do we know that it wasn't an elaborate suicide even?' This was part of the pattern the three had. They would bounce ideas and theories off each other, spurring the other on to think harder, to really dig deep for a solution.

'That set-up was definitely for a date,' said Chris. 'Believe me.'

'I don't doubt you there, Chris,' joked Kennedy with a heavy dose of irony, 'since a handsome lad like you is off on a date every night of the week.'

Chris rolled his eyes and concentrated on picking the shriveled tomato out of his salad. He was as health conscious and fit as Reilly was.

'Well, we just have to dig deeper into the victim's life. Friends, family, habits. You know the deal.' She didn't want to discuss Chris's love life, any more than she wanted to talk about her own.

The truth was, she had been feeling a little off throughout lunch. The sight of Kennedy's burger leaking grease was enough to turn anyone's stomach. She had been back at work for a week now, after her extended Florida stay, but still wasn't over her jet lag. It was unusual for her, but she thought she would get back to normal after a few morning runs and a couple of early nights.

Though if she was being honest, Reilly would hazard that thoughts of Todd Forrest had been keeping her awake at nights. Their affair had ended so abruptly, and he hadn't reacted at all when she told him she would be returning to Dublin.

Perhaps it was best in the long run. A relationship that straddled two continents was bound to fail. But there had been so much about Todd that appealed. Not to mention all they had been through together over those few weeks. She'd been drawn into an investigation that was deeply personal to him and his father, her old Quantico mentor Daniel. 'Put it out of your head,' she warned herself. She'd made her choice and now here she was back in Dublin and back in the heart of a brand new investigation.

That was part of it, she guessed, that Todd symbolized sunny, fresh Florida. His tan skin and white teeth instinctively reminded her of her native California. They had both grown up around beaches. He knew what it was to watch a game of baseball. He knew how to make a Chimichanga. He had memories of Thanksgiving, just like her. She had thought herself reconciled to life in Ireland, but being in the US last month had revived her, in more ways than one. Now, back in grey and drizzly Dublin, everything seemed tiresome and complicated.

Back in the lab at the Garda Forensic Unit, she felt more comfortable. It was easy for her to lose herself in her work anywhere. This was the reason she got up in the morning, and if she ever faltered, she had good reason to pick herself up and keep going.

It was good to be back working with Chris and Kennedy too. She didn't have the same fraught relationship with them that she'd had with the American equivalents she'd worked with in the past. Though it had taken a little time in the early days (especially with Kennedy), after over two years working side by side they were respectful of the way she did things, and she in turn was open to their ideas.

They had proven themselves in the past, not only as investigators, but as colleagues she could rely on. Friends almost, if Reilly was the kind of girl who went in for that kind of thing.

Later at the lab, she looked up to see Lucy hurrying over to her desk. 'Welcome back. I can't believe I missed your first week.'

Reilly was fond of Lucy Gorman. She was the daughter of senior GFU investigator Jack Gorman, but that didn't win her an easy ride in the unit. On the contrary, Jack would have wanted his daughter anywhere else but working in forensics. But both he and Lucy had special reason to be here, in this job. Lucy's sister, Grace, had gone missing ten years before, and the case had never been solved. Never even a reliable lead.

Until recently.

'Thanks. Did you enjoy your time in Scotland?' She was glad the younger tech was back from her holidays; her own leave of absence had been hurried and she hadn't had an opportunity to talk to Lucy before she'd left for Florida.

And they had much to talk about.

Reilly knew what it was like to have loved ones snatched away from you. She knew what it was like to feel that every day you did this job you were avenging something. She also knew how it could take you over, each and every case feeling like it had personal meaning. Reilly didn't have a very fulfilling personal life, and she didn't want to see that happen to Lucy as well. She had promised that she would push the task force investigating her sister's disappearance at every opportunity, but she hadn't had the opportunity to do that while away in Florida.

Now that she was back, she would redouble her efforts to try and get closure for the Gorman family. Something about Lucy reminded her of herself when she was younger. Back when she was a little softer.

Lucy shrugged and her face darkened, obviously thinking of the same thing. 'Good to get away from this place for a bit I suppose.' Then she forced a smile, obviously eager to move on to happier subjects. 'You look so tanned though.'

'Not for long, I'm afraid,' said Reilly. 'I'll be pasty again in two weeks, no doubt about it.'

They were interrupted by the shrill bleat of Reilly's phone. 'Reilly? It's Karen. I've got the results on the Armstrong autopsy if you want to come over.'

Dr Karen Thompson was one of Reilly's favorite people. It wasn't just that she was another strong woman in a male dominated work force, but that she was impressive on merit alone. Driven, capable and extremely detailed, Reilly trusted her implicitly. She sometimes wished she knew Karen outside of work; that they could sit and chat over a glass of wine. But that wasn't how either of them did things.

'Thanks, I'll be over in about half an hour. Let me check with the lab first and see what, if anything, we have.'

As she made her way down the hallway, Reilly ran into Gary. At the moment he was doubling up on IT duty while Rory, the GFU's resident cyber whizz was on holiday.

His boyish face broke into a grin. 'Just to let you know that I've got your vic's laptop, so you can expect some dirt in….oh, I don't know. An hour?'

'Don't strain yourself, Gary. I wouldn't want you to miss something important.'

'Have I let you down before? I'm trying to break my personal best.'

'We'll see what you come up with,' she said, trying not to smile. 'I'll reserve judgement until then.'

At the morgue, on the other side of the city, the air was brittle with cold. Reilly, Chris and Kennedy all donned masks and nose plugs. Reilly was especially sensitive to the smell of death, even when a corpse was this fresh.

There was something about a body being cut open to the air, things that should not see the light being exposed. Everybody, no matter how clean living, had a musky rotten smell to them in death. Dr Thompson was used to it and went without a mask.

'Well,' the doctor said, 'your victim was in good health overall. Note the lack of fatty tissue, the good condition of the muscle. She was in perfect health, really. I was very quickly able to rule out death by natural causes.'

Reilly, Chris and Kennedy nodded. Thompson was good at her job, but she liked to unveil her results slowly. All medical examiners had this slight theatrical tendency, Reilly thought.

'There had been no sexual activity prior to death, though your victim had fitted a diaphragm, indicating that some was perhaps expected.'

Dr Thompson lifted the sheet up to obscure the victim's body, leaving only her face visible. A face that was once quite striking, now leached of peachy skin tones, simply thin flesh stretched over a skull.

'There is no sign of a struggle. No bruising, no flesh under the fingernails, nothing to indicate the victim was aware of being killed. What is interesting though,' she said, 'is your victim bit down quite hard, on the left side of her tongue, before death. I may have attributed this to mere accident while eating, were it not for the powder, the same substance recently encountered by you Reilly.'

Thompson now pulled the sheet all the way up and turned away to retrieve a sample of the powder.

'As we already found from our previous situation, the powder is once again antimine,' she confirmed and

Reilly nodded, expecting as much. 'Good to have had this previous encounter as it doesn't usually show up in your average toxicology test. It is derived of a natural product and comes from the seeds of a fruit called Joker fruit. The fruit itself is not poisonous and is a delicacy in Asia. But the seeds are extremely poisonous when eaten in large quantities.'

'This is indeed what killed your victim. I have run analysis on the food that was prepared, and it was present in huge quantities in one plate. The meal was duck confit with a salad of Asian greens. It would have been undetectable to the palate.' Dr Thompson was finished. 'There you have it,' she said. 'That's all I was able to gather for the moment.'

'Thanks, Dr Thompson,' said Chris. 'Brilliant as usual.'

Reilly noticed that Dr Thompson blushed slightly at the compliment. She was warm-blooded, after all.

'That antimine again stuff narrows things down at least,' said Kennedy afterwards. 'We have a list of importers from the last time, so we can start looking closely again at anyone who can get their hands on it.'

'Bound be hard work,' Reilly said. 'Considering you're still running into brick walls with it from the last investigation. Plus, we can't be sure that someone hasn't smuggled it in either. I want to go over the crime scene again on iSPI, make sure we haven't missed anything.'

Kennedy held up his hands. 'If you're talking about a late night, count me out. I've got my anniversary dinner tonight. I can bring a note from the wife tomorrow,' he joked. 'I'm more afraid of her than I am of you.'

Reilly smiled. 'I wouldn't want Josie coming after me, lovely as she is. Chris and I will take care of it. Unless you have other plans?'

'Nothing but the gym and a spot of reading,' he said. 'In other words, I'm free as a bird.'

Back at the GFU, they ordered some takeaway Thai food and set themselves up in the Visual Equipment Suite. Technically, you weren't supposed to eat in here. Technically, you weren't supposed to do quite a lot of things.

It was one of Reilly's gripes about the job that her fitness suffered because she so often had to work late and ended up eating takeaways. But it had been a while since she and Chris had done it.

Eyeing the food, they grinned conspiratorially at each other. 'We can work it off tomorrow,' said Chris.

'Yup. Can't be all work and no play,'

'True,' said Chris. 'I certainly feel I'm too much of one, and not enough of the other lately.'

Personal revelations from him were rare enough. Reilly had worked with him for two years, and still only knew that his parents were dead, he had the same commitment to keeping in shape as she did, and if he was doing anything at the weekends, it was usually going to the gym or spending time with his friend Matt and his family. He was godfather to Matt's four year old daughter Rachel, and Reilly knew that he enjoyed seeing her and being part of a family. For all their joking with Kennedy about his wife, Reilly got the sense that Chris actually envied that close knit relationship, having someone know you so well. She wondered if she carried around the same aura of loneliness, the same air of having been wounded in the past.

They switched on the iSPI equipment and ate in companionable silence over the whir of the computers.

'So,' he said eventually, between bites of chili chicken, 'how was Florida?'

She shrugged. 'It was…nice to be home - sort of. I didn't realize how much I had missed the US. Sometimes I feel like a fish out of water here.'

'It's what makes you stand out, though. You're like a breath of fresh air. Something colorful in a room full of gray.'

'I've already had comments about my tan, thank you.'

She had a way of automatically shutting down anything suggestive like that. She knew it would be so easy to fall into something more and to completely ruin the strong working relationship they had. She knew that other women in the force talked about Chris. He was handsome, mysterious and people wondered what he was like away from the confines of work.

They'd shared a lot in their working relationship so far, including a revelation about Chris's health that now seemed under control, and she wasn't sure if this had hindered or improved their relationship since the earlier days, when they'd become uncomfortably close during their first investigation.

Jennifer Armstrong's living room sprang to life on the screen before them and Reilly's thoughts returned to the present. Their murder victim had lived the life of someone rarely at home. There was a small table that doubled as a desk, a cross trainer, a book shelf that held a few ornaments, but no books. It was a room that gave away few clues about Jennifer herself, or the person who killed her. Or the reason she was killed.

'Pretty bare,' said Chris.

'Reminds me of my own living room,' Reilly commented truthfully.

They zeroed in on the kitchen. 'This is where the meal was prepared,' said Chris. 'You can still see the dirty chopping board, the pans, the knife…wait a minute,' He zoomed in on the knife. 'Taking into account what Karen said earlier about the meal, it sounded quite specialist. And that doesn't look like the kind of knife a woman like this would keep in her kitchen. It's of very high quality and it doesn't match anything else.'

'Maybe she just likes a sharp knife.'

'No,' said Chris. 'She barely has anything else in the kitchen. Why this one expensive utensil?'

'So, you're saying we're likely looking for someone who brings his own tools?'

'Exactly,' said Chris, and as they continued to discuss and hypothesize, soon Reilly felt like she'd never been away.

She couldn't find sleep easily that night though. The events of the day were going around in her head. The detectives would start interviews tomorrow, find out more about this girl. And she would follow up with Gary to see what personal revelations about the victim her team could bring to the table. Despite his boasts, he hadn't got back to her with any information about Jennifer Armstrong by the end of the day.

Added to that was the newly re-opened Grace Gorman missing person investigation. Reilly knew that Lucy was hopeful she could get things moving on that. But where did you even start to dive back in to a case that's been dead this long? A piece of jewelry left in a house was a flimsy piece of evidence when taken alone. There was always the chance that the necklace could have been lost somewhere else, or been sold and resold a hundred times in the ensuing years since its owner's disappearance. Of course, there was the fact that it was found in that terrible place. Somewhere where bad things had clearly happened. But so far, the man who had occupied the long-dead pensioner Martin O'Toole's house, had been untraceable.

And then there was Lucy's hope – she really believed that her family might get some closure at last. She wanted that for her parents. But she should know how rare that was, in this line of work. Lucy worked in crime scene investigation—she knew better than most that there was rarely a happy ending. Not after this long.

Reilly had an awful feeling that maybe no one would ever know what had happened to Grace. The answer had to be somewhere, though. It always was. But sometimes that somewhere was a place they could never go, or with witnesses who would never talk.

Disappointment on top of disappointment.

Well, Reilly would do what she could. She would talk to the task force and check out the files and see what if anything she could bring to the new investigation. It was all anyone could do.

And it was the kind of thing she did every single day.

THIS WASN'T MY FIRST TIME, of course. The girl with the green eyes, staring at me onscreen like a personal challenge. "Come and get me," she seemed to say. As if she wanted to see you try just so she can push you back. So that she can list your failings later to her friends: here's all the reasons I could never love him.

I've heard those before, the reasons. Too clingy. Too demanding. "You want too much. It's like you want to climb inside my mind or something."

No, it wasn't the first time. But it was the best yet. The first I've felt confident enough to leave for others to find. The others were clumsier. I had to choose those who weren't so one-minded and cold-hearted. Who might almost be capable of arousing pity, if they weren't necessary sacrifices?

I don't like doing things randomly, pointlessly. All has a climax, an ultimate end goal. But it has to be perfect. It has to be exactly the way I planned it.

Reilly went into work the following morning feeling better than she had in days, a banana smoothie in hand. She wore a blue roll neck jersey dress, and had her blonde hair up in a high bun. She had got up early enough to run around the park near her flat before work and was feeling energized for the first time in days since her return. The jet lag seemed to be finally abating.

'OK…OK,' called out Gary as she walked into the lab. 'You hunted me down.'

'You gave me the impression I wouldn't have to look for you, actually,' she replied drily. 'But what have you got?'

She took a chair by Gary's workstation and Lucy joined them on the other side.

'Well, ladies, prepare to have your minds blown,' said Gary and Lucy rolled her eyes.

Reilly said nothing while the two younger techs bantered. Was it only her that didn't need to bring a sense of fanfare to her work?

'OK,' said Gary finally, 'here's what I've got. Jennifer Armstrong had pretty good security protection on her laptop, probably because she does PR for some big clients. You wouldn't believe the kind of stuff I found there. Scandal. But that's another story. The deal on your victim from her computer is that she works long hours, emails her mother and friends quite a bit, and kept a lot of photos from a past romance. From the looks of things I would say she still holds a major torch for this guy and it's been her one really serious relationship.'

'Possible perp?' Lucy ventured.

'Wait, there's more,' he said. 'Our girl was a regular on dating sites. Loveforever.com, Firestarter, Matchbook – she had accounts with all of them and she wasn't afraid to use them. Unfortunately it'll take longer to look in to any private conversations she had with these guys. But I do have a list of matches she's had.'

'Wow,' said Lucy. 'That's a lot. I've never had that many.'

They both looked at her and she shrugged, blushing. 'I dabble.'

Reilly thought it if it wasn't so pitiable it might almost have been funny to watch Gary deflate.

'Well, you might want to be a little more careful,' he said. 'Some of these guys aren't safe, obviously.'

'I wouldn't have one over to my apartment, thank you. Like I don't already have an overdose of parenting in the work place, I don't need you adding to it.'

'Anyway,' said Reilly. 'Can we get back to the matter at hand?'

'Well, that's almost all for now. Jennifer Armstrong dated frequently. She would email her friends and say: "I have a date tonight," but no details beyond that. So it's hard to figure out who she might have been seeing the night she was killed. I'm going to try to access her conversations, but those places have major security.'

'It's a start at least,' said Reilly. 'But I'm not sure how we're meant to find these guys. "FunnyBunny213", "Bigboots24"? It's a bit beyond me.'

'I've got faith, boss,' said Gary. 'And I've seen Batman and Robin work miracles before,' he added using his favorite nicknames for Chris and Kennedy. In the meantime, I'll try to find out more.' Reilly got up to leave. 'Oh, one more thing, she liked fancy restaurants. Over the past six months, she's had reservations at some of the poshest spots in town. I'm talking *Amuse Bouche,* L'Ecrivain, Hammer and Tongs. She didn't mind dropping the big bucks for some wild boar or whatever.'

Reilly wondered if this meant anything taken with the specialist knife that she and Chris had noted at the crime scene. She asked Lucy to follow her to her office afterwards.

'About the other case …' she began hesitantly, when they were alone. They would surely both know she was referring to the Grace situation. 'Any word from the task force?'

'Useless.' Lucy shook her head despondently. 'They're at a dead end from what I can tell. As much as I wanted the necklace to break the case wide open, I know myself that there's a long road ahead.'

'Well, I wondered about going over old ground again; this time with fresh eyes. You'd be surprised at how people sometimes remember key things years later. Little details that they didn't think were important at the time.' Reilly had an inkling of something last night lying awake thinking about it, but she didn't want to reveal the notion to Lucy just yet. It was enough to let her know that she hadn't forgotten about her.

'Do you mean re-interview some of the witnesses?'

'For a start, yes.'

'I've got to warn you, Reilly, Dad might be upset. He won't like it if old wounds get reopened.'

'I know,' she said. But Reilly knew better than anyone that until you knew what happened, those same wounds never got the chance to heal.

That morning Kennedy and Chris went to interview Jennifer Armstrong's last serious relationship, Cormac Lister.

'I don't think he's our guy,' said Chris on the way from the station, 'but he could give us some useful insight. We don't know anything about this girl so far.'

He watched the inner city scenery go by. Living in a more affluent side of Dublin, you might not even believe this other part existed: the housing estates and apartment blocks where terrible things happened every day. Mostly not the kind of things his unit Serious Crimes was involved in: these were crimes motivated by poverty and desperation, and the perpetrators were easy to find.

What he and Kennedy dealt with often revealed an uglier side of people. The cases they handled were usually people hurting others for no reason at all, or for reasons that were not fathomable to anyone else—often borne of huge egos and delusions of grandeur; people who believed that they had a right to trespass on the lives of others. Many garden variety killers felt remorse, but not these guys. They wanted fame, some of these killers, and the sad thing was they often got it.

The landscape changed into more genteel suburbs now, leafy and pleasant as they approached Southside Dublin suburbia. 'Here we are,' said Chris when they pulled up to a very Victorian brick house with planter boxes of chrysanthemums along the window sills.

Reilly had sent over the information from Jennifer's laptop earlier that morning, and the handsome man that had been most prevalent in her collection of photos ushered them in. The house inside was in the kind of mess that could only be created by children, and Cormac Lister had clearly been trying to clean up before they came in.

'Sorry about this,' he said. 'My wife works. Seems like I haven't been able to think straight today or get anything done since the news about Jenny.' He sat down on the couch with a thump. 'I'm sorry,' he said, putting his face in his hands. 'It's been a huge shock.'

Chris almost shook the guy's hand and left at that moment. He was completely innocent. He had seen a lot of perps act out grief: believable performances, to be sure, but he could spot them now. Lister was genuinely upset.

'We just need to ask you a few questions,' Kennedy said, expertly ignoring the guy's distress.

'Of course,' the man said, visibly pulling himself together at Kennedy's tone. 'I just need to keep an ear out in case one of the kids wake up.' He indicated a baby monitor.

Chris knew that in situations dealing with fragile or volatile people he really came into his own. He let people speak in their own time, not getting impatient with them as Kennedy did. 'You were in a relationship with Jennifer for 4 years, is that correct?' he began.

'Almost 5. We broke up 18 months ago.'

Chris looked around at the domestic mess surrounding them and resisted the urge to frown in confusion. How could all this happen in just 18 months? There was a photograph of Lister with a woman and two babies on the mantlepiece.

He caught him looking and explained. 'I met my wife about a fortnight after I left Jenny. Things moved pretty fast: we wanted the same things. She was pregnant after a couple of months and we had twins. They're seven months old and she has a three year old from her first marriage. Hence,' he gestured at the toys and bottles around the sitting room, 'this mess.'

'Did you and Ms Armstrong split amicably?' Kennedy asked.

'No, not really. She was very upset. She kept up a long campaign of contacting me afterwards, even after the twins were born. I asked her many times to stop, but she wouldn't listen. The last time I made it very clear that she was frightening my wife and that I would take measures if she didn't cease.' His face hardened then, and Chris suddenly wondered if he had been wrong. Lister looked like he had every reason to be angry with Jennifer Armstrong.

'What kind of measures?' he asked.

'Like going to the police. That wouldn't look right for her, not in her line of work. But she backed off after that. I didn't hear from her, or anything about her really, until the terrible news yesterday. I had heard she was dating again, and I was happy for her.'

'Where were you on Friday night?' asked Kennedy. He obviously thought this was a dead end too but wanted to rule it out. Chris knew his partner had no patience for the intricacies of the case.

Lister shrugged. 'I was here, cooking dinner for my wife and family. You're more than welcome to check with her. The truth is, that's what I can be found doing most nights.'

'Do you have any reason to believe that someone would want to hurt Jennifer?' asked Chris. Unlike Kennedy he preferred to use the victim's first name so as to make the questioning feel more personal and less official. Make it more comfortable and it would be easier for subjects to let their guard down.

'No. I can't think why anyone would do this. Jenny was a lovely girl. She was fun, she had lots of friends. She liked to go out a lot, she lived a very busy life. That was the reason we split really. I wanted a quieter kind of life, but Jenny's career was all-important. She didn't have room for anything else, barely room for me. Perhaps a disgruntled client…? But, no. I can't think of anyone who would want to hurt her.'

'OK,' said Kennedy. 'One last thing though, can you confirm if Jennifer had any favorite restaurants, places she liked to go to in particular?'

He smiled. 'If a restaurant was written up in the *Irish Times*, or if one of her clients recommended it, then Jenny would be there in a heartbeat. She has been to every good restaurant in this city, and she's had cooking classes with many of the Michelin star chefs. Not that she cooks herself, really. She just loves food.'

Sadly for Jennifer Armstrong Chris thought, as they finished up the interview and said their goodbyes to Cormac Lister, it the very thing that killed her.

'What was with the restaurant question?' asked Kennedy when they were back on the road. 'That came out of left-field.'

'It makes sense, when you think about it,' Chris replied. 'Jennifer was killed because of a gourmet meal. She frequented high class restaurants with different men. We can check their bookings, see if their reservations list features Jennifer or matches any of the guys on her dating sites. It's a long shot, but at the start of a case like this, everything is, you know that.'

Kennedy sighed. 'Things were much simpler in my day. When I was courting Josie we just went down to the pub for a pint and a packet of crisps and that was as fancy as things got. Now, everyone's going out for miniature bits of steak on a bed of baby food. Last night for our anniversary she takes me to this place where the waiter wrestled my coat off me, sat me down and practically wiped my mouth. I said to her: "If this is fine dining, then the whole world has gone to the dogs."'

'Looks like it'll be just me and Reilly checking these places out then,' Chris joked, not altogether put out by the prospect.

'You'll get no complaint from me,' his partner agreed. 'Now if your woman had been going to burger places, that would be a different story.'

4

DESPITE ITS PROMISING START, THE day did not get any more fruitful. Gary was still unable to get the real identities of the men on Jennifer's dating sites profile, but had promised that he would stay late to work on it.

'Julius identified the knife in the kitchen though,' he told Reilly when she checked in with the lab on her way home.

'And?'

'And,' Julius, the more senior lab tech on the team replied, 'it's not your garden variety kitchen knife. These are made in Italy. They're for top of the line kitchens, for people who are really serious about cooking. Nothing else in your victim's kitchen even comes close.'

Julius didn't expect his boss to show much enthusiasm. She was notoriously cool and calm. He suspected the only thing that really got Reilly Steel excited was seeing a killer get cuffed. Other than that, she was the consummate professional.

'Ok, thanks guys,' she said. She didn't tell Gary not to stay too late. Hadn't she put in long hours at the start of her career? She was putting them in still. It was part of the job.

Reilly had stopped by the shops in Ranelagh on the way home and picked up some fresh shrimp. Now she had a paella simmering on the stovetop, and an Adele CD playing low on the stereo. The female vocalist crooned through the speakers, making Reilly feel like she had company.

There was a storm wailing outside, rain lashing her apartment windows. With the lights turned low and the aromatic smells from dinner wafting through the room, it seemed like the perfect set up for a date.

She recalled the evenings in Clearwater she spent with Todd and Daniel, drinking wine, eating Daniel's cooking and forgetting about casework albeit only briefly. It had made her feel a little more like she had the balance in her life right.

Now, she was about to sit at the table and eat her dinner while poring over files. Such was the reality of her working life in Dublin.

It wasn't that she wanted Todd to come here and for them to resume their relationship; that wasn't an option, and in any case she still wasn't exactly sure how she felt about him. They had a brief and tumultuous affair, made even more intense by the personal nature of the case they were working. They had been very physically attracted to each other that was for sure, but she didn't know if a real emotional connection lay under that, or whether it was the situation they were in that had made things feel so intense.

The trouble was, Reilly wasn't very good at sorting out her feelings about her personal life. That's why she threw everything she had into work; it was just easier. The only person she really needed was her father. Mike was her only remaining family, and while she'd originally come to Ireland to keep an eye on him, he'd since returned to the States. At least in Dublin, even if they didn't see much of each other, they'd shared the same night and day. She knew the bond she shared with Mike was stronger than she would ever have with another person, and was borne of their shared grief and anger about her mum and Jess, as well as their loneliness and guilt at being the ones left behind.

She worked out a plan of attack for the Armstrong case. Because a piece of evidence had been identified in a previous case (the one that had necessitated her leave, but remained unsolved), the detectives already had a list of places in the city that used anitmine aka Joker fruit, and lists of those who had licenses to use it and import it. It was a logical place to start. It was decided that she and Chris would visit the restaurants that Jennifer had been to, to check out the antimine angle, and if their victim had been there with the same person, or whether any of her dates were traceable.

Meanwhile, the rest of the team was still scouring trace evidence found at the murder scene. There must have been something else useful left behind; it was just a matter of finding it. Movies gave the impression that these things were discovered straight away, but in reality it was a long and arduous process.

So while the substance and its food-related equivalent wasn't much of a start, it was something. Reilly was confident that they would get a decent lead soon, but given that it hadn't been all that long since the previous finding, she worried that the killer would strike again before they found him. It was that kind of case. There was no violence in Jennifer's killing; it was clinical, academic. They were dealing with someone who killed for pleasure, not out of passion. They had to get their sights on him before he got brave enough to try again.

Her paella was ready. Perfectly cooked, the edges slightly crunchy. She contemplated pouring a glass of wine to accompany it and then thought better of it. She had work to do and the jet lag still lingered.

She sat down at her small table, and took out Grace Gorman's missing person file. Since the discovery of the necklace, she must have read it tens of times by now, but she still thought something might jump out at her.

There was the distraught mother, the angry father. There was the boyfriend, strangely ambivalent, but then he was just a kid. She thought about what she'd said to Lucy about things jumping out after so many years, and decided that Darren Keating should be re-interviewed: it would help to know what kind of person he had grown into. He may remember things that he was scared to reveal then. If he and Grace had been in any trouble for example, he might not have wanted to say at the time. But now it would be different.

Then there were the interviews with Lucy herself. Short and gentle, because she was so young. Also because Jack Gorman would have hung, drawn and quartered anyone who upset her

Did your sister have nice friends?

I don't know. I suppose so. They laughed a lot.

Did you like her boyfriend?

I don't know…not really. He always told me to go away, get out of the way.

Did you ever see them doing anything naughty?

I don't know.

Did your sister ever tell you that she had a secret? Something she didn't want your parents to know?

I don't think so. Sometimes she got angry with them.

Why did Grace get angry with them?

They wouldn't let her go out at night, down to the shops.

Do you like your parents? Are they good to you?

Yes.

That was it. Nothing of great value there, unless you knew how to read between the lines.

The sisters had been reasonably close in age, but eleven year old Lucy was just young enough to have been a nuisance and perhaps sometimes a confidant. It could be that she knew more than she thought she did. It was hard to get information out of young children, Reilly knew.

Most adults were very suggestive and it was easy to get them to remember things that they had never seen. If you asked a person: 'Did you see the man in the blue hoodie?' they would remember that, even if the man was wearing red.

But it was even easier with children. You had to be very careful not to influence them. Their testimonies were often not reliable in court. But it might help to talk to Lucy again now, to find out if she had buried something down deep. Some clue that might help. After all this time, it might even help to have her hypnotized. Reilly didn't always put much stock in that kind of thing, but while on an FBI task force back in the States she had seen people remember a lot when they relaxed their minds a little. It could have remarkable results.

She took a couple of bites of paella, felt the firm flesh of the shrimp squeeze and pop beneath the pressure of her teeth. She suddenly thought of all the tiny capillaries and veins visible through shrimp skin, its flesh-like pinkness. Suddenly, the food had turned repulsive in her mouth and she felt as though she couldn't eat another bite. She got up and scraped the rest of her bowl, and the leftovers into the bin.

It was probably all this thought of food, mixed in with death. Maybe she was getting softer as she got older.

Reilly took a long bath instead, remembering the drawn out Florida heat, all the while trying to forget Todd Forrest's hands on her body as they made love into the night.

5

THERE ARE MANY LAYERS TO the body, and each has its own particular use and value. The protective outer layer, a tell-tale of age and quality. Underneath the layer of subcutaneous fat, most to be cut away with a flinching knife, leaving just the finest coating. Then the working muscles, the flesh and blood that lets us all move around, hurting others with careless movements and thoughtless words.

What happens to the body when it is poisoned? Oh, all the things you would expect. The discoloration of surface skin, the dilating and then shrinking of the pupils. The heart speeds up, pumping poison to the extremities faster as it struggles to comprehend what is happening. The veins shrink like rivers in drought. Eventually the muscles begin to harden, the tongue lies fat and heavy like a sated slug in the mouth.

I have no desire to mutilate these women. I am a clean person. I always teach my trainees the importance of keeping a tidy workspace. If I hadn't been interrupted the other night, I would have cleaned up after myself. A tiny bit of sloppiness which won't be repeated next time.

These women have done enough to make themselves unattractive. I need not peel back their skin, take the bones out of the putrid flesh. I can see below their deceptively firm and lustrous skin to the merciless harridans they are. Obsessed with only themselves, and with getting ahead. No time to stop and love someone. No time to see what a person might have to offer them.

They think they have it all, until the moment they realize it's all being taken away…

When Reilly woke up the next day, it was to the grey, rain-misted Dublin skyline. She had dreamt of the Gulf Coast's white beaches and palm trees, the sun's warmth enveloping her limbs. Wishful thinking.

She dressed with less enthusiasm than she had the day before. It was too late to go for a run, and too wet in any case. She studied her body for a long moment in the mirror. Florida was gradually being leached out of her limbs, leaving them pale. Despite the fact that she had been neglecting exercise since her return, her body was still slender and strong. Her hair fell shining and blonde to her shoulder blades. She looked the same. She looked good. So why did she feel so different? As if she wasn't quite sure whether she belonged back in Florida or here?

In any case, she had to keep going. Murders didn't solve themselves. She would take a round of Vitamin C and soon be back to normal.

And this terrible Irish summer weather was enough to give anyone second thoughts about coming back.

'OK, so here's the lowdown,' said Gary later at the lab. 'I've managed to trace most of the dating accounts Jennifer was communicating with.'

Gary, Chris and Reilly were going over the identities of the men Jennifer had connected with recently. They were in the poky little conference room down the hallway from the lab. Reilly couldn't help but be acutely aware of Chris, right next to her, emanating warmth and that woody scent he had. He had freshly showered before work she knew, his hair slightly damp and citrus smelling.

Then she caught herself, horrified. What was she *doing*? She couldn't believe she was thinking like this. Her mind was all over the place.

'The trouble is, a lot of these people set up bogus email accounts, with fake names. Some of them are married, but obviously we know some of them have even more sinister reasons for doing it.'

'So what can you tell us then?' Chris asked.

'Honestly? Not that much. I've got two names of guys that she was seeing a while ago, who seem to have set up their accounts with real names. But according to their online conversations, they went out on a couple of dates and that was it.'

'We'll follow up anyway. At this point, everyone who's ever spoken to the woman is a suspect. We've got nothing else.'

'I'm going to do my best to see what else I can find. If these guys used the same email accounts for anything else, I might be able to get a name.'

'OK, thanks, Gary,' said Reilly. 'It's a start.'

'Hey, one more thing. Lucy mentioned you wanted to help out on the task force for her sister.' He paused a little, rare for him. 'Do you think I could help too? I … ah, don't have much experience with cold cases and I'd like to get some.'

'I'd need to know that your personal feelings wouldn't cloud your judgement,' Reilly said, seeing right through him.

'What personal feelings?' said Gary, assuming an innocent face. 'I barely have feelings at all.'

'I'll let you know,' said Reilly. 'But right now this investigation is our priority.'

'Of course. But I'm ready whenever.'

'OK thanks. In the meantime, keep your mind on the matter in hand,' she told him, aware that she sounded a little like Jack Gorman. 'For this one, we need everything you've got.'

Outside in the hallway, she said to Chris: 'I wish people wouldn't fall in love with their colleagues. It makes everything so complicated.'

She was joking but his reply was surprisingly serious. 'People have to fall in love with someone, I suppose.'

Later in the lab, Reilly looked through the team's analysis from the crime scene.

'Any promising hair samples?'

'A few,' said Lucy. 'We've definitely got some that aren't from the victim.'

'And the bed thing is interesting, don't you think?' Gary piped up, referring to the imprint he'd noted on the mattress.

'Interesting, yes,' she replied. 'I'm not sure what it really tells us, though. The perp got tired? Has intimacy issues?'

'There are two more things,' he told her.

'Feels like Christmas,' said Reilly with uncharacteristic snark.

'OK boss, seems you brought back more than a tan from Florida,' Gary replied good-naturedly. 'But look at this.' He moved to a nearby laptop and brought up an enlarged image onscreen. It was of some wood, crisscrossed with gouges. 'It's the victim's chopping board. You can see the old marks where she had been chopping with a blunt knife. On top of those are really slight, short marks. I'm willing to bet that they were made by the knife at the scene.'

'So, in other words, someone really knew how to use that expensive knife,' Reilly mused.

'Exactly. I'm not sure how much it helps, but the evidence seems to be building up to someone who likes to cook and has at least some expertise in that area.'

'What's the other thing?'

'I managed to get into the victim's phone. Not too much of interest, but she did have six missed calls from a friend the night she was killed. A person called Helena Burke.'

'The detectives are talking to her, actually' said Reilly, remembering Chris mentioning that name. 'What time were the calls?'

'Around 9:30pm.'

'Perhaps the perp was interrupted or spooked somehow?' she mumbled, almost to herself. 'That's good work. Thanks, guys.'

'One more thing: the place had been wiped clean,' Julius put in quietly. 'He might have left some things undone, but surprisingly there are no prints, not even a partial. Even the phone was wiped clean, which indicates the unsub may have picked it up to see who was calling. He did leave behind that imprint on the bed Gary spotted though, and we're analyzing trace on the bedclothes now.'

'We don't know that *he* left that shape, though,' Lucy pointed out.

Reilly nodded. 'At this stage, everything is up for speculation.'

6

LIKE EVERYTHING IN LIFE, PREPARATION for this kind of thing amounts to a recipe.

First step: Find the main ingredient. If you wish to continue the recipe analogy, you could liken this to harvesting, or selecting the right product.

It can't be just any ingredient. When you pick fruit, you pick that which has ripened perfectly, that will bear up to the treatment required. You pick something firm, but not too hard. You pick something with the exact right color, the right smell.

The right subject must be one who is supremely confident. You must trawl through hundreds of these infernal profiles, looking for someone who is so confident they don't believe that anything bad could happen to them. She must look straight at you. She must be beautiful. She must not be so young that she hasn't had a chance to make choices. She mustn't be so old that she has had a chance to regret them.

It's a fine line, you see. The wrong ingredient can strike a sour note through your whole meal.

Even after you select the subject, you might chat with her for a while and find that she is not the right one after all. You have to start all over again.

I will not waste my talents on just anyone. Not anymore. My days of apprenticeship are over.

For now, I think I have another in my sights. She seems perfect, but of course more work must be done. Now I begin the slow process of getting to know her. She must invite me into her home for the first date. There can be no prior meetings, this just increases the probability that she will talk to a friend about me.

You might think that I don't enjoy getting to know to my subjects, that, since I am planning to kill them, I must not want to waste time talking to them. On the contrary, I find it enlightening. I want to know what made them the way they are. I want to have no reason at all to feel bad for them.

I think of the things I will say to her to make her trust me. I think of these things as I run. I run so fast people might think I am running from something. I run until my lungs are burning like coals in my chest. I run until I can feel my blood pulsing in my fingertips. I run to take the edge off my needs, to train myself in patience and discipline.

Revenge is a dish best served cold. Sometimes the old adages are indeed the truest.

Chris and Kennedy sat in Helena Burke's perfect living room. It was almost comical, how uncomfortable Kennedy looked, sitting on a pristine cream couch. He was perched as though to move would be to smear grease all over it. The whole place appeared startlingly clean, which was strange, as Helena and her husband had two children. They must be angels, thought Chris. Or else their mother must keep them in a cupboard somewhere.

He was trying to appear more relaxed than Kennedy, but they were just the wrong size for a room like this. Helena Burke had gone to fetch them coffee, despite them saying that they didn't need anything. Chris got the feeling that Helena was the kind of woman who couldn't let you leave her home without having been offered something.

'Mate,' he whispered, 'You look like you're about to snap.'

'This chair is not made for sitting,' Kennedy grumbled. 'It's an instrument of torture.'

Helena breezed back in with coffee and biscuits laid out on a tray. They went through the milk and sugar preferences and then it was time to ask some questions.

'Did you know Jennifer well?' Chris began.

'Well, yes,' said Helena. 'She did some work for my husband and we became quite close. It's a terrible shock to me.' While she spoke, the woman showed some textbook signs of emotion. She dabbed at the corner of her dry eyes, looked down at the floor and then made eye contact with each of them in turn. Chris guessed that she didn't really feel strong emotions: she may have been shocked at first, but now she was excited to be part of an investigation. They saw it often. People getting a kick when their lives were touched by a tragedy that wasn't too close.

'And you continued to see each other after she stopped working for your husband?'

'Yes, we went out for dinner a lot. We both enjoy fine wine and food. Jennifer was quite confused and looking for love. I was able to guide her a little.'

'Guide her?'

'Yes, well, I have a successful marriage, children. Jennifer was looking for that kind of happiness.'

'Everything we know about her indicates that she was dedicated to her career,' said Kennedy. He took a bite of the dry biscuit that Helena had served him and froze in the action as crumbs scattered all over the floor. Chris bit back a smile.

'Yes,' said Helena, coldly, eyeing the crumbs, 'she had been. But lately she had been talking about settling down. She had been going out on these ridiculous dates. With complete strangers.'

'Did you meet any of the men she was dating?' Chris asked. Kennedy was surreptitiously trying to pick up each individual crumb.

'No, she was quite secretive. I got the feeling that they didn't work out well, or mostly amounted to flings.' She said the last word distastefully, as though she couldn't bear to think of anyone enjoying sexual congress. Chris studied her. Helena was a beautiful woman, no mistake. Her amber colored hair sat in a lustrous bun on top of her head and her skin glowed. But she seemed cold. He couldn't imagine wanting to touch her. It seemed like a freezing blast of air was waiting inside her, to flow out on any offending parties.

'Our records show that you called Jennifer six times on the night she was killed. Can you tell us why you were so urgently trying to contact her?'

Helena turned her head in Kennedy's direction. 'You can leave that,' she said, referring to the crumbs. 'The cleaner will handle it.' She turned back to Chris. 'I called her because I was worried. I had received a voice message from her saying that she had a date that night. Someone she hadn't met before was coming to her house to cook her dinner. It seemed like a preposterous idea to me. Sadly, it seems that I was right.'

'Why do you say that?'

Helena looked at him as though he was mad. 'Well, obviously. The details might not be in the paper yet but it's clear she was murdered.'

Chris noted a tiny hint of triumph in Helena's voice. Maybe she did have some emotion after all, but she certainly wasn't grieving for her "friend".

'Can we hear the message?'

Helena flicked her hand dismissively. 'I deleted it.'

They would have to check with the GFU to see if it could be traced. It seemed like there was nothing else for them here, in this strangely unfriendly pastel tinted room. But he felt something else was going unsaid. The house itself smacked of discord. There was no comfort to be found here, and Helena herself was stretched tight as wire.

'Did your husband have a close relationship with Jennifer?' he asked suddenly. Out of the corner of his eye he saw Kennedy slump back down on the couch with a look of resignation.

'A working relationship,' said Helena a little haltingly. 'Yes.'

'Did they remain close after she stopped doing work for him?'

'I suppose so. He saw her when I did. I don't see what this has to do with anything…'

'Everything at this stage of the investigation is important to us,' said Kennedy but Chris knew his partner wasn't sure where he was going with this line of questioning.

'How long did Jennifer do PR for your husband?'

'It was a short contract,' said Helena. 'Three months.'

'Are you happy in your marriage?' Chris asked then and Kennedy's head snapped up.

'I don't see what that has to do with it,' said Helena, again. Her neck and chest were becoming a mottled red. 'Not particularly. My husband is a bit of a prick. Happy?'

Chris didn't enjoy upsetting her, but he needed to know what was happening. This could be a breakthrough.

'Did your husband and Jennifer Armstrong have an affair, Mrs Burke?'

'Yes,' said Helena, through clenched teeth.

'Was it ongoing at the time of her death?'

'I'm not sure,' said Helena. 'Perhaps, but I got the feeling that they had cooled off.'

'Were they aware that you knew?'

'No,' she replied. 'In any case, Jennifer may have felt bad but my husband wouldn't have cared.'

'Ok. I think that's all we need from you,' Chris said, making a move to leave.

'You won't get much out of Blair,' said Helena. 'He's a snake. He won't want to be involved in a murder investigation.'

'I'm afraid he doesn't have a choice,' said Kennedy, standing up. The crumbs in his lap fell to the floor.

'She was a stupid girl,' said Helena savagely. 'She thought she could have anything she wanted and look where she ended up.'

'One more thing,' said Chris, unimpressed by the theatrics. 'What does your husband do for a living?'

'He owns a bloody, stinking restaurant.' Helen Burke told them.

Chris's blood was pumping with the kind of exhilaration he got after a decent workout. This was the first major lead. All it took in a case like this was one thing to crack the whole investigation wide open. Jennifer Armstrong and Blair Burke had been lovers. Blair Burke owned a high end restaurant, which indicated some kind of knowledge of fine food, even if he himself wasn't a chef.

'Why did she become friends with the wife, do you think?' said Kennedy, clearly befuddled. 'Why would any woman befriend the girl who's having her husband on the side?'

'I think it was perhaps a case of keeping your enemies closer. In any case,' said Chris. 'We've finally got a lead.'

They soon arrived at La Boca, Blair Burke's restaurant in the centre of the city. It served Mexican fusion cuisine, made from locally sourced ingredients. Word had it that the food here was truly good, truly authentic.

Under other circumstances, Chris would have liked to eat there.

'We're closed,' said a young waiter who was setting up chairs on the terrace outside.

'We don't need you to be open,' said Kennedy, flashing his badge. Of either of them, Kennedy was the one who occasionally enjoyed coming off like your typical TV cop, mainly to scare young people like this one.

It worked. The boy snapped up straight and looked at them with a kind of terror. Chris guessed he was wondering if it was wise to bolt for the street.

'We're not interested in you and whatever you're putting up your nose, kid,' said Kennedy. 'Is your boss here? Burke?'

'He's always here,' said the boy, relieved but still slightly shaken. 'Come in.'

Blair Burke was noticeably drunk. The detectives could tell this even as they walked across the room. He was slouched at the bar, a bottle of red wine beside him, and his voice was booming throughout the cavernous restaurant. He appeared to be shouting at no one in particular. At least, no one that Chris could see. He heard Kennedy sigh beside him. He agreed. It was going to be a long afternoon.

Once they had made themselves known to Blair Burke, it was clear that he was not going to cooperate. 'I don't have to talk to you,' he said again and again. 'I want my lawyer.'

Eventually they took him in for questioning. He could have his lawyer, but he was going to have to dry out first. He stunk of booze and Kennedy sat with him in the back of the car to make sure that he didn't cause any trouble, but he appeared to have passed out. As they left the restaurant, the waiter had told them: 'This happens every day.'

They needed to send someone from the GFU to examine the kitchen, but would need a warrant. They could get on that back at the station. Burke was going to need a few hours at least to sober up before he could be questioned.

Still, Chris felt optimistic that they may well have found their man.

Reilly was on the way back from the lab towards her office when Jack Gorman, her elder GFU counterpart waylaid her in the hallway. She'd seen very little of Lucy's father since her return and given her fractious relationship with the man, that was exactly how she liked it.

'A word, Steel,' he commanded, in his typically gruff manner.

Suppressing a sigh she followed him into his office. Jack was a good man, she knew, and was still grieving for his daughter. He would probably be grieving for the rest of his life. But he was a pain in the neck sometimes. He had only recently been accepting of her as an asset to the GFU. Previously, he thought that her and her "American notions" simply complicated things and had rejected her right from the outset.

Today he didn't beat around the bush. 'I hear you're checking up on the task force. There's a competent team already in place Steel; it's not necessary.'

She exhaled. 'Jack, having spoken to the detectives, my worry is that they're not really looking at the case in its entirety, and simply following up the new lead with the necklace. The key to Grace's disappearance lies at the beginning of the investigation, I'm sure of it.'

'I've been over those files myself, a thousand times. If I thought there was anything of use there, anything at all, then I would break the rules, even risk my own career to follow it up. But there's not.'

'I still think it's worth going over. Perhaps if we re-interview, follow up with some of the witnesses, someone might remember something.'

'I don't want it all stirred up again. It would kill my wife - she's still trying to come to terms with the latest find. We need something definite, not the probing of old wounds. Bloody hell, Steel, don't you have enough to do anyway?'

'I promised Lucy,' she said stubbornly.

Jack Gorman sighed. If he had an Achilles heel, it was Lucy. He wanted his remaining daughter to be happy, so much so that he had indulged her most dangerous wish: to work in law enforcement.

'If you must,' he said, and she couldn't contain her surprise. Obviously the new find had affected him as much as it had his wife and Lucy. 'But try not to step on toes. And I don't want you speaking to my wife either.'

'I just want to help Jack, not interfere,' she told him softly. 'You never know - there might be something, something small that might just…'

'I know that,' he mumbled, refusing to meet her gaze. 'My worry is that all of this is sending us back to square one, back to that terrible place. Just when we thought we were moving on.'

Chris and Kennedy were about to begin the interview with Blair Burke. His solicitor had since shown up and made a fuss, and if they weren't going to file a charge, he had told them, they had better let his client go.

So a bedraggled Burke was brought into the interrogation room at Harcourt Street. Even his solicitor seemed to balk at the foul smell emanating from him. He had been sweating heavily, the stains under his arms almost reaching the waist of his pants. Chris tried not to breathe through his nose. It was hard to believe that someone as attractive and successful as Jennifer Armstrong should want to have an affair with this man. It was hardly surprising that his wife appeared to detest him.

'I didn't do anything,' Burke slurred as soon as he sat down. 'I loved her.'

His solicitor bristled. 'It's best if you don't say anything, actually, Blair. I'll handle it.'

'How long did your relationship with Ms Armstrong go on for?' asked Kennedy.

'I was waiting for her all my life,' said Burke. 'Forty three years.'

'How long were you having a sexual relationship with her?'

'That's none of your goddamn business! Get the hell away from me, pigs!'

Chris could already tell that this would be useless. They would have to let Burke go, interview him another time, when they could catch him sober. His solicitor seemed to be at a loss too, frantically whispering in his ear.

Kennedy tried one last time. 'How long were you seeing Ms Armstrong?'

Burke sprung up, took a hold of his chair and swung it at Kennedy. For a big man he ducked surprisingly easily but as the chair completed its arc, it hit the solicitor in the face. Blood poured forth almost immediately. The man demanded to be let out at once.

'Find yourself another lackey,' he hissed at Burke through the blood coming from his nose. 'I'll send you a final bill.'

Chris was almost relieved at the debacle. At least now they could book Burke for assault and keep him for questioning until he sobered up.

'Do you really think this is our guy?' Kennedy asked him.

'Could be,' he said. 'But he seems too stupid, too volatile. Every indicator we have shows that this wasn't a crime of passion. It was so well planned. This guy looks like he couldn't plan getting up in the morning.'

'And,' Kennedy pointed out, 'La Boca isn't one of the restaurants that imports or uses Joker Fruit.'

'Doesn't mean he couldn't get hold of it,' said Chris. 'He's got the right connections.'

'Let's interview him in the morning,' Kennedy said yawning. 'I'm sorry that someone had to get their head busted in, but at least Burke will be sober enough to answer our questions then.'

'Tomorrow, so,' Chris agreed. 'Bright and early.'

7

DESPITE WHAT HIS COLLEAGUES THOUGHT, Chris Delaney did not mind being alone. For years, he had enjoyed his own company. He had built up a cosy life for himself. He had good friends, and was godfather to Rachel, his best friend Matt's daughter. And he had his work of course. If he ever watched the relationships of Kennedy and Josie, or Matt and Emma and felt jealous, that was a feeling that could usually be worked out of his system at the gym. He often turned to a rigorous workout to cure all ills, and it had worked for a long time. Although a more recent ongoing ill had to be cured in different way, but that was another story.

Lately however, he was finding it harder and harder to stay satisfied with solitary life. Given the nature of his work and his past relationship issues, he had always believed that he would be better off single. He couldn't bring the complexities and the sheer harshness of his work life home with him. But recently he thought that perhaps he had a duty to seek out and create any warmth he could, as a kind of rebellion against the darkness and cruelty he encountered every day. He imagined teaching his children about right and wrong; ensuring they grew up to be good people. He imagined coming home to someone who loved him, someone who understood what he faced every day.

Chris sighed and pushed the weight bar out parallel with his chest. It was an impossible dream, he knew. You couldn't teach children to be good people. Procreation was a game of Russian roulette: he had seen many good families be devastated by an evil seed in their midst. People sometimes were just bad; there was no real reason for it. Of course, that wasn't to say he hadn't seen many potentially good kids ruined by terrible upbringings. It was risky all round, having children.

As for the relationship business, that was just a pipe dream. One after the other of his past romances had been ruined by his work and the effect it sometimes had on him. It was hard to believe in love when you knew what people would do in the name of it, never mind that such was a sick, twisted kind of love. More about possession than anything else.

He pushed the weights harder and faster, until his biceps, shoulders and chest muscles strained. It's no good thinking about Reilly the way he had been lately, either, he told himself. Reilly didn't think that way about colleagues and certainly not about him. He wondered who she did think that way about though, and suspected that something had changed in her since her return from the US.

Had something happened there? Not with Forrest, he guessed, for starters she viewed the guy as a second father, and for another he was way older.

Yet *something* had happened though, Chris reckoned. And Reilly was only human after all.

Me: Hi there.

Her: Hi yourself.

Me: You'll have to forgive me for being a little overwhelmed. I don't usually speak to women who look as good as you.

Her: This isn't really speaking LOL. Wait until you meet me in person. I'm used to that kind of response.

Me: I'll bet. You're a very impressive woman. How is it that you're single, if you don't mind me asking?

Her: I haven't really focused on love. There's been more important things for me. There still are more important things, LOL. I guess you'd better know that straight up. I don't want to waste your time.

Me: I don't think I am.

Her: I think we'll get on just fine then, LOL. Just as long as everyone knows where they're at.

It starts like this. Lies and flattery will get you where you need to be.

Only I need to caution myself: slowly, slowly. To rush is to scare your prey.

To rush is to lose, and I no longer lose.

The detectives interviewed Blair Burke early the next morning.

It was 8am, and Reilly's hair was still slightly wet and fragrant from her post gym shower. She wanted to sit in on this interview and get a sense of him as a potential subject and it was fine to do so, since Burke hadn't actually been charged with anything.

'I see you brought the arsenal with you this time, boys,' said Burke, eyeing Reilly. 'You couldn't do this all by yourselves? Had to bring the little lady in with you? I'm more likely to end up coming on to her than confessing to her.'

Reilly didn't react. None of them did. But each one of them knew that this would be a hard interview. Hard for Burke that was.

'How long were you having intercourse with Ms Armstrong?' she asked.

'You interested in all the gory details, love?' asks Burke. 'Want to see what you're missing?'

'Are you sure you wouldn't like a solicitor?' Chris asked. 'Without representation of any kind, I have the feeling you are going to sink like a stone, Mr Burke.'

'Don't need a lawyer,' Burke scoffed. 'I've done nothing wrong.'

'Well, the evidence might suggest otherwise. Answer our questions please.'

'How long was I with Jen? How long is a piece of string? Every time I tried to call it off she was begging or more.' Burke leaned back in his chair, hands in his pockets so the fabric of his pants stretched tight across his crotch. Reilly felt a sudden nausea. This guy was a creep.

'Were you aware your wife knew about the relationship?' asked Kennedy.

He shrugged. 'If Helena's aware of something, it's only between 6am and 10am, before she's doped to the gills.'

Already Reilly was frustrated. This interview wasn't going as planned. Burke was not going to give them anything except more smart answers.

'Why did you engage Ms Armstrong's services in the first place? Why did you need someone in PR?' probed Chris.

'Restaurant stuff. We were growing, needed a bigger profile.'

'From what I gather, Ms Armstrong didn't deal with small time things like that. She was more about damage control, which leads me to believe that you had some kind of trouble.'

'Believe what you want.'

Burke was still leaning back in his chair when Chris's palm hit the table top between them. 'Give me some straight answers and I might be able to,' he said shortly. 'Keep messing me around and you'll end up with a murder charge hanging over your head. See what that does for business.'

Burke swallowed, and brought his chair down on all four legs. 'We had some problems,' he admitted, sounding less cocky now. 'We hired her to smooth over some bad press we were getting. My ex-business partner had … unpleasant connections and we were accused of muscling out any competition. There had been a few incidents. For the record, I wasn't involved with any of that. My partner and I went our separate ways and I cleaned the place up, made it what it is today. I couldn't have done it without Jenny's help.'

'When did your relationship change from business to more romantic in nature?' asked Chris.

'Pretty soon after we met. She had no qualms about mixing business with pleasure. She was hard-line, knew how to get the job done. In all respects,' he said, with a return of his smirk towards Reilly. 'I make no bones about liking an attractive woman.'

'Were you serious about your relationship with Jennifer?' Chris asked, trying to keep him on topic. 'Did you plan to leave your wife for her?'

Burke became serious. 'I couldn't leave Helena. We have shared business interests. I told Jen that from the start. At first she was fine with it, but then…it wasn't just a fling,' he spat. 'We loved each other.'

'Were you still seeing each other at the time of her death?'

'How could I be seeing her when she bloody well wouldn't let me? Wouldn't have a thing to do with me? Seeing all these other men and letting me know about it, too. It broke my heart.' His voiced cracked, an intimate sound that surprised them all. 'If we were still together then she wouldn't be dead. She'd still be here and eventually she would come around. We had a good thing. A good, warm thing.'

'Have you ever heard of antimine?' asked Kennedy suddenly.

Burke looked truly surprised by this question. He had no idea where it had come from. 'Like, protesters against mining and stuff?' he asked. 'I've seen them on the telly. What's that got to do with anything?'

'Where were you the night Jennifer died?' asked Chris.

'With Helena. Ask her; she won't lie, even if she is devoid of all feeling.'

Reilly had a sense that his alibi would check out. She thought that they were looking at a scumbag, but not a killer. She exchanged a look with Chris and knew he was thinking the same.

'Ok,' he said. 'We're going to take a break.'

Outside, the three of them watched Blair Burke as he held his head in his hands. He seemed truly upset by Jennifer Armstrong's death, even if he was a horrible person. He treated her like a possession, thought Reilly. People are always upset when their things got broken or taken away.

'Let him go?' Chris suggested.

'I wouldn't jump the gun,' said Kennedy. 'I agree that this doesn't look like our guy, but you can't be too sure. Best to bring the wife in and check his alibi.'

Reilly sighed. She hated to admit it, but Kennedy was right. It did pay to be careful, where you could. The last thing they needed was Blair Burke skipping the country if he was the one who had killed Jennifer.

'I'll get Helena in,' Chris said. 'She could have saved us a lot of messing about if she had just told us he was with her in the first place.'

Later, after watching the interview with Helena Burke, Reilly felt more drained than ever, and strangely dirty. She'd had enough of humans and their problems.

Burke's wife had been diminished by the stark reality of the interview room. Chris and Kennedy had interviewed her, but Reilly had watched through the one way mirror. Helena had kept glancing at her own reflection, as if surprised at how small and scared she looked.

'Was your husband with you the night Jennifer was killed?' asked Chris.

Helena nodded.

'I need you to say it. For the record, please: was your husband with you the night that Jennifer Armstrong was killed?'

'Yes,' said Helena. 'He was with me. We were at a charity gala. He used my phone to call Jennifer.'

'Did he go home with you?'

'Yes, we went home together. He was drunk. He fell asleep on the couch and was still there in the morning when the children got up. I don't think he could have moved, to be honest. Not even to take his shoes off.'

'Why didn't you tell us this in the first place? You have taken up precious resources of this investigation by withholding,' Kennedy chided.

'I'm sorry.' Helena lifted her eyes in appeal. 'I just wanted him to feel a tiny bit humiliated. Having the police show up at his restaurant…you can't know what he's put me through.' The mask of perfection had slipped, and anyone could see how desperate and scared the wife really was. Reilly watched as Chris turned off the tape recorder.

'Why don't you leave him?' he asked.

'I wouldn't know where to begin,' said Helena. 'I've been with him since I was sixteen. I don't have the first clue how to get by without him.'

'He won't change,' said Kennedy.

'I know,' said Helena. 'But if he keeps drinking, maybe he'll die first. That's what keeps me going.'

Reilly thought it was a slim hope to live on. A life that was barely a life at all. She felt sad for the whole lot of them. Jennifer, Helena, Blair Burke: what kind of loneliness drove them to do the things they did?

'Not a nice thing to end your days with,' said Chris, when he got out of the interview room.

'We've seen worse,' said Reilly. 'It's just all so…sad. I used to be better at handling this kind of thing, letting it slip away. But at the moment I get home and feel it needling away at me. I think about it, and it keeps me up at night. Maybe the older I get, the softer I get.'

Chris laughed. 'I'm not sure it's that. Maybe as you get older you start to realize how precious everything is, how fragile. It's happening to me too. Things that used to be like water off of a duck's back give me nightmares now.' He shrugged. 'Maybe we're just becoming more human.'

'Well,' said Reilly, 'if it gets in the way of me doing my job, I'd rather be a robot, thanks.'

'At least we've got dinner at Amuse Bouche to look forward to tomorrow,' said Chris. 'Bring your appetite. I haven't looked forward to a work outing like this for a long time. Good food, good company… I even think Kennedy is starting to feel a little left out.'

'You know, it's not strictly protocol that we do this,' said Reilly. 'Actually dine at the restaurants serving Joker Fruit, I mean. I'm starting to feel a little guilty, not to mention nervous. I know what that stuff can do.'

He grinned. 'What? Give up the opportunity for a slap-up meal on the job with the department picking up the tab? You must be nuts.'

He left the station then, slinging his gym bag over his shoulder. She watched him go. Everything Chris did was so effortless. Watching him move was like watching a silverfish in water, or a bird gliding in the sky. He was in his natural element wherever he was. She wondered if he had been flirting with her just now. If he had, it was effortless too.

Just enough to make her wonder.

8

'NO OFFENSE, REILLY,' SAID LUCY, later that evening when they were finished at the lab, 'but I can't really see how this is going to be of any use. I wasn't there when Grace disappeared. I can't know for sure where it happened.'

'It doesn't matter,' said Reilly. 'I just want to go over the route she would have taken home. It's all important, especially if you remember something.'

They drove through the leafy streets, slowly following the route that Grace would have taken the day she went missing. The houses were small and pretty, with gardens out front. A few kids were out playing in the front gardens or cycling around the paths outside their houses. It wasn't hard to imagine Lucy and her sister living here and being happy, feeling protected. It wasn't hard to imagine that if you lived here, you might think that nothing could hurt you.

Lucy sighed. She seemed very reluctant to do this, and while Reilly understood that it brought up painful memories for her, she was the one who had asked her for help. She would get Reilly's help, but on her terms.

'OK,' she said, walking around the neat suburban estate they'd driven to. 'This is Grace's best friend's house?'

Lucy nodded. 'Yeah, Georgina Davidson. They were really close.'

'And did you know Georgina?'

'I knew her,' she smiled a little bitterly. 'But we weren't friends.'

'Why not?'

'She was a nasty sort, really. Whenever she saw me, and Grace wasn't around, she was mean to me. They called themselves "The Two G's". It was really stupid.'

'What kind of stuff were they into? What did they like doing?'

Lucy shrugged. 'The normal kind of teenage stuff. They listened to music, went down town on Saturday and bought CDs. They liked older boys.'

'Did Grace ever get into any trouble?'

'Not really. Before she disappeared she had just started to act out, but it was normal teenage stuff. She would come home late or climb out our window. I had to swear to her not to tell mum and dad. After she left, Dad found out that his gin and vodka bottles had been emptied and filled with water. But all the kids drank down at the park. Not me, though. Can you imagine? I was barely able to walk to the shops on my own after Grace disappeared.'

Reilly could picture it. She felt a fresh stab of pity for Lucy, who would have spent her teenage years being so heavily supervised, hardly able to go out and experiment like everyone else. Reilly knew how difficult it was to be the one who was left behind.

'But she was good at hiding stuff. Mum and Dad were totally convinced if she ever got in trouble, it was someone else's fault. She was so smart. She would have done something really good with her life, I know it.'

'Did you ever spend time with Grace outside of the house and away from your parents at this time?'

'A little bit. We would walk to the shops for ice creams or something and she would tell me about her boyfriend Darren. She was really into him.'

'Did you meet him?'

'I saw him once, when I was walking home from hockey. They were standing by the side of the fields, talking. They didn't see me. After she disappeared I would see him around with this older guy, but if he knew who I was, he didn't acknowledge me. Sometimes… sometimes she came home crying,' said Lucy suddenly.

Reilly didn't say anything, it seemed like Lucy was almost in a trance, remembering things that she hadn't thought of in years. 'She would climb in our window after midnight and she would be crying. Once I asked her what was wrong and she said "Why does he have to say horrible things? Doesn't he know how much I love him?" But she wouldn't say anything else. I should have told my mum and dad. If I told them what she was doing, they would have grounded her and she wouldn't have gone missing.'

Tears began to run down Lucy's face.

'It's not your fault,' said Reilly. 'You know that, deep down. Even if your parents had found out, she would have rebelled against them anyway. It's what teenagers do. None of this was in your control, Lucy.'

She waited in silence until Lucy had stopped crying. They were pulled up outside the Gormans' old house. The family had moved away soon after Grace's disappearance. Reilly could see the window that Grace would have climbed through. The oak tree that used to stand next to the window had been cut down, probably to stop someone else's daughter doing the same thing.

'I know,' said Lucy, once her tears had subsided. 'I know that it's not my fault. People have been telling me that for years. But I just feel so helpless.'

'I want to ask you to do something,' said Reilly. 'Something that you may not be comfortable with. I'm not even convinced it will give us results, but it's worth a shot. I want you to undergo hypnotherapy, to see if there's anything that you've blanked out. Talking to you now it seems as though you've repressed your memories of that time. There might be something else.'

Lucy shook her head. 'I've told you everything I remember. I told the investigators right at the start what I knew. You've read the files. No way am I doing that, Reilly. I'm sorry, but it's just not going to happen.'

Reilly nodded. She wasn't going to argue with Lucy yet. People were afraid of what their psyche held. She would be afraid. But she had a feeling that Lucy might change her mind. This was more important to her than anything else.

She just needed some time.

The following morning, Reilly went for a run before work. She liked the feeling of being among all the others at the park trying to outrun the mundanity of their lives, trying to outrun the gray Dublin day.

Trying to feel something real before they were plunged into their lives, even if it was just the desperate beating of their hearts. She knew she was in her element here. Her body soaked up the impact of her feet on the concrete, turned it into something powerful that she could use for the rest of the day. Her eyes focused on something ahead of her, something invisible and it cleared her mind, made her feel like she was above everything, able to pick up on the smallest of details. She could smell those around her: clean, sharp sweat, deodorant, the scent of people. Their blood rushing to their skin. It was a good sense, of people being just human. Not being monsters.

None of this was easy. There was nothing easy about what she did for a living all day long. Her young GFU team might think they knew that now, but it was nothing compared to what you saw once you had been working forensics for years. Sometimes Reilly saw kids like Lucy, Gary and Rory and wanted to tell them to get out of this line of work. Go be a schoolteacher, she wanted to say, or work in a bookshop. Go do something useful that won't leave you hurt and lonely.

But that wasn't her place, she knew. They all had their reasons for being there, just like she did. Her job was to make them the best she could, and attempt to guide them through the many obstacles that this job threw in their way.

There would be times when they wanted to give up, when the darkness of the world seemed too much for them. She had been through it, and her mentor, Daniel Forrest had dragged her through. It had all made her stronger. If she was worried about losing her edge, she only had to look back at some of the hellish cases she had endured. She could do it again, she knew.

So the run was a good way to start the day, before it got clouded with the mess that she dealt in. Today was a full day: interviews with Jennifer's friends and family, and two of the men that she had dated that had come forward.

They just had to find the killer before something else happened. Every morning Reilly woke up knowing it was one day closer to when he would feel brave enough to kill again. They needed to get ahead of him. She ran faster and faster, as though the killer was ahead of her and she was trying to catch him physically.

When she reached the gates of the park she realized that she had almost run herself to exhaustion. She stretched up towards the sky, fighting the impulse to curl into a ball. As she fought to control her breath, she thought once more about the day ahead. They would make progress, today, she told herself.

They just had to.

'Reilly! You're here, finally,' Gary rushed her like an eager puppy as soon as she got in the door.

'It's 7:55am, Gary,' she said. 'I wouldn't say I overslept or anything.'

'I know, I know. It's just, last night I was thinking about the case and I couldn't sleep. So I came in at around

5am…I know, I know, it's crazy,' he said in response to her stern look. 'But I was thinking about the bed in our victim's house. And I'd been going over cold cases for days and finding no similarities. But I just needed to have another look. It was playing on my mind. And Reilly,' he said, 'I think I found something.'

Reilly, Chris and Kennedy waited patiently as Gary set up the viewing equipment. Crime scenes had only started being transformed into 3D a few years ago, so there was still something of the magical about it for Reilly and the two cops.

But it was now just the everyday for Gary. He would never know what it was like to spend painstaking hours recreating an older crime scene from photos alone.

Reilly could see that he was excited. She knew how it felt, early on, when you made a connection or discovery. It was a rush, a high. It was easy to believe you were simply solving a riddle sometimes, looking for clues. You had to forget that you were dealing with the minutiae of people's lives, or you would go mad.

'OK,' said Gary. 'Besides the Armstrong case and the previous one that knocked out Reilly, there have been no other antimine poisonings that we could find. So I started to look at poisonings with other substances, instead. Over the past few years, there has been a significant rise in people being injected with large amounts of heroin; trying to make murder look like a suicide. But I had this perp figured for something a little more sophisticated. Whoever this guy is, he's not out trawling backstreets to score dope.'

Reilly saw Kennedy surreptitiously slide a snack bar from his pocket. She and Chris exchanged a grin;

Kennedy caught it and blushed, then shrugged. His colleagues knew his vices all too well.

'But there was this one unsolved case that kept coming up when I ran a search for poisoning. A few months ago. A girl, living in a one room bedsit in Rathmines. Aspirations to be an actress, she had a couple of tiny parts in plays. 24 years old, she was found dead one day by her landlord. She worked part time as a waitress in town and she hadn't shown for a week. But no one worried too much, because waitresses are always slipping the net. So she was in a pretty advanced state of decay. They couldn't figure out if it was homicide or suicide.'

He brought up two images side by side. The decomposing body of the girl on one side, and the recreation of her flat on the other. Reilly felt a stab of pity. Who would want four people dispassionately analyzing the contents of your life when you were dead? Everything this girl had was in this grimy little room. You could see her dreams in the theatre prints on the walls, her hopes in the obsessive neatness of the room.

'They eventually landed on murder, because the pills she had taken hadn't been swallowed whole, but crushed up and added to the food she was eating.' He paused for a moment to let that fact set in. A third deadly dinner.

'Added to that, it was clear that someone had been in the room with her. Neighbors had heard talking and laughter but no struggle of any kind. The place was clean. But, if you look here,' He enlarged the recreation of the girl's room and zoomed in on the bed. It was rumpled, indented. Someone had been lying there. 'Same kind of thing as in the Armstrong case. Someone lay down in the bed. Someone that was heavier than the victim.'

The victim herself lay neatly on the couch, as if slumbering.

'Looks like we've got a repeat offender then,' said Kennedy. 'If there's been three, and he's got away with it, there's probably more.'

'And he'll be looking to try again,' Chris agreed.

'We'll look into the restaurant where she worked,' said Kennedy, 'see if we can make a few connections. Seems too good to be true that she worked in the restaurant business.'

'This place doesn't exactly match any of those that Jennifer Armstrong went to, though,' said Reilly. 'This is basically a burger joint.'

'That's why this one is mine,' said Kennedy triumphantly. 'The two of you can have your tiny pieces of duck liver or whatever it is. I'm going to eat some real food. And, if there's information to be had, I'll come back with it. Let's see who has the most productive day, eh?'

'You're on,' said Chris. 'If you make it back to work, that is. You'll probably give yourself killer indigestion.'

Kennedy laughed. 'Josie made me a salad for lunch,' he said. 'Anything's better than suffering through that.'

'We'll meet you back here at 3pm,' said Reilly. 'Compare notes.'

'Sure,' said Kennedy. 'Just let me know if you want me to pick you up a burger. I get the feeling you won't be quite satisfied.'

9

IT WAS A BEAUTIFUL EARLY summer's day for a change, and Reilly and Chris had an outside terrace table at Amuse Bouche, the first restaurant on their list licensed to import and use Joker Fruit, aka antimine.

Reilly had changed out of her work clothes into a simple black shift dress and high heeled boots. The whole point of her and Chris visiting was to not look like law enforcement. Kennedy would have stood out like a sore thumb but Chris had scrubbed up too, replacing his usual work uniform of T-shirt and jeans for a light blue tailored shirt and chinos.

'Nice to see a bit of sunshine for a change.' said Reilly. 'I don't think we've had one sunny day since I got back.'

'You Americans, always complaining about the weather,' said Chris. He couldn't help but admire how she looked under the golden sunlight, though, her hair falling in glossy waves, her skin soft and bright. Then he cursed his mind for straying in that direction. You're here for work, he reminded himself sternly.

'What do you think of Gary's little show this morning?' he asked, determinedly steering the conversation towards work.

'It looks promising,' she said. 'But it's flimsy at best. Not admissible of course. We need a real, concrete lead.'

'At least we're building a decent psychological profile,' said Chris. 'Seems he has control issues. He's a perfectionist. Cold and calculating. But obviously he's needy too. Needs the comfort of a woman's bed, but not sexually. It's more of a nurturing thing.'

Reilly raised an eyebrow. 'Maybe you should apply for the new profiler's job, Chris. You seem pretty clued in on all this psych stuff.'

He winked. 'Must've learnt from the best then. But I do think this kind of thing is important. We'll cover all avenues of course, but it lets us know that we should concentrate our efforts on more professional, educated possible suspects. This isn't a case of a jealous lover, or a revenge killing.'

'You're right,' she said, 'but I still want something hard and cold in my hands. If we're going to catch this guy, I need to know where he is, not just what makes him tick.'

'I'm with you there,' said Chris. 'And with Kennedy's hard-line, no nonsense, "let's get the baddies" attitude, the lot of us make a pretty fearsome trio don't we?'

'I'll toast to that,' said Reilly. 'if only we weren't still on duty. I've just seen a white from Napa Valley on the menu that I'd die for. A taste of home.'

'You know I did my undergrad degree in psychology don't you?' said Chris, unexpectedly. 'I did kind of want to go down that road, what Forrest does. Or did,' he added, remembering that Reilly's FBI friend was now retired.

'Why didn't you then?'

'It just seemed too taxing, being in the minds of these guys all day long. Almost being them, trying to understand what motivated them to do such horrible things. I wanted more action, wanted to be the person who put them away.'

'But you analyze them, anyway,' she said, understanding. 'You can't get away from it. Every case we're on, you're following the perp like he's drawing you a mind map. I get that all too well.'

Chris shrugged. 'I suppose I managed to avoid it for a few years,' he said. 'It was all about cuffing them. But lately I have been thinking about the cases a bit more deeply. I don't see the value of throwing these guys in jail without knowing why. How are we supposed to stop it happening again?'

'Sometimes you can't stop evil,' said Reilly. 'It's that simple.'

'Do you really believe in evil though?' he asked. 'Even after all we've seen, evil seems to me a kind of fairy tale construction. People are crazy, mean, motivated by uncontrollable desires. They're ignorant of their own souls. But I don't believe in evil.'

'I do,' said Reilly. She looked thoughtful. She didn't often have this conversation with people. 'Maybe it's got something to do with my…family. I believe I've seen evil.'

'I'm sorry,' he said, temporarily forgetting that what they were talking about was deeply personal for her. 'I didn't mean to …'

'No, it's fine' she said. 'I know that my own experience sometimes clouds me, makes me believe that there is no redemption, if you like. You know, even my dad has a greater capacity to believe in goodness than I do. He's always cautioning me: "Try to see the good, honey."'

'Good advice.'

'Hard to follow, though. But I do see some very good things on this menu,' she said expertly changing the subject.

'You're not wrong there. I hope you don't object if I go for the full three courses? I worked out in anticipation of this,'

She laughed. 'Me too.'

The restaurant was styled like a cottage: wisteria growing along the trellis on the terrace, the ceilings inside were low and the tableware was delicate and floral. Reilly generally preferred a cleaner more modern look, but this was interesting. Their waitress kept shooting little glances at Chris, but he seemed immersed in the menu and talking to her. It was quite pleasant, she thought. She and Chris never really got to chat like this anymore. They'd done so quite a bit in the early days when they were just starting to work together and get to know each other, but more recently their relationship had cooled a little. She'd surprised herself by how much she'd missed his company while she was in Florida and was happy of the opportunity for a proper catchup now that she was back.

Of course the only reason they were here was because Joker Fruit was used in the food, and when Reilly flipped to the dessert menu, she saw the dish: "*Joker's revenge: a molten white lava cake with a puree of the most dangerous fruit you'll ever eat. Only if you dare.*"

There was a note at the bottom of the page explaining that every care had been taken to prepare the food safely, but you still ate it at your own risk. Reilly had already suffered at the hands of a very mild dose of antimine and felt that diners here were really taking their lives into her own hands. She knew it wasn't worth the risk. Nothing tastes quite that good. She smiled as she recalled her earlier statement: "I'd die for a glass of that wine." Not quite.

'It's nice to see you smile,' said Chris. 'I get the sense that you've been a little low since you got back from the States.'

'I have, actually' she admitted, touched that he'd noticed. 'Just a bit blue and irritable. For some reason I can't seem to get my groove back. Everything feels a little blurry …like I can't quite get a handle on things.'

'You wouldn't know it to look at you,' said Chris. 'You seem as sharp as ever.'

'Yes, well. I'm confiding in you only,' she said laughing lightly. 'I can't have the rest of the team thinking I'm not on top of my game. Especially not Kennedy.'

'You don't always need to be a superwoman, Reilly.'

'You don't cut yourself much slack either,' she replied pointedly.

Their first course arrived just then. Reilly had seared tuna on Israeli couscous with a garlic asparagus puree.

Chris had an ostrich burger. 'You might as well have gone and had one with Kennedy,' she joked.

The waitress topped up their water glasses and Chris continued their conversation where it had left off. 'I don't need to cut myself any slack,' he said. 'My life is pretty simple. I've whittled it down to the bare necessities. It's basically work, exercise, and hanging out with little Rachel.'

'You really enjoy seeing that little girl don't you?'

'I love it,' said Chris, taking a bite of his slider. 'She's one of the things about life that just makes me feel that it can't be all bad. You've met Matt and Emma; they are so happy. It's hard being a family in this day and age, but they make it work. And Rachel's a dote. I took her to the beach a little while back and she buried me in sand. It was freezing. I had sand in my ears, not to mention other places, for days.'

Reilly cracked up laughing. It was funny to think of him in such a precarious position. 'Seems like she's really got you wrapped around her little finger.'

'She does.' He smiled. 'I'm helpless.'

'Did you ever…' Reilly wasn't unsure if she should ask. Too personal? 'Did you ever wonder about, you know…'

'Reilly,' he said. 'Just ask the question. We've known each other a long time now. Yes, I did think about having kids at one point. When I was younger, but of course after Mel. … it just seemed crazy to even think about anything like that anymore, bringing a child into the world. But it's a good thing for some people. The world needs more parents who love their kids. What about you?'

Reilly was really enjoying herself. The tiny bite of the tuna she had was delicious. She cut off another piece. "Me? It's never really been on my agenda. I think it would be great, I mean, like you said I think it's great when other people do it. But I just don't know how people like us could do our jobs and have a relationship, never mind a child.'

'I guess it's a choice. Maybe you can't do both.'

'If it's a choice, then I choose this,' she said. 'I think I make a better CSI than anything else.'

'Don't sell yourself short,' he said. 'I think you'd be just as good with unwashed hair and vomit stains on your sweatshirt. Sleep deprivation would suit you down to the ground.'

She balled up her napkin and threw it at him. 'Very funny. I've heard fatherhood can be pretty rough too. You wouldn't have time to work out, and soon you and Kennedy would look like twins.'

'That should be enough to put anyone off,' he chuckled. Then more seriously: 'Ah, I don't know if I would mind all that much. I've lived this way long enough, I sometimes think if everything else was right, I might not mind letting some of the rest slip.'

Reilly nodded. The conversation was becoming intense. She wasn't used to this kind of openness from Chris. She wasn't used to being open herself. It made her feel naked, like she was walking on a platform that might give at any moment. She wondered if it was a carry-over from the emotional intimacy with Todd, as well as that overwhelming, all-consuming sex. Unbidden, she felt a stab of desire in her lower stomach as the thought of it flashed into her head. It was strange to be thinking of that now, here with Chris. It made her feel confused. Chris was attractive, anyone could see that. But they were workmates. Simple.

Still, she was glad of the distraction when their mains came.

Chris had ordered steak, which she thought was a bit boring, but she had to admit that it looked good. It was a couple of inches thick, still rare and running blood in the middle. It was garnished by a potato which had been carved into a kind of torpedo shape and fried. Then vegetables and a wedge of blue cheese sat on the side. Simple, but effective.

She had stuck with the seafood theme and ordered the restaurant's take on an old English classic: fish pie. Hunts of tender white fish and prawns lay under a crust of sweet potato and parmesan. She pierced the top and a creamy white sauce flowed out. She was still starving and began to eat with gusto.

'You have to try this,' said Chris. 'Here.' He held out his fork to her, a bite sized piece of steak on the end. Reilly was momentarily flustered, unsure whether to take the fork and feed herself, or let Chris place it in her mouth. It all seemed very intimate. She didn't want to seem like she was making a big fuss, so in the end let him place it in her mouth.

'It's fantastic,' she said. In turn she gave him a bite of her meal. A woman at the table next to them smiled at them indulgently. Did it really matter if people thought they were a couple? She had to get the conversation back to safe territory.

'So the chef is going to come and talk to us after lunch?'

'Yes, it's all arranged. Let's hope he hasn't figured out why we're here. He might have laced the food.'

'At least then we would have a lead,' she said.

'Are we going to have this dessert then?'

'What? Are you serious?'

'Of course. It seems a pity to go to all of this trouble and not. It's what we're interested in.'

'Thanks, but I've already had my share. Not to mention that I'm almost full enough to burst.'

'I'll chance it then,' said Chris, signaling to the waitress. 'I want to see what all the fuss is about.'

10

AT REILLY'S REQUEST, GARY WAS trying to track down the boy Grace Gorman had been seeing when she went missing, Darren Keating. The guy had maintained that the relationship wasn't serious. Of course it wasn't. Grace had only been fourteen. Keating was fifteen. Nothing's serious at that age. But it didn't mean the guy didn't know anything else about her disappearance.

Reilly had given him this work shortly after the meeting that morning. He felt like she was almost rewarding him for finding the third meal-related murder. He had been pleased to work on anything to do with the Grace Gorman cold case though, even something as mundane as this.

The truth was, he had dreams of being some kind of hero to Lucy. Anything that would finally get her to notice him in a way other than just her idiot workmate. He knew she wasn't that kind of girl though; she would rather be her own hero. She didn't go in for acts of chivalry. If he opened a door for her she would just stand and wait for him to go through it. But if he had anything to do with finding out what happened to her sister, she would definitely thank him.

But finding out what happened to Grace Gorman would be its own reward, too. Gary remembered what it was like to be fourteen; to be overwhelmed by the rush of feelings you suddenly had about everything, to be on the edge of everything beginning and to be unable to wait for it to happen. That shouldn't be taken away from anyone. He had been bullied mercilessly when he was a geeky teenager and the joy and relief he felt when he came out the other side and realized those people had nothing to do with his life any more or how he felt, was immense.

Grace's old boyfriend had a couple of aliases. He had been in and out of juvenile detention, and then prison. Gary had put in an ID request to the related justice departments to find out where he was now. He did an internet search to see if the guy was on any social media under any of his names, but there was nothing. Gary wouldn't know what he was in for until he got the information back, but whatever it was, it didn't seem to be big enough to make the papers.

He thought back to the house where they had found Grace's necklace a few weeks back. It had just been a routine search, at first. Someone had reported an abandoned house, but the cops who searched it thought there was something off about it, and they had brought in the GFU.

By sheer luck, it had turned out to be himself, Reilly and Lucy who had searched the place. Well, maybe it wasn't luck. Now Lucy would always have first-hand memories of that place: its starkness, the blood on the wall shining blue under the luminol, the boxes of wigs and the mannequins stacked up in the attic like bodies. Most creepily, there had been the trinkets hidden in the wall. Things belonging to women that had been picked up like souvenirs. Watches, hair clips, scarves, little things like that. The wigs themselves had been made of human hair. They were still being analyzed and matched to missing persons. It was a long process, and they didn't know yet if any of the DNA found in the house matched Grace Gorman.

Gary refreshed his email and something from a friend at the Criminal Justice Department popped up. It read:

"Gary, my man, haven't seen you in ages. Meet us for drinks on Thursday in town sometime? Re your boy Darren Keating, aka Derek Freeman. This guy has been in and out since age fifteen. Juvie records sealed as per norm but I'll try to get something for you by end of week. He's been arrested under a few different names so it's hard to get a read on his sheet, but basically: armed robbery, assault of domestic partner, petty drug dealing and possession. He's doing a longer stint in Mountjoy for battery and assault, again of his partner. Nasty bit of stuff. Will send through proper records by end of day plus any new info that comes in."

Well, it wasn't great news, but at least now they knew where Keating was. It would be easy enough to go over to Mountjoy Prison and interview him, if that's what Reilly wanted. The bad news was that Lucy's sister had been hanging around such scum before she died. Gary felt bad that Grace Gorman should ever have been in the same room as someone like this guy.

A knock on his door startled him out of his reverie. It was Lucy. 'Want to go and grab a sandwich?' she asked. 'I've been doing background on the Armstrong case and it's driving me mental.'

When they were sitting in the GFU café downstairs with egg sandwiches, milky tea and a blueberry muffin to share, Gary asked: 'So, what's getting to you about the Armstrong case?'

'Just that Reilly's having me go through all her emails. No offense to this girl, but they're boring as hell. I know there's some more salacious ones about her PR clients but those are blocked. I'm just doing the personal ones. They're mostly like this: "Saw X last night. Funny guy, but a little lacking in other departments, LOL." Or "See you for margaritas on Friday. Need to blow off some steam." Rubbish like that. Nothing really revealing. Reilly's going to be disappointed.'

Gary laughed. 'You forget that I had to go through those emails too. But I have to say, I didn't give them the same excruciating attention. However,' he said, 'I did get a look at some of the more interesting ones about her clients.'

'Don't hold out,' she said.

'I am a bastion of professionalism,' Gary teased. 'No way are you getting actual names. But let me say this: a daytime RTE talk show host, who has made his empire on advising others? Has fallen off the wagon, and is into gambling and drugs in a big way. *And*, an actor from our most beloved TV soap has been caught cheating on his wife, again. It was all pretty grim stuff. No wonder the girl needed to blow off some steam.'

Lucy shook her head. 'I just feel like it takes someone fairly shallow to do a job like that. Half of those people shouldn't have their dirty business swept under the rug for them. Why shouldn't they have to face up to the things they've done, like everyone else?'

'You're probably right,' he agreed. 'They don't deserve more of a break than anyone else. I don't think Jennifer Armstrong was shallow though. Everyone has an inner life that's inaccessible to everyone else Luce. She probably felt just as lonely and confused and disgusted with the world as everyone. But she had a job to do.'

Lucy stared at him. 'That's pretty philosophical, for you.'

'Ouch. I'm not all good looks and laughs, you know. I do actually think about things now and then.'

'Yeah, I see that now. I know you're right. I'm just easily distracted lately. Thinking about my sister's case makes everything else seem petty.'

'Yeah I can't imagine how difficult it must be. But Reilly's really trying to help. She's got me working on some stuff as we speak. She's looking out for you.'

Lucy blushed a little. 'I know she does. I know she's trying to help me… but I feel like she's asking too much of me. It's hard enough to go through all of this again without her asking me to do hypnotherapy. I feel like I'm being accused of something.'

'That's not Reilly's way and you know it. You were a kid when Grace went missing, but you were closest to her. You know from our work with kids that they often blank things out, especially unpleasant things. No one's blaming you.'

'It's just, when we went for that drive, out to my old house, I started to remember all this terrible stuff that happened. How unhappy Grace had been and stuff like that. If I remembered that, just from going for a drive, what will happen if I undergo hypnotherapy?'

Gary took her hand gently. 'Maybe nothing. Maybe there is truly nothing else for you to remember. But if there is something, even if it's horrible for you to think about, if it helps find out what happened to Grace, it's worth it. That's why we are all here, Lucy. To find things out, so people can get on with their lives. You and your family deserve that too.'

'I know,' she said. 'I just wish it wasn't so damn hard.'

11

WHEN THE RESTAURANT'S POTENTIALLY LETHAL dessert arrived and was set with reverence on the table between Reilly and Chris, they both hesitated. Reilly could see the unnatural yellow of the fruit oozing over the lava cake.

'Well, it certainly *looks* toxic,' said Chris. 'I'm game if you are.'

He raised his eyebrow at her, and suddenly deciding to throw caution to the wind, Reilly couldn't help but take up the challenge. Wielding her fork, she said: 'OK see you on the other side.'

Normally she wasn't much of a dessert fan. But this, this was something else. The tart bite of the fruit set off the white chocolate cake perfectly. When their forks pierced the middle, molten dark chocolate flowed out onto the plate. It was luscious. Reilly completely forgot that they were eating a fruit that was potentially poisonous.

'Well, that was pretty amazing,' said Chris, when the plate was clean. 'I thought you were going to stab me with the fork for that last bite.'

'I would have,' said Reilly, 'but …' Her temperature soared as suddenly, an intense feeling of nausea washed over her. She got up from her chair and moved quickly to the bathroom, where she was afraid she might throw up. Could the antimine still be in her system from before, and the desert had re-activated it or something? But no that wasn't possible.

The wave subsided and she splashed water on her face in the sink, the cold of it reviving her somewhat. Then, her temperature returning to normal, she looked in the mirror at her pale face, feeling much better.

When she got back to the table, a large man was sitting with Chris. He was dressed head to toe in a black uniform. Reilly guessed this must be the chef.

Both turned to her with a concerned look. 'Madam,' said the chef, 'I hope you were not unwell. Is everything is ok?'

'I'm fine,' she lied. 'I'm just recovering from a tummy bug and probably shouldn't have eaten quite so much, but your food was delicious. Please, let's continue.'

The chef looked somewhat mollified but Chris continued to give her worried glances throughout the rest of the conversation.

'We've sought you out because you are one of the most knowledgeable authorities on this particular substance,' said Reilly. 'I understand that you went to Asia to receive personal training in the preparation of Joker fruit?'

'Yes,' said the chef. 'My wife and I went there ten years ago. She cooks also.' Chris and Reilly exchanged a glance. A female killer perhaps? Not exactly part of the profile. But you never knew. Plus, not to make too many assumptions, but this guy looked like a teddy bear. It was hard to imagine him cooking up deadly potions for young women.

'Do you use the fruit often?' asked Chris.

'Only in season. In Asia they mostly use it in savory dishes, to provide a sweet counterpart. It is very popular in Cambodia especially. There are many accidents though. It isn't regulated, so any person can serve Joker Fruit and sometimes it is prepared poorly.'

'People die?'

'Some,' said the chef. 'The poison works very slowly, so most people are able to realize the symptoms and have their stomachs pumped. But it can cause bad nerve damage once it has stayed in the system for some days. Some people are never the same.'

'A few days?' said Reilly. 'How much would it take to kill someone in a matter of hours?'

'I can't say for sure,' said the chef. 'I studied it for culinary purposes only. All I learnt about the seed is that you should throw it away. But it does have a reasonably strong outer shell that encases the poison. Once in the stomach, the shell is worn away by stomach acid and the poison begins to seep in slowly.'

'Have you ever seen it made into antimine?'

'No. I have not seen it in that form, though I've had the process described to me. The shells must be cracked open and discarded, the poison poured out. It must go through a process of purification, where it is mixed at a high speed and made very, very fine. It is hard to do.'

'Can you show us the Joker fruit?' asked Reilly.

The chef nodded. 'Come with me.'

They followed him into a kitchen that was not like a usual restaurant kitchen. Smaller, cozier, more like someone's kitchen at home. He picked up a large, thick-skinned fruit and held it out to Reilly. It was an odd, ridged shape, almost square.

'I am the only one who can prepare it in our kitchen,' said the chef. 'It is not dangerous if you know how to do it.'

'Where were you last Friday night?' asked Reilly. Already she knew the question to be pointless. This wasn't the killer.

'I was here,' said the chef. 'I finished early and then I took my wife and children to a movie. Am I in some trouble?'

'No, no trouble at all,' said Chris. 'Thank you for your time. It's been very informative.'

'So,' said Reilly afterwards, as Chris navigated the late afternoon traffic back to the GFU. 'Let's go over what we know so far. Our victim, Jennifer Armstrong, was a career woman who frequented dating sites. She was killed after eating a well-prepared meal laced with antimine. The fact that her death was reasonably quick indicates that the antimine was prepared professionally. There were no seeds in her stomach, which backs up this assumption. We have two previous instances from before, which were sloppier but still hold some of the same calling cards:

professionally prepared meal, non-violent death, potential fetish held by the killer for the victim's bed. Not much to go on.'

'I think the bed thing is less of a fetish, and more of a compulsion,' said Chris.

'OK Freud,' said Reilly. 'Still, we need something else. I'll check in with the crew when we get back, see if they've come up with anything from the trace. We just have to keep ploughing through.'

He looked sideways at her. 'I would tell you to go home and rest after that little incident back there, but I have a feeling you won't take to that too kindly.'

'You're right about that,' she said, embarrassed afresh. 'I don't want to hear another word about it. I'll admit I was worried for a minute but I must just have a stomach bug. I don't need to go home and rest. I need to get something concrete in this case before it drives me mad.'

'I hear you,' said Chris. 'Maybe we'll strike it lucky. Maybe Kennedy actually did something useful at lunch, other than eat the biggest burger he could find.'

In fact, Pete Kennedy had discovered a thing or two while eating at Jumbo's. He had found the burger restaurant he had been missing all of his life: the burgers there were big, juicy and delicious and they came with a serve of beer battered chunky fries. If this was heaven, then he was in it.

While he ate his burger, he got chatting to the waitress. Kennedy could always get a pretty girl to talk to him. His intentions were pure: he just liked to chat. He wasn't threatening or sleazy.

'You like working here?' he asked the waitress.

She looked young, with curly brown hair and full pink lips. He had the feeling, looking at her sleepy eyes and the agitated way she kept moving her hands that she might not look young for much longer. A user.

'It's all right,' she said. 'Better than some places. They don't shout at you here.' Her accent was thick.

'You from England, love?'

'I am, yeah.'

'Whereabouts?'

'Manchester.'

'Great place.'

'I miss it,' she admitted. 'I thought that I'd come to Dublin and something good might happen, but I just fell in to this job, these people. It's just like being back home, only I have no money and no family.'

'You could go back,' he said. 'No shame in that.' She smiled hopelessly, and he leaned forward. 'I heard a girl who worked here got killed a couple of months ago? Do you know anything about that?'

'You the grease, or something?' Her demeanor changed suddenly, she got suspicious.

'No, nothing like that,' Kennedy lied smoothly. 'Truth is, her father was a friend of mine and I'm just asking around for him. As you can imagine, he's disappointed that no one's been arrested.'

'Well,' she said, relaxing again. 'We all are, aren't we? 'Specially as we know who done it, an' all,' Her accent slipped into her Manchester vernacular now that she was familiar with him.

'Who was that, then?'

'Harry McMurty. Used to work here. Real piece of work, he was. Used to try and get into all our pants, but only Rose would let him. She must have been mad. I mean, he's handsome, sure, but just a real rat?'

'Yeah, I know the type,' said Kennedy. 'So why didn't the cops get him?'

'Bloody fluff couldn't catch their own arses if you ask me,' she said. 'Useless as anything.'

'I agree with you,' he said staunchly.

'They said they hadn't enough evidence. But here we all were saying it weren't no one else but him. And they let him go. He's got some fancy job over at Hammer and Tongs now. Smooth talker.'

'Hammer and Tongs? What's that?'

'Real fancy place over on Baggot Street. Tuck your napkin into your shirt, wipe your nose for you that kind of place. He's the head waiter or something. Wants to be maitre'd.'

'Well, thank you,' said Kennedy. 'You've been a real help.'

'I hate that bugger, I do,' the girl said with sudden vehemence. 'I know Rose wasn't much and a dreamer to boot but she were one of us and she didn't deserve what happened. I hope that rat gets it.'

'We usually get what's coming to us, pet,' Kennedy said, getting up to leave.

'Not that I've seen. It's them willing to walk over the rest of us that get the cream.'

Kennedy left her a big tip. She would need it, poor girl. He'd seen so many like her, heading for disaster, but having two young daughters himself, he wanted to save them all.

The world was a harsh place, sucking in and spitting out kids like that who were too young to stop it. It was a terrible shame.

Back at the GFU, he met up with Reilly and Chris in the lab.

Kennedy didn't have anything against the blindingly impressive results that DNA could give them. But he still favored good old-fashioned detective work. He preferred to think of the stuff done here as a kind of alchemy, something magic. Not anything that these kids had to put hours and hours of work into, just to extract the DNA from a single hair.

'OK,' said Gary, filling them in, like the show-man he was. 'We managed to extract a single piece of hair from the bed at Jennifer Armstrong's, and compared this to the DNA of the two men who came forward and admitted to dating Jennifer. No match. But,' he said, 'and this is where you'll want to give me a big kiss, it does match the DNA taken from the previous crime scene with the bed imprint in common. It's a match. Your guy was at both scenes. And who knows how many others. Nothing from last month's anitimine-related one unfortunately. Problem is we don't have enough trace left to keep testing. We need to keep the rest to match against any real suspects.'

'You're a magician all right,' said Kennedy. 'Are you ready for that kiss?'

They all laughed. Reilly was relieved to have something to go on finally, but it only confirmed her worst fears.

With a stab of familiar resignation in her stomach, she acknowledged that they were dealing with a serial killer.

12

ONCE SHE GOT HOME THAT evening, Reilly made herself a quick salad and sat down at her table to work. At times like this, it would be nice to have a cat or dog. Or something for a little companionship. Most of her colleagues were out having a post work drinks and she was at home, trying to concentrate on old case files and keep up to date with emails.

The truth was, her mind kept wandering to the lunch she had with Chris. They had strayed into the territory of the personal today, and it had been strangely comforting. She knew, had known for a long time that Chris was someone she could really tell things to.

That's why she had to be extra vigilant around him. She'd learnt that lesson with Todd. She didn't need anything complicating her work relationships. Especially not now, when they had made the biggest break-through of the case so far.

What Gary had found today would help. They would be able to make stronger hypotheses about the killer, able to track his state of mind more easily. There might be yet more clues to be gleaned from the earlier crime scene, Rose Cooper. The two victims were very different. Jennifer was reasonably wealthy, having had a successful PR firm of her own making. She was sophisticated, savvy, independent. She knew what she wanted and had no problem taking it. This other girl, Rose, was much less sure of herself. She was a single mother, hailing from a working class family who lived outside of Dublin, in the Midlands somewhere. She had left school at sixteen, become pregnant and then came to the city and began working as a waitress, trying to pick up acting gigs at the same time.

Family and friends said that around the time before her death she had been feeling discouraged and was depressed. One of Rose's close friends had said that she was not sexually confidant, but was quite shy with men and seemed to date only men who didn't treat her well. Reilly saw the name Harry McMurty pop up a few times. An old colleague. She wondered if Kennedy had found anything out on his solo expedition to her workplace. He hadn't said anything that afternoon, but then they were all excited about the new findings.

She opened her laptop and clicked on the email from Gary and frowned. Darren Keating, Grace Gorman's ex-boyfriend was in jail, in Mountjoy Prison.

She would go over there after work on Friday if she could spare the time. The prison was only a stone's throw across the city but she wasn't exactly overjoyed at the thought of it. The guy sounded the very opposite of charming and she was sorry that Lucy's sister had got mixed up with a kid who was clearly trouble. The question was, did he have anything to do with Grace's disappearance?

According to the case file, Keating had been interviewed a few times immediately afterwards, but had been less than helpful. He had tried to diminish the relationship, saying that it was just a casual thing, that he hadn't really known Grace that well. But other friends indicated that they had been together all the time; that they were practically inseparable. Reilly always felt that there might be more to tease out there, but from what she could tell the new task force wasn't focusing on past acquaintances. Hell, she didn't think they were focusing on much at all and the investigation was more about appearances than anything else. The lab had got practically nothing from the house and the other trinkets, so what had seemed like a breakthrough at the time had simply led to other frustrating dead ends.

Lucy was another problem when it came to the re-examination of Grace's case: she'd barely spoken to Reilly since they had gone out to her childhood home the other day and she had broken down.

Reilly felt that she was actively avoiding her. She needed to talk to Lucy, to make her feel safe again. But she couldn't help but feel that her reaction merely proved that she knew something, whether she was aware of it or not. She didn't think that Lucy was lying, or hiding anything deliberately. The mind was a powerful thing, and would do what it could to protect a person from harm.

In the excitement of the day before, Kennedy had neglected to update the others about his exploits at Jimbo's. He was starting late that morning, so he decided to drop into the fancy restaurant on Baggot Street the waitress had mentioned and check out Rose Cooper's old workmate Harry McMurty before considering it seriously as an avenue.

Hammer and Tongs was just opening when he walked in at eleven a.m. He guessed it was the very antithesis of the place he had been in the day before. It was an old warehouse, with huge high ceilings and the sound in the room flew about and bounced off the walls like a panicked bird.

'Can I help you, sir?' A waiter rushed him as soon as he walked in, seeming alarmed at the sight of a man who looked like he really should be out ploughing a field, darkening the door of one of the best restaurants in Dublin.

'I'd like to speak to Harry McMurty, please,' said Kennedy.

'I'm afraid that Mr McMurty is working right now, and can't entertain friends.'

'This isn't a friendly visit,' Kennedy replied gruffly, annoyed by these hoity toity places. 'You'd do well to sit yourself down and entertain the law. You're wearing a name-tag, you gobshite. '

McMurty blushed but remained defiant. 'What's this all about? I've had enough of you guards. I already told you everything I know about Rose.'

'How did you know I'm here about that?' asked Kennedy.

'Girl I used to work with rang me up and told me you'd been sniffing around.'

'I got the impression she wasn't a fan,' said Kennedy, surprised. 'What's she doing ringing you up?'

'They all hate me until they need something,' he sneered.

He was handsome, Kennedy supposed, but underlyingly threatening. He had a face that was smooth and unblemished, glossy black hair and was slim and lithe. A tiny diamond glinted in his earlobe and tattoos peeked out from beneath his sleeves. His eyes were the only thing that gave him away. They were a deep blue, but shot through with red. He obviously didn't get much sleep.

It was the ones who looked like this who were often the most trouble, thought Kennedy. Their good looks reeled people in, made them trust them. They should come with a bloody warning sign.

'Just sit down,' said Kennedy. 'I won't take up much of your time. Not if you behave yourself.'

McMurty threw himself into a chair like a sulky child.

'You were seeing that girl, weren't you?' asked Kennedy.

'Which one? Pick a number,' said Harry. 'I was seeing all of them. Easy, the lot of them.'

'What did they see in you, I wonder?'

'What do you think?' he replied with a grin, making a vague gesture to his crotch.

'Don't give me that. Those women were desperate for something all right, but it wasn't that.'

Harry sighed. 'You know this is all on record already don't you? You could just do your job and read the reports.'

'I want you to tell me.'

'OK, I was giving them stuff, wasn't I? Something they wanted for something I wanted. A simple trade. It didn't hurt anyone.'

'I'd beg to differ,' said Kennedy. 'That girl ended up dead.'

'Not by my hand, granddad,' said Harry getting back up. 'I've got a job to do. You've got nothing on me. Come back when you do.'

'I will, believe me. I get my kicks out of putting slime balls like you in jail.'

'Things have a funny way of happening to silly 'oul fellas like you,' said Harry. 'So, I'm not too worried. I think you'll change your mind.'

Kennedy laughed loudly as he left the restaurant. He had been threatened by dirt bags like this one before. They didn't have the backbone to go through with it. They only liked to hurt people who were weaker than themselves.

13

CHRIS CAUGHT UP WITH REILLY at the GFU lab later in the morning. 'Are you feeling better after yesterday?' he asked.

'I'm feeling fine,' she said shortly, her expression tight. 'Have you been over the interviews with Jennifer's family and friends yet?' she added, straight back to business. 'Anything there?'

'I've read them,' he said, taking her cue. 'Nothing new: vibrant, full of life, beautiful girl, lots of friends, the usual. Like to have a good time. The men she dated revealed that they went out once, had dinner at a fancy restaurant and then went back to her place for sex. It was all very business-like. Jennifer told them that she didn't have time for a relationship.'

'But she told Blair and Helena Burke something different,' said Reilly, looking thoughtful. 'Said she was looking to settle down.'

He shrugged. 'Maybe she was looking for a particular type of guy. These guys were younger. Not in the same place in life. Maybe she wanted someone with a bit more success.'

'Maybe. Seems like a study in contradictions, though.'

He grinned. 'No such thing as a simple woman, Reilly.'

'Now you sound like Kennedy,' she said.

'So when are you free to check out the next antimine supplier on our list?' he asked. 'Friday afternoon would be best for me.'

'It'll have to be next week then,' she said. 'I'm leaving the office early on Friday.'

'Oh? Romantic weekend away?'

'Hardly. No, unfortunately it's work stuff.'

'If it's work stuff, shouldn't we be invited?' he wheedled.

'Stop being such a detective,' she said, trying to hide a smile. 'If you must know, I have to go up to Mountjoy to talk to Grace Gorman's old boyfriend.'

'Ah, and you want to keep that quiet, because if Jack finds out, he'll have your head on a platter.'

'You're very good at this,' said Reilly. 'Maybe you should be a cop or something.'

'I'll go with you,' he said. 'Mountjoy is not for the faint-hearted.

'No need. It's not even official business per se. I'm just doing it for Lucy.'

'Then I'm doing it for Lucy, too. It makes sense. Going to a prison on a Friday evening will be its own special kind of hell believe me.'

'OK,' she exhaled, surprising herself. 'I'll owe you a favor.'

The rest of Reilly's day went by in a blur. She reviewed the witness statements with Jennifer Armstrong's friends and family, and then the ones with Rose Cooper's. No real similarities other than that they both liked good food, but only Jennifer was actually able to afford the kind of places that Rose aspired to.

According to her friends, Rose had wanted a job in a better restaurant. Somewhere "fancy". They both seemed to date rather loathsome men. Blair Burke and Harry McMurty were both scumbags. But there was nothing pointing either of those men to the murders. They hadn't completely ruled out McMurty yet, but based on what Kennedy had told them, Reilly didn't think he fit. He was just a regular, run of the mill loser. He had given Rose Cooper drugs and then fed on her addiction.

'Reilly, can we talk?' said Lucy, as she was gathering her stuff to leave.

'Sure,' said Reilly, evenly, easily guessing what this was about.

'OK,' the younger girl said, closing the office door behind her. 'I need to "level with you". Isn't that what you say in America?'

She smiled. 'That's what we say, yes.'

'I've kind of been avoiding you.'

'No kidding,'

'You knew?'

'Lucy. Come on. A blind man could have figured out that you were giving me the slip since the other day. Let's be real.'

'I'm really sorry. It was stupid. It's just that being back there brought up a lot of painful stuff for me. You were right. I remembered some stuff that I didn't know that I knew. Or that I just pushed away. I've had years of therapy and all it's taught me to do is repress.'

'Don't be so hard on yourself,' Reilly soothed, understanding all too well. 'This is hard stuff. For anyone.'

'I know. But I'm the one who's been pushing you to look at this. I should have been prepared to do whatever you asked me to. I think I am now though,' she added, taking a deep breath. 'I'm going to make myself ready for what you suggested. I know I need to do this.'

'You shouldn't push yourself,' said Reilly. 'I won't make you do something you're not ready for. But I really do believe hypnotherapy might be a good way forward.' Reilly admired her. She was tough. She didn't want to mention anything about Grace's old boyfriend just yet. Not unless the prison visit threw up anything. And also because technically she couldn't really discuss it with her. When it came to Grace's case, Lucy was still officially a witness.

'I think that's wise,' she told her. 'Let me make a few calls and we'll work out a time for your first session.' Reilly knew of a good hypnotherapy person the force used for some victims. It was not always reliable, and often didn't give the results you were looking for, but it was worth a shot. 'But I just want to ask you one thing,' she added, before Lucy turned to leave, 'do you remember where Grace got that necklace to begin with? The one we found in the house?'

'It was a present from Darren, her boyfriend. I don't think he bought it himself though, Grace said he "found it" which I thought was a bit cheap, but she was thrilled.'

Reilly nodded. The boyfriend again. More roads leading to Darren Keating than were comfortable, yet nobody seemed to have paid him much heed at all during the initial investigation.

Well, he wasn't going to get away so lightly this time.

14

SO THEY'VE GOT THEMSELVES A lead. Cops blundering around the restaurants, asking stupid questions.

I've got myself a lead too.

There is no question that she is beautiful. Long blonde hair, green eyes, skin like an English rose. I love that creamy skin, love the way it flushes so easily, the capillaries underneath filling up and flooding at the slightest provocation.

I imagine how she will look when the poison sends her off to sleep. Her lips slightly open, face flushed, hair a little messy. I wonder how she will smell? Musky and cloying, or fresh and scrubbed? I will bathe in her scent, lay down beside her and suck up that sweet smell. The scent of a woman is a seductive thing. We become addicted to it in the womb, it is fed to us in our mother's milk, and then we seek it out in lovers. One after the other, seeking that perfect blend of pheromones.

I have been communicating with this woman every night. Her name, which I won't write here, for fear of jinxing my plans, means "pleasant". She is far from pleasing, though. She embodies everything that I hate. She has made it clear, that when we meet, I am to be used for her pleasure. Fine, I say. I can't think of anything better.

Her interests are listed as: fitness, fine dining, movies. We have so much in common! I tell her. She has been to my restaurant, just LOVES the food there! Soon I'll tell her I'll make her the meal of a lifetime, something she truly can't pass up. And it will be the meal of a lifetime, in so many ways.

I've been experimenting with a few things. I won't use the fruit again: too risky. I want to use more natural substances, things that are harder to track. Those cops would never have picked up on what it was if I hadn't had to leave Jennifer's. Her cellphone ringing, then her landline. Some drunk idiot threatening to come over. I deleted the message, but I should have left it, thrown out a false lead for them.

It just shows that I'm still prone to panic. I need to refine my actions. I need for everything to go very smoothly.

I do have a little something up my sleeve, though, thanks to the idiocy of that cop. It's still in embryo form this idea, so I'll just nurture it until it becomes fully fledged.

I've tried mushrooms, large amounts of nicotine, nutmeg, all the usual things. It has all been enough to kill a dog or cat in an hour. Slightly larger doses for a person, I think. Plus I will have to travel further afield for the animals. I don't want my neighbours comparing notes about missing pets. I don't feel bad about it. An animal is an animal. Made to be eaten. Bred to die.

My running times continue to be astounding. I feel as though I am imbued with energy. I leave all the others behind in the dust. I have to caution myself not to get too eager, not to get sloppy in my excitement. I would do this all the time if I could, but I have to keep up the pretense of my life.

Lately, I've felt strong enough to begin looking into my past, to find her. It is my feeling that she will be a wasted old harridan, and I will rejoice in this. She is oddly hard to find, though.

I'll keep trying.

Reilly woke with a start and sat bolt upright in her chair. Chris jumped away from her.

'You were asleep,' he said. 'I just touched your arm to wake you and you sat up like you'd been shot.'

'Sorry,' Reilly muttered blearily. 'Oh my god, I feel like I've been asleep for a million years. What's the time?'

'Just after 2pm.'

'Did anyone see me?' she asked, horrified.

'Everyone seems to be having long lunches,' he said. 'Friday and all that. Are you sure you're still up to going to Mountjoy today? You might be better off taking an early -'

'Give me ten,' she interjected. 'I'll meet you in the car park.'

When Reilly reached the car park she was feeling slightly more awake. Chris didn't mention anything more as she got in the passenger seat, but she could feel him shooting her concerned glances.

'I'm fine,' she says.

'You've been saying that a lot lately.'

'Because it's the truth.'

It wasn't long before they were stuck in the snarl of city traffic heading north.

'Something's on your mind,' said Chris. 'You might as well tell me. We'll be here for a while.' He popped open a bag of crisps and offered them to her.

'A secret junk food addict,' she replied. 'I never would have guessed.'

'Just a little motivation for the drive. And don't change the subject.'

After a pause, he put some music on the stereo.

'MC5?' she asked. 'That's pretty far out, for a Dubliner. Very American.'

'I'm from Wicklow remember? And I was a pretty cool teenager,' he added wryly. 'I knew my stuff.'

She laughed. 'I can see it now. Chris Delaney, hanging out at de corner shop in a Clash T-shirt, smoking a fag and chatting up the gurls.'

'Your Irish accent is terrible, by the way,' he said. 'But the rest is pretty spot on. What were you like? You never mention your childhood other than …' He left the rest of the sentence hanging but she knew what he meant. Her childhood mostly consisted of her stepping in as mum to her younger sister Jess and watching out for their alcoholic father, when their mother walked out on them.

'Sooo earnest,' she said, laughing a little. 'Braces. Hair in plaits. Not cool at all. I listened exclusively to country music and tried to learn the banjo once.'

'And did you succeed?'

'No.' she said. 'I don't like to talk about it but Mike could tell you about that time, with great glee. Although at the time he was mostly telling me to go outside and practice.'

'As you've trusted me with such precious information, I'll tell you a secret from my own embarrassing past,' said Chris. 'I used to do Irish dancing.'

'I'm not even sure what that it,' says Reilly, 'but it sounds hilarious.'

'It is, not so much for girls but definitely for lads. I used to get kitted out in a kilt and long socks and fling my legs about to accordion music every Friday night.'

'OK, yours sounds definitely worse than mine,' she chuckled.

They passed the journey in comfortable silence for a while after that, until Chris spoke again. 'How is your dad by the way? You haven't mentioned him in a while.'

'Good. Did I tell you he met someone? They're in California now, and looks like they might stay on for good.'

He stared at her. 'Seriously? Does that mean that you're thinking of …'

'Following him back across the Atlantic again? I don't know, I think he's done with me looking over his shoulder at every turn. Besides I'm pretty sure he's sober for good now. The woman, Maura is good for him. I'll miss him of course but we're still close and I know now that he's always there for me, always on my side. You need at least one person like that in your life.'

'I don't know if I have that,' Chris said thoughtfully.

'What about Kennedy?'

'Of course I know Kennedy's got my back. But he's my partner and while he's my friend too, it's his job to look out for me. I think what you're talking about is someone who really puts you at the centre of their universe.'

'Yeah, I guess that's what I mean.'

There was a heavy silence as they were both lost in thought at the notion. For Reilly the conversation was becoming uncomfortably personal again and she struggled to move it on to safer territory.

'You think that if Jennifer Armstrong and Rose Cooper had someone like that they would have ended up dead?'

'No,' Chris replied. 'But I do think maybe they went looking for it in all the wrong places.'

Darren Keating by all accounts, did not start the bad news he grew up to be. He had a steady home life, though his father left when he was three, but his mother had remarried and he got on well with his step-father.

His older brother had gone to live with the father when his parents spilt. The year before Grace Gorman went missing, two things happened: Darren's older brother Brendan came back to live with his mother, and Darren started to get into trouble. This was also around the time he started seeing Grace. It was small time trouble at first: stealing CDs from the store, breaking car windows and the like, but Reilly could see that it spiraled out of control. She couldn't help but feel that the brother, Brendan Keating, had something to do with it. There was the barest mention of him in the files. He hadn't sparked anyone else's interest, apart from as someone who knew Darren well.

But somehow between then and now Darren had ended up in the country's main prison.

Mountjoy itself was huge and imposing; it was a marvel of its time, and built with a central observation deck, so that the prisoners never knew when they were being watched. Theoretically, they were being watched all the time. It was based on the philosophy of Foucault: if a man feels watched, he will begin to self-police.

'Pretty grim, isn't it?' said Chris as went through the security booth to the car park.

'You can say that again. Gives me the creeps just looking at it.'

Given his last-minute offer to accompany her, she hadn't been able to secure an interviewer's pass for Chris in time, only for herself. Despite all her years in US law enforcement, she had never actually interviewed a criminal inside a correctional facility before. It made her feel strangely vulnerable, like she was going to their house, having to handle things on their own turf.

It was silly. She was perfectly safe.

Inside, Mountjoy prison smelled like all the bad dreams Reilly had ever had. It was fetid bodies, overlain with greasy, fried food. Added to that was the stink of rage, of despair, of violence. These men were caged animals, pacing their cells for hours of the day. She imagined the kind of things that took place whenever they poured out into the yard.

A guard led her to the private room where the interview would take place. Well, not private. As the guard explained, there would be two other guards present. It was just separate from the other visitors, so that Reilly could question Darren Keating in private. He would be cuffed, the guard told her, but if she felt uncomfortable at any time, she should just raise her hand and the interview would be terminated.

'I should warn you,' said the guard, 'he's not exactly a nice guy.'

'Are any of them?'

'This one is especially nasty.'

Darren Keating may once have been handsome. Reilly thought if she felt safe enough to squint, she might have been able to find traces of the good looking kid that had once attracted the attention of Grace Gorman.

But no longer. He had a tattoo of a scarab beetle under one eye, the wings shimmering green and appearing to move whenever the muscles in his cheek moved. His face was overlain with scars. This is what happened when you spent so much time in jail: you had to prove yourself again and again by fighting those who were stronger than you. Reilly thought that Darren had probably proved himself by now. His knuckles were a mess of fatty scar tissue, pink and obscene.

'Did the warden finally shell out for a pro?' he asked, as she sat down. He leaned back, surveying her.

She regarded him with a blank stare and switched on her voice recorder. 'I'll be taping this,' she said.

'I like a woman who wants a souvenir,' he said. 'Nothing you do will be a problem for me, darlin''

'Cut the crap,' she said. 'You know why I'm here.'

'I haven't actually been informed of that little tidbit, no,' he said, looking genuine. 'I get dragged from my cell and told to be on my best behavior, but they don't tell me why.'

'I'm here to talk about Grace Gorman.'

'Grace….Grace Gorman. Doesn't ring a bell.'

'Don't play with me.'

'I'd like nothing better than to play with you, actually. But I reckon you might not like my brand of playing.'

'Answer my questions,' said Reilly, standing up. 'Or I'm leaving.' She thought it would work. These guys didn't get a break from the mundane sameness of every day. If nothing else, this encounter would be something for Keating to think about later, although she hated to think of him carrying her image in his mind.

'You were seeing Grace Gorman at the time she went missing, eighteen years ago.'

'I was seeing her, yeah. But do you have any idea how many women I've "seen" since then. You'll have to forgive me if my memory of this one is a little foggy.'

'I'm sure we can get you to remember a few salient facts. How long did you go out with Grace?'

'We were kids. We went to different schools so I didn't see her that much. Weekends, mostly. Her parents were very strict.'

'Were you happy together?'

'What kind of question is that? I was fifteen. I wasn't happy with anything. I thought she was kind of cool. We liked the same music. But she was just a girl, one of many.'

'Was your relationship sexual?'

He sneered. 'Yeah. I bet you'd like to know just how much wouldn't you? Give you something to think about later.'

'Answer the question,' said Reilly.

'No, it wasn't. Not like that. She was a bit innocent that one.' His face softened a little and this surprised her. 'We just messed around, a bit of a feel here and there. Nothing to rock your world. Don't think like that. It wasn't like that with her. It wasn't dirty.'

Taken aback by his vehemence, she noticed he was breathing deeply, no longer as assured and controlled. 'Did that upset you?'

'I just wanted you to understand that no matter what came after, Grace wasn't like that. I just liked to be with her, to talk with her, you know? She was more of a friend.'

'Okay. Did your brother … Brendan know her?'

His head snapped up and his grey eyes seemed to look right through her. 'What's that got to do with anything? What's he got to do with it?'

'You tell me. Did he know Grace?'

'Yeah, he knew her. She was round our place sometimes.'

'Did he like her?'

He shrugged. 'I don't know what he thought of her. Didn't care.'

'Do you and your brother have a close relationship?'

'I haven't seen Brendan in years,' he said.

'Before that. Were you close?'

'Yes. He looked after me. He stood by me. He knew what was best.' He sounded almost like he was reciting a lesson.

'How did he know what was best for you?'

'He knew how things worked. Knew that my mam and Frank were just out to get me. Wanted to send me away to school. Brendan looked after me.'

She guessed Frank was the mother's new husband, Darren's stepfather.

'Where is Brendan now?' she asked.

'No one knows. He must be dead though, because he wouldn't go and take off somewhere without saying something. Someone must have got him.'

'Did your brother have lots of enemies then?'

'Sure,' said Darren. 'People were afraid of him. They wanted him dead.'

'Were you afraid of him?'

Darren looked away. 'He would never hurt me.'

'Were you afraid of him?'

Still he didn't reply and Reilly sat silently for a minute. She could feel the guards waiting behind her, staring at her and Darren. She had the feeling that if she waited, he would say more.

'Did my brother hurt me? Yeah,' he said. 'Plenty of times. He would hit me. He killed my dog. He would tear up my schoolwork, piss on pictures of my girlfriends, my family. Yes, I was afraid of him. But everything he did was love. Everything. See this burn?' He pointed to a long burn down his forearm. 'He did this with the blade of a knife he had held in the fire. Every time he hit me, or took something from me, he did it to make me stronger. Because he loved me.'

Reilly was overwhelmed. She felt ill. 'Did your brother try to take Grace from you?'

Suddenly a stream of filthy words and invective flowed. The man who had spoken to her so reasonably a minute ago was now going crazy. He threw his body over the table between them. His teeth were bared in a yellow rictus, his hands made into claws. Reilly shot her body backwards, sending her chair flying. The guards were on him in seconds, but she had felt the hot air of his breath, felt his words land on her like blows.

Outside, she gulped for air. She still had her recorder grasped in her hand, thank goodness. She didn't remember picking it up, didn't remember being escorted from the premises. She stumbled back to the car park, where Chris was waiting, leaning against the car.

'Reilly my god, what's wrong?' He held out his arms to steady her, and she fell against his chest. 'It's all right,' he said, 'It's all right. It's all right.'

The strength of his arms around her seemed to trigger something in her, and before she realized it, Reilly found herself wrapping her arms around him.

Then without warning, she raised her head and pressed her lips against his, trying to fill herself up with the smell of Chris, the taste of him, anything to block out the events of the past hour.

15

PETE KENNEDY WAS WAGING HIS own private war against Harry McMurty. Chris seemed to think he was a dead end in the investigation, but he just had a feeling about this kid that couldn't be ignored.

He found out where McMurty lived and followed him there. He watched him leave his house and go running in the mornings, and he watched him leave for work, perfectly groomed and strutting down the street like he owned it. He watched him flirting with girls at the restaurant, and had no doubt that he was up to his same old tricks.

He hadn't seen him do anything incriminating, yet. But Kennedy had no doubt, if he kept watching, that McMurty would slip up.

Reilly would rather have done anything else than go into work on Monday morning. She thought about calling in sick. She thought about just crawling back into bed and ignoring the world. Instead she gave herself a talking to, one of the variety her father might have given her: You just lift your chin up honey, and get back to work. I didn't raise you to hide under a rock whenever you did something stupid.

Because she *had* done something stupid. Appallingly stupid. In that moment of emotion, she had kissed - practically *jumped on* - Chris Delaney, sending years of a good working partnership straight down the toilet.

Yes, he had responded, but how could he not, given the circumstances? She had basically been distraught. She was mortified about running into his arms like a scared little girl, but there had just been something about the encounter with Darren Keating that shook her to the core.

It wasn't just that he tried to attack her. It was that something under his exterior was so hurt, so badly damaged that it made her afraid. There was something else to this story, Grace's story, but she hadn't stayed in the room long enough to find out.

Eventually she'd come to her senses and quickly pulled away, mumbling a quick apology and shutting down any conversation about what had just happened.

She knew he had been just as stunned as she was, and the journey back across the city had been excruciating. Every time Chris tried to speak to her she had started to talk about the Armstrong case; details they had already been over. She couldn't stand to hear any of his platitudes, or his "I'm flattered but I don't think this is a good idea speech". She already *knew* it wasn't a good idea.

They were scheduled to go to a restaurant called Hammer and Tongs today to enquire about their use of antimine, and to look into any links with Rose Cooper's former workmate Harry McMurty. There would be no cosy lunch this time, though. Reilly would keep things strictly business. She didn't know how to begin to repair her relationship with Chris, to make him feel safe around her again.

Now she just had to get through the day.

But if she thought it was going to get any better, she was sadly wrong.

She had a stack of emails and messages from the lab waiting and now she could see someone making a beeline for her office. Couldn't they just give her a minute to hang up her coat first?

But she would have happily talked to anyone, over what happened next. Jack Gorman walked past her in the hallway. "Steel. My office. Now."

She knew it wouldn't be good, and it wasn't.

'We talked about this,' said Jack. 'We talked about this and I set out the ground rules and you agreed to them.'

'Yes, I did.'

'So why don't you tell me, if you understood and agreed to those rules, why my daughter was undergoing hypnotherapy on Friday, while conveniently enough you were in Mountjoy interviewing a former witness? What the hell is wrong with you Steel? You were interviewing a witness who has been questioned a hundred times! Do you know how this looks?'

'I just needed to -'

'I don't care if you needed to bloody well dance on the table tops. I don't care what you need at all, Steel. The point is, you shouldn't have been there. You shouldn't have been anywhere near Keating. There's a task force in place and now I've got my colleagues, the ones who are actually supposed to be working this case, breathing down my neck.'

'They might be breathing down your neck, Jack, but they're not helping you find your daughter.'

'And as of now, neither are you. We've got a job to do here in the GFU and that's what I want you to be doing. No flitting off on Friday afternoons on a wild goose chase.'

'I resent the implication that I was ignoring my work, Jack. That's not true. And further to that, you don't control what I do in either my work or personal time. I made a promise to Lucy to help and I'm sorry, but I'm going to act on that promise whether you like it or not. You weren't there the other day with Keating; there might be something ...'

Jack Gorman was so angry that for once Reilly didn't follow through on her argument. She could almost feel the heat coming off him. He had a right to be, she knew. She had expressly gone against his wishes. But with good reason.

'Please, Jack. I really think I've got something. I just need more time. I'll keep a low profile.'

'According to you,' he said, 'I can't stop you.' Then his voice softened a little. 'I appreciate you trying to help our family, but your job isn't going over old ground Steel, it's covering new.'

'That's what I'm trying to do, Jack. You know I'm good at my job.'

'I know you used to be. But since you've got back from your leave of absence I don't think you've been on your game. And I'm not the only one who's noticed. So I'm warning you now, as a colleague and a friend: Do your job.'

She was almost shell-shocked when she left Jack's office. Was he right? Had she been off her game? Sure, she had been jet lagged for longer than usual, and was definitely finding it harder to get back into the swing of things, but she thought that was visible only to her.

She would just have to push herself harder. She would go down to the lab herself this afternoon, to go over the evidence. Something mundane like analyzing trace might help her to focus her mind; really narrow in on something.

He was right about one thing, she really did seem all over the place since she'd come back, the ongoing murder investigation, the cold case, her relationships …

Her mind shutting down at the thought of what had happened with Chris, she thought again about what had Jack had said about the cold case. She shouldn't be meddling. But how could she stand by and watch the task force scratching their asses, when she now knew that there was more to Darren Keating than met the eye? It would be a different story if she trusted the other detectives to do the job. But she didn't. And she didn't care what Jack said; Lucy was relying on her, and she wasn't going to give it up. Not while there was a sliver of hope, however faint that might be. She owed it to Lucy.

Reilly turned to her emails and with a deep breath, began to methodically sort through them. From Gary was some background information on Brendan Keating, which she'd requested before heading out to the prison on Friday. She would read that later. It wouldn't do for Gorman to walk in and see her reading it. From now on, she would work on Grace's case outside of work hours and in her spare time only.

From Julius: "More promising evidence in the Armstrong AND Cooper case." Well, that was some good news, at least.

The last one from Chris, she almost deleted without reading. Don't be silly she told herself. It's probably something about work. But something stopped her and she was just about to click on it when another email right below it caught her attention.

It was from Lucy's hypnotherapist.

It could be because of the amount of time that has passed, it read, *or because of the extreme effort that Lucy has put into forgetting this particular event, but it is hidden very deep. I will need to go very slowly with her, to avoid traumatizing her completely. I have no doubt that there is something to be found, but I don't want to harm the patient in the process of extraction. You might consider the consequences if we uncover something damaging. Audio transcript attached.*

Reilly downloaded the audio file and put her headphones in. She listened to the therapist put Lucy into a sleep-like state, a place where her defenses were lowered and she could free associate. Whatever was in her unconscious wouldn't come up against the same barriers as it did when she was awake.

Once she was under, the therapist began to ask questions in her low and pleasant voice. Reilly felt like she was listening to something very private. She didn't have the right to intrude on someone else's memories. But Lucy had consented beforehand, agreeing that it was necessary.

'Are you happy with your sister?'

'No, I am angry with her.'

'Why are you angry with her?'

'You know,' says Lucy. *'Because she won't tell.'* If Reilly didn't know better, she would think she was listening to a recording of an eleven year old. Lucy sounded so young, so childlike.

'Won't tell what?' asks the therapist.

'The thing. In the house. You know,' she says again, insistently.

'Why don't you tell?' The therapist tried a different tack.

'If I tell, they will do it to me, as well. That's what she said. Don't tell.'

'What will they do to you?'

'You know,' said Lucy. *'You know.'*

'I don't know. Perhaps you told me, but now I don't remember. Please tell me.'

Lucy begins to whimper and cry. *'I can't tell,'* she says. *'I can't tell, or something bad will happen to Grace. I can't tell.'*

16

LUCY WAS AT HER DESK with her headphones in, and she jumped a meter in the air when Reilly tapped her shoulder.

'Reilly. Oh my God, you scared me!'

'Sorry. I just came by to tell you, if you don't want to do this anymore, it's OK. The hypnotherapy I mean. I'll keep working a few angles, but you don't need to be involved if you don't want to. It's probably too much.'

Lucy looked taken aback. 'No, why would you think that? Of course I want to keep going. I'm not that soft that I would change my mind after one session.'

'But I thought … I got the impression from your dad that you didn't want to do it anymore. Because it upset you.'

'It did upset me. But Reilly, you were right. I know something is there. I know that there's something I've blocked out. I talked to Dad because I thought he might remember something himself. I asked him if he remembered Grace being particularly distracted or down in the dumps before she went missing, and he got so upset. He thought I was blaming him and mum, which of course I wasn't. And he's adamant that Grace didn't run away or had maybe done something ... herself, and he thought I was implying that.'

Reilly felt like a heel for putting the family through all this again. There was little question of Grace having committed suicide though, given that no body had ever been found. And that her necklace had been. 'You're sure you want to keep going?' she asked Lucy again. 'The therapist says it will be really heavy going and it's only going to get harder.'

'I want to keep going,' she insisted. 'Gary helped me see that it could actually be good for me. All this energy I'm putting into keeping a secret from myself? I'm sick of it, Reilly. I want to be free. Don't worry about Dad. I'll handle him, ok?'

'The thing is,' said Kennedy, who had appeared in Reilly's office when she got back. 'I just know this guy's up to no good. I want to put a closer watch on him.'

'They'll never agree to it. We've got nothing on McMurty, and those are huge resources.'

A plate of pastries wobbled between them. Reilly did have a weakness for pastries and she was steadfastly trying to ignore them.

'I've just got a feeling about this guy. You understand those feelings don't you? He might not be smart enough to be our murderer...but maybe he is. He's into all that dating stuff on the internet too. I had Gary check.'

'I'll try and get you something but I've already got O'Brien playing target practice with my head. He wants something solid from the evidence. And: so far we've just got bits and pieces.'

'Well, what does the chief bloody well expect? For us to pull something out of a magic hat? If our jobs were that easy there would be no murders. I saw Gorman stomping around your desk earlier too, like a big, red bull. Someone should shove a pin in his backside, see how he likes it.'

Reilly couldn't help but laugh. There was no love lost between Gorman and Kennedy. It was strange, because they were both of the old-school way of doing things.

'OK,' she said. 'But I think you should go to the restaurant with Chris this afternoon, despite your dislike of fine dining. There will be no eating today, just business.' She knew she was bottling it, but what else could she do? She just couldn't face Chris today.

'Grand. We'll see if we can't get a read on this fella.'

Before he left, Reilly gave in and split a pastry with Kennedy. What was life for, anyway, if you couldn't comfort yourself after the morning from hell?

So,' said Julius, positioning a slide under a microscope, 'whoever was lying on Jennifer Armstrong's bed, was wearing a material that didn't shed. But it did leave a residue of a chemical called magnesium stearate.'

Reilly immediately recognized this as the finishing agent on spandex. 'So basically, tights, exercise gear, things like that.'

'Yes. Because it's so thin, I had hoped that we might be able to get a skin sample though the fabric. Or maybe semen, if the unsub's reaction was sexual one. But I don't think it is. Anyway, along with DNA from the hair, we also now have the fabric agent linking these two crime scenes. The same trace occurring at both scenes.'

'OK. What kind of person wears spandex…someone who exercises obviously. Or…' she continued, her brain suddenly spinning into familiar overdrive. 'It might be a very smart thing to wear to a murder. Like you said, it doesn't shed fibers as such. So what if the killer wore normal clothes to the murder site, took some clothes and changed into exercise gear to run home in? He wouldn't be noticed. There's thousands of people running to and from work in the city.'

'You're right, it's completely anonymous. No one would think twice.'

'Another thing. If the unsub was on or in the bed, and we could get something from his clothing, then why wasn't there more trace left behind?'

'My theory is that he was wearing a head covering of some kind. This guy came prepared.'

'Any treads?'

'Very vague,' Julius said, pulling out the tread imprints. 'Guy's light on his feet.'

'And a runner would be light on their feet too, wouldn't they?' Reilly moved in to look at the treads. The footwear in question looked to have a strong raised arch, and thick ridges, the same indentation disappearing every centimeter.

Her face brightened as finally some of the puzzle was starting to come together. 'I think our guy was wearing running shoes.

17

HAMMER AND TONGS HAD A cold, clinical feel to it. Chris didn't like it at all. He was glad they weren't eating here.

But he was taken aback and more than a little worried that Reilly had cried off on the visit today. Especially given what had happened on Friday…

To say that he was shocked was the understatement of the century. He had no idea what had happened in the prison, but the sight of her when she came out … he'd automatically moved to comfort her. And then, when she'd turned her face up at him like that looking so vulnerable, so unlike her … He shook the thought away and tried to concentrate on the task in hand.

Harry McMurty escorted them to the kitchen. He smirked when he saw Kennedy again. 'Come to arrest me then, have you?'

'All in good time, mate.'

In the frantic kitchen, they were greeted by a tall red headed woman. 'Better make it quick,' she said. 'I've got a full house today.'

'Are you the Chef?' Kennedy asked.

'No, I'm the bloody Queen of England. What do you think?'

It occurred to Chris that this woman was probably used to being harassed in the workplace. The restaurant business was short on female chefs. Cooking at home was a supposedly woman's business, but being a chef required the strength and creativity of man. Or so the theory went. You needed to rule the kitchen with an iron fist.

'Are you the only chef here?' he asked, the woman who eventually introduced herself as Gemma Collins.

'I'm the daytime chef. The owner, Nico usually does the night work.'

'Popular, isn't it?'

'Best food in Dublin,' flashed the woman, proudly. 'Tony and Nico are doing amazing things.'

'And you use Joker Fruit?' Kennedy asked.

'Not any more. We did once or twice ages ago, but it's a bit old now, isn't it? In this restaurant, we don't need to put poisonous foods on our menu to impress.'

'Well when you did use it, were you involved in the preparation of it?'

'No, Nico did all of that. He's licensed.'

'And is Nico here?'

'Sleeping, probably. He works until very late. You can catch him in the evenings but I don't think he'd welcome you. We don't have problems with drugs among our staff, if that's why you're here.'

'Why would you think we were here because of that?'

'Everybody who works in hospitality takes amphetamines to stay up. Long hours,' said Collins. 'But our staff don't deal. They're good kids.'

'What about Harry McMurty?' interjected Kennedy.

'Harry? Yeah, he's a bit of a snake all right. But he can cook. Nico's mentoring him. Lets him into the kitchen and teaches him things.'

Kennedy shot Chris a triumphant look. *This* was the link he had been looking for.

'It's solid,' he argued after they'd left the premises. 'He murders one girl he's seeing with sleeping pills, starts working at this fancy place and murders the next one with something harder to trace. I don't know why we didn't bloody book him the first time round.'

'Patience. We'll get him in for questioning. But I don't know if he's the right fit for both. He's so young for starters. Too young to date Jennifer Armstrong.'

'Don't be too sure of that,' Kennedy said. 'Too young to have a relationship, maybe, but not too young for something casual.'

'I agree that this guy seems cocksure. Too in your face. By Julius's assessment, this unsub is supposed to be a loner.' He sighed. 'We'll bring him in for questioning tomorrow. But I just don't think he's the one.'

That afternoon Reilly studied the background report on Brendan Keating. It didn't make for pleasant reading.

When their parents split up, Darren had been 3 and Brendan 7. Brendan went to live with his father, a truck haulier who took his son with him to work. By age ten, Brendan had seen all of the country, and much of Europe, but had also been witness to the worst of his father's vices: women, alcohol and speed. It was no secret that truck drivers, like hospitality workers, often took drugs in order to work the long hours they needed to.

At age ten, Brendan Keating's father considered him old enough to stay at home by himself. Young Brendan started getting into the kind of trouble that you might expect from a sixteen year old: robberies, vandalism, intimidation. He was sent to foster homes and correctional facilities for youth, but to no avail. The damage was done. He had a list of convictions as long as Reilly's arm. There were three charges of sexual assault that had been dropped before they went to court. Interestingly, Brendan's criminal history stopped at age eighteen, around the time when he reconnected with his brother. Reilly couldn't put this down to Brendan turning over a new leaf, however, since this was when Darren started to get into trouble too. She thought that Brendan had still continued to commit crime, but perhaps had used his brother as a scapegoat.

Soon after, Brendan Keating dropped off the map. His brother had been doing a short stint in jail, and when he got out, Brendan had disappeared. The official theory was that he had been killed, but a body had never been found.

Reilly couldn't help but increasingly feel that Brendan was involved somehow in Grace's disappearance. From the sound of things, Darren Keating had been a good kid until he turned up. She needed to do two things: dig deeper in to the pasts of the brothers, and see if Lucy's hypnotherapy sessions turned up anything else in the meantime.

At the moment all she had was a hunch, but it was a strong one.

She picked up a photograph of Brendan Keating and studied it. Like Darren, he had also been a good looking kid. He had a scar running down the side of his face from an accident he'd been in. His father's truck had flipped on the ice on a windy road up North. Miraculously, they had both survived.

Reilly had a sinking feeling it would have been better for Grace Gorman if he hadn't.

18

LATER THAT EVENING, KENNEDY WAS happy enough to sit in his car and watch Harry McMurty. He was in one of the seedier parts of Dublin. Josie had her book group this evening, which generally consisted of too much wine and shrieking, so Kennedy thought it was a good chance for him to escape the house. He had just ordered a burger from the fast food place he was parked next to, and had put a Johnny Cash CD on.

McMurty was lurking about in a bar across the road. Kennedy knew it to be a notorious hangout for dealers of amphetamine. If nothing else, he could probably go in and nab McMurty on a possession charge. But that wasn't the way they did things. You had to respect the turf of others. He and Chris were homicide detectives, and they had done their stints in Vice and Narcotics. You couldn't go stepping on people's toes. There could be an operation here that he didn't know about.

Chris had offered to come with him but Kennedy had told him not to bother. Surely a young buck like Chris had other things to be doing. Though he knew Chris's life wasn't quite as exciting as it should be. He should have women climbing all over him, that fella. Well, maybe he did and he was just quiet about it?

And Steel was no better. Why did a good looking woman like that spend her nights alone? He didn't understand what people were up to these days and his thoughts drifted back to the murder victims.

Why spend your time looking for love on a computer when there were thousands of people out there, just waiting for someone special. He had met Josie at friend's wedding. That's how it should be done.

Kennedy's reverie was interrupted by a knock at his window. A man stood there holding a bag from the chipper he had ordered his burger from. He rolled down the window.

'Thanks,' he said.

'You're welcome,' said the man, with a quick grin.

Funny, thought Kennedy. He didn't look like the guy he'd ordered from. He was a little older. And come to think of it, he was wasn't wearing the uniform either. Maybe he was the manager or something.

He unwrapped his burger and took a bite. Delicious – wait, no, there was something not quite right. He poked around in his burger and found the culprit. A mushroom. He hated the things, wouldn't let them near the house. Smelt like an unwashed drawer of socks.

Kennedy didn't like complaining, but the mushroom had tainted the whole burger. He was sure they would give him a replacement. He got out and walked through the chilly air to the fast food place.

An odd feeling assailed him as he walked. Kind of like he was being squeezed out of his body. Like someone had a hold of him and was trying to crush him. Pete Kennedy made it inside the door of the chip shop before he crashed and fell, the hard linoleum floor feeling like a balm to his burning skin.

Reilly's phone rang in what felt like the middle of the night. She sat bolt upright and found herself at the kitchen table, a document from the Gorman missing person file stuck to her face. She ripped it off and madly rummaged through the papers to find her phone. A glance at the clock told her it was just after midnight.

'Hello?'

'Reilly. It's Chris.' Immediately she was flooded with discomfort, embarrassment … but then she heard something in his voice. This was nothing to do with … 'Something's happened,' he continued. 'It's Pete, he's had a heart attack or something.'

'Oh my God. Oh no -'

'He's all right. The hospital won't let anyone but Josie in now but I'm going to see him first thing tomorrow.'

'I'll meet you there,' she said, automatically.

'Are you sure? You don't have to, I just wanted to let you know.'

'Of course, I want to.' Kennedy was her colleague, her friend, the guy she'd been sharing pastries with the day before. She thought then about his terrible eating habits. Had his love of all things fried finally caught up with him?

A black fear gripped her heart. Chris had implied he was out of danger but what if he was wrong? If Kennedy died, it would be like losing … a good friend, she realized.

When Chris and Reilly met at the hospital the next morning, it was like they had run into mirrors of their own tiredness. It was also the first time they'd come face to face since the episode on Friday.

She'd finally opened his email after crying off on the restaurant visit. And when she did, she felt even worse for doing so.

Reilly, whatever happens, we are friends first and foremost. Don't shut me out. Out and about this morning but see you at the restaurant at one. It'll be a relief to escape from Kennedy for a bit. He's gnawing my ear off about this McMurty guy and you know what he's like. Dog with a bone …

She'd felt a flush of shame when she read it. He was so good. Here she was, trying to avoid him, and he was just trying to make her feel better. Thank goodness he'd been able to just laugh the whole thing off. Now maybe she should do the same.

'Rough night, huh?' she commented, trying to make her voice sound casual, easy, the way it used to be between them.

'I honestly thought the morning would never come. I can't believe it. Kennedy of all people. We both know what he's like but honestly I thought he was so bloody stubborn he'd end up outlasting the lot of us. Josie said he collapsed in a chipper. Obviously his bad habits caught up with him.'

It was exactly what Reilly had been thinking.

They quickly waylaid a nearby nurse to find out the location of Kennedy's room and both swept through the doors.

'Bloody hell,' he admonished. 'A man might need a private moment or something. Fat chance of that with you two around.'

Reilly could have cried with joy to hear him speak like that. He was still the same. A little gray, maybe, but sitting up in bed like a king entertaining his subjects, Josie by his side.

'Yes,' his wife admonished. 'We've all been worried. You gave us a terrible fright. Now it's time for you to listen to me and give up that rubbish you insist on eating. I told you didn't?' She turned to Reilly and Chris. 'He was in the chipper when he collapsed. Imagine that?'

'Now love,' said Kennedy, rolling his eyes. 'They still don't know that it was a heart attack. They're running tests.'

'What else would it have been? No, from now on it'll be steamed veg and skinless chicken for dinner.'

'I might as well be dead, then,' her husband moaned. 'Would you be a pet and go and get these two a cup of coffee? They look worse than I do.'

'Secret police business, I presume,' Josie said shaking her head indulgently. 'Yes, I'll leave you in peace for a bit. As long as you promise not to slip him any doughnuts or anything.'

They promised, and Reilly thought for a second that Josie might make them turn out their pockets. She would have made a good cop.

When she was gone, she turned to Kennedy. 'We were so worried,' she said. 'Thank goodness you're OK.'

'You should never have gone out alone,' said Chris. 'I told you I'd come with you.'

'Blah, blah, blah' said Kennedy. 'Save it for my funeral, kids. I need you to do something.'

'Of course,' said Reilly. 'But you shouldn't be thinking about work right now.'

'This was no accident—seriously' said Kennedy. 'My car's still on Sheriff Street with any luck. Here's my keys. I want you to get the remains of the burger and have Julius run his fancy tests on it. Mark my words, something will come back funny.'

19

'WHAT DO YOU RECKON?' SAID Chris, as he drove them both to collect Kennedy's car.

'Seems a bit far-fetched,' said Reilly. 'But we have to check. Maybe he's just embarrassed. It's a big thing for a guy like Kennedy to feel vulnerable. He probably just wants there to be another reason for this, other than his health and age.'

'Maybe you're right,' said Chris. 'I'd probably feel the same. He seemed pretty certain it wasn't a heart attack, but then again he's got nothing to compare it to, has he?'

By some kind of miracle, Kennedy's car was still where he left it. Not exactly *as* he left it though. It was up on bricks, the four tires removed.

'No surprise there,' said Chris. 'You can't drop your trousers in this part of town without them getting stolen.'

Reilly bit back a smile. 'Speaking from personal experience then?'

He chuckled, realizing how it must have sounded. Then he unlocked Kennedy's door, and sure enough, there was the burger, with a single neat bite taken out of it.

Reilly put it into a specimen bag, ready to go to the lab.

'Better get someone to come and get the car before it gets impounded,' Chris said. 'But right now, we're both late for work.'

In the car, they fell into the uneasy silence Reilly had been dreading. She bit her lip, and took a deep breath, deciding she might as well attack it head on. They were stuck in traffic. Neither of them could run away.

'I'm really sorry about … the other day, Chris. I was upset. I didn't mean…I didn't mean…anything,' she finished lamely.

He took a long time to reply and when he did he wouldn't meet her eyes; he kept looking straight ahead at the line of cars at the traffic lights in front of them.

'Just a mistake - of course.'

'Yes.' A huge weight was suddenly taken from her shoulders. He got it, he knew it was something crazy, a huge spur of the moment thing. It didn't mean anything to either of them. 'A huge mistake. A major mistake,' she mumbled, laughing nervously. 'So don't worry, we can just be normal with each other again. The usual, OK?'

'The usual,' Chris repeated, his tone giving nothing away. 'Of course. No worries.'

'Great,' said Reilly, feeling better than she had in days. 'Sounds perfect.'

Julius was running analysis on a burger that Reilly had practically shoved in his face first thing and told him to put before everything else. Not that he didn't have a million other things to do, but when the boss said jump…

He pulled apart the separate pieces of the burger, and extracted a small piece of the beef. It smelt rank. He didn't know how people ate this stuff. Julius had recently converted to vegetarianism and had never looked back.

He ran the morsel of beef through a simple solution that tested for poisons. It only picked up common substances, so if he didn't find anything, he would have to do more intensive analysis. He did the same with the cheese and the bread. Then he turned to the mushroom, and took a closer look at that. Holy hell, he thought immediately taken aback. This was no run of the mill Portobello. Where exactly had this burger come from?

All the tell-tale signs were there. The flesh of the cap was pink not white, and the cap itself was not curved and smooth, but bulbous and blemished. He was about to put a call through to Reilly when Gary came in.

'Man, did you hear the news about Pete Kennedy? Guy almost died yesterday. Heart attack while he was eating a cheeseburger apparently. Not so much Batman but Elvis.' He chuckled at his own joke.

'Well, if happened to be this burger,' Julius replied, his tone grave, 'it was no heart attack.'

Poor little fat man. He took it so trustingly, like a child. Only thinking of his own pleasure.

It was so easy. All I did was walk into the place, and tell them I was picking up my uncle's order, and they just handed it over. Such sloppiness. I slipped in the prize ingredient, wrapped the thing back up and knocked at the guy's window. It was such a temptation to wait around and watch him gasp for air, stuck in his car like a thrashing fish. But I couldn't do that.

Such a pleasure to know that the cops are running around, dealing with my chaos, while I calmly prepare for tonight. Chopping, slicing, marinading.

Just because it will be her last meal doesn't mean that I can afford to be lax. It should be perfect. She should die in a paroxysm of pleasure, only realizing at the last moment that the air is receding, that the edges of her vision are going black.

Tonight will be perfect. No distractions, everything perfectly prepared. I have become good at this and I can only get better.

Good isn't good enough, *she used to say to me.* You have to do better.

If only she could see me now, top of my game in all respects. I wonder does she think of me? Wonder what happened to the weakling she used to know. I think of her. I'm closing in on her.

Soon I'll know what became of her repulsive life after I left it.

20

'BUT HOW WOULD SOMEONE GET the mushroom into the burger?' Chris asked Reilly. 'Wouldn't the restaurant have delivered the food to the right customer?'

'Well,' interjected Julius. 'I know the place. Restaurant is maybe too strong of a word for it. It's a rat infested shithole, basically. I don't think they would care who the food was delivered to, as long as they got their money.'

'So,' said Reilly. 'It's not a stretch to think that someone, maybe McMurty, maybe someone else, collected Kennedy's burger, shoved a toxic mushroom in it and delivered it to him?'

'We need to talk to Kennedy again,' said Chris. 'See if there was anything odd about the delivery. For all we know, the restaurant might just be so bad they don't know their poisonous mushrooms from their button cups, or what have you.'

Chris's phone rang and he turned away to answer it. Reilly continued to talk to Julius. 'I want you to test the oil used to cook the mushroom and compare it to the one used to cook the meat,' she said. 'We need to find out if they were prepared separately.'

'That would be extremely difficult,' said Julius. 'It'll be cross-contaminated once they're put together.'

'Just try it,' she insisted. 'You're the best in the business. I know you'll find a way.'

Chris ended his call and turned back to her. 'The guy Kennedy was watching, Harry McMurty? He's just been found dead.'

When Reilly and Chris pulled up to the apartment block not far from Sheriff Street, they could see police cars around the entrance. Residents milled about too, looking intrigued and slightly disturbed.

'Delaney.' A tall, sandy haired man waved at them from behind the police cordon. 'Over here.'

'Reilly, this is James Costello from the Narc Unit. Not sure if you've met.'

'From Chris's days down with us lowly bunch,' the man finished. 'Looks like we've got a suicide here, mate, but I called you in because it could be related to that murder case.'

'Which one?' said Chris. 'The Armstrong girl?'

'That's the one,' said Peter. 'Come on up.'

The elevators in Harry McMurty's building smelt of spilt liquor, vomit and urine. Her nose was able to pinpoint each one with deadly precision and it was all Reilly could do to keep from throwing up.

'Almost there,' said Chris, looking sideways at her. He understood that her sense of smell could be both curse and gift.

McMurty's apartment was small and dim, much the same as Rose Cooper's. It was a single room, with a bed that pulled down from the wall. The windows were not clear glass, but instead they were a kind of foggy fiberglass material. There was no view to be had, and with the lights off, only a dim and murky light filtered through.

'Here you have it,' said Costello. 'A suicide note.' He picked up a single sheet of paper that was bagged and put back in its original position. The note was badly written, in a cramped and ugly script. It read:

'I did them murders. The girl Jennifer Armstrong and the other one Cooper. I hate women, those slags. I fed them poison and pills in their food. Killed the cop too."

After that, the note slid into incomprehensible scribbles. Chris and Reilly looked at each other. 'Not exactly Shakespeare, was he?' said Chris.

'We need to find out what his reading and writing level was,' said Reilly. 'It looks like he could be semi-illiterate.'

The corpse of Harry McMurty was slouched over the little formica table like a man gone to sleep at dinner. He was clutching his stomach. Reilly didn't want to look too closely until she had scoped out the rest of the room.

The walls were mostly bare, apart from a few pictures of Harry with different groups of people, male and female. Holiday shots, by the look of them. Young kids having fun in the sun. McMurty was always at the centre of the action, with the prettiest girl on his arm. Reilly recognized Rose Cooper in one of them, her hand held under her chin like a starlet, her red lips pursed in a kiss. The last picture Reilly had seen of her, she had been a dead, sold corpse. If only she could reach back through time and warn her: Get out of there.

The carpets stank. Dirt and filth had been ground into them. Cigarette burns littered the floor like gun casings.

The bathroom was full of beauty products. Moisturizers, hair oils, cleansers, toners, concealer. The guy had more products that Reilly did, that was certain. McMurty may not have cared about what his apartment looked like, but he sure cared about his looks. Reilly guessed he probably stole these from the girls he was with. They were high end products, a lot of them.

'We already did a quick sweep of the bed,' she could hear Costello saying to Chris. 'It looked as though he hadn't washed his sheets in years. We found a stash of meth in the bathroom, and pills under the bed. He was a known dealer, but small time. We were watching him, seeing if he would lead us anywhere big.'

'Did the neighbors hear anything last night?'

'Haven't talked to them yet. People here are pretty loathe to talk to cops. Plus, what would they hear from a suicide? The guy crying or something?'

Reilly sighed. It was this kind of sloppiness that led to things being missed.

'Let's call in our guys,' she said, coming out of the bathroom. 'I want them to tag and bag this place.'

Half an hour later, Lucy and Gary were at the flat, going over everything with a fine toothed comb. 'We're lucky those narc cops didn't completely trash the scene,' Reilly commented.

'We're lucky those narc cops called us,' Chris pointed out. 'And you're going to have some explaining to do to the chief about why the GFU are here, cleaning up a suicide.'

She looked at him speculatively. 'You can tell me that you're one hundred percent sure that this was suicide?'

'I'm not,' said Chris. 'I'm not as convinced as you are, that's all. But it's not me that you have to convince.'

'Leave O'Brien to me,' said Reilly. She leaned over the body of Harry McMurty, trying to get a glimpse of his face, which was curled into the shadow of his chest. She saw something glinting in his dark hair. Taking a cotton bud, she dragged it over his scalp, then raised it to her eye and saw that it was a tiny speck of red glitter. It was present all through the hair. 'Look,' she said, 'he's got glitter in his hair. So he goes to a party, then comes home and just kills himself?'

'Stranger things have happened,' said Gary, who was dusting the floors and surfaces for prints.

Reilly crouched down again and studied the dead man's prone form. Karen Thompson would do an autopsy, of course, but Reilly wanted to know if the body could tell her anything from the outset. A bottle of pills lay prone on the table. The suspected suicide weapon.

As she looked at the creamy smoothness of Harry McMurty's skin, Reilly noticed something at his temple. A redness, an indentation.

'Lucy,' she called. 'Get the camera.'

She lifted Harry's glossy hair while Lucy took some close ups of the marks.

The forensic sweep of Harry McMurty's flat was taking a long time. Chris, who was supposed to be concentrating, found himself distracted by Reilly. She was completely focused of course, going over the scene like it had something urgent to tell her, something that was just for her.

And it did. She had found something.

Last night, when he got the news about Kennedy, Chris had felt his whole world tilt on its side. He took Kennedy and his partner's solidness, his humor and his reliability for granted. More than ever, he had wanted someone by his side to share his distress with, and the only person he could think of was Reilly.

Since her return they had been growing closer, he knew it. He had always liked how tough she was, how smart, how you could joke around so easily with her.

For a long time he had told himself that he simply admired and respected her, and that was it. But when she was away in Florida, he found that he had missed her. He missed their daily banter, the little glances they exchanged when they had both zeroed in on a clue or inconsistency in a case. Pete Kennedy had a heart of gold, but catching his eye didn't give Chris quite the same thrill.

When Reilly came back, he had cautioned himself not to be over eager. But he found that she seemed a little more open now, almost as if she was allowing him to get closer. Something had happened in Florida. He wasn't sure exactly what, but he liked the effect it had.

And then the other day … Whatever part of Chris that had still been trying to be careful, to hold something back, had been completely overwhelmed by that kiss.

But then she had pulled back. He had been more disappointed than he cared to admit when she'd called it a "major mistake." She had laughed about it, as if the mere thought of being with him was hilarious. Well, he would back off. He had never been in the habit of chasing women. If Reilly wanted to be friends, then he would be friendly.

Now, she was on her hands and knees taking hair samples out of the carpet with Lucy. He didn't envy them. That carpet was beyond the pale.

Gary began spraying some of the hard surfaces with luminol. The chemiluminesence was visible to Chris from across the room. He had closed the curtains, so the rest of them stopped the work they were doing and watched instead. There were some smears on the wall next to the bathroom. 'Ugh,' said Gary. 'Ten points for guessing what that is.'

'Blood surely?' said one of the narc cops standing nearby.

'Well, my friend, you could be right. I would hope, actually, that you are. But luminol will show the presence of faecal matter in exactly the same way that it shows blood. From the placement and the patterning of this, I'm picking the former.'

'That is so disgusting, Gary,' said Lucy. 'No need to be so graphic.'

'Man's just trying to learn something,' muttered Gary and Chris felt sorry for him. It seemed as though he and

Gary were in the same position: pining after women who didn't want them.

'But this,' Gary continued, pointing to the countertop. 'This is definitely blood. Or at least the sign of someone trying to clean up some.' He turned to the other cop. 'Luminol also reacts with bleach. So if someone has tried to clean this surface of blood, that could be what's showing up.'

Chris shook his head indulgently, wondering why all forensic investigators felt the need to show off their encyclopedic knowledge.

'Looks like there's been an accident in this spot for sure,' said Reilly, examining the area that Gary had indicated. 'But I imagine that lots of bad things happened here. Whatever the victim was, he was no saint.'

They were at the crime scene until late in the evening. McMurty's body was removed and taken to the city mortuary. The team packed up the hundreds of trace samples they had collected for analysis. The fingerprinting alone would take days. Hundreds of people had probably come through this flat, and all of them had left behind a tiny piece of evidence. It would be a difficult scene to wade through for that very reason. There was too much trace. It was like swimming through a cloudy pool, with millions of pieces of debris floating around you. Hard to know what to concentrate on.

21

CHRIS CHECKED IN ON KENNEDY on his way home. He was feeling much better, but still a little sleepy.

'I'll be back on the job in no time,' he said.

Chris filled him in on the events of the past few hours: the results from the mushroom, and Harry McMurty's supposed death by suicide.

Kennedy shook his head. 'I knew there was something off about that delivery guy,' he said. 'I should have listened to my gut.' He laughed. 'Actually, I was listening to my gut. And it told me to eat.'

Chris frowned. 'What was wrong with the guy who delivered the food?'

'He wasn't in uniform. Just normal day to day clothes. The stuff before I passed out is a little blurry, but I remember thinking it was weird.'

'Do you remember his face?'

'Not particularly. But I do remember noticing that his feet squeaked on the wet path as he walked off, like he was wearing something with plastic soles, runners or something.'

'Let me know if you think of anything else. I'll come and see you tomorrow.'

'I'm being discharged in the morning,' said Kennedy. 'But wait, why does this matter? Sure Harry's the guy isn't he? He just got one of his lackeys to deliver me the burger. And you said he wrote a confession.'

'Reilly's not convinced about the suicide and to tell you the truth, I'm not either. There's definitely something off about it, the note in particular.'

'For football sake,' said Kennedy. 'Just when a man thinks it's safe to come back to work ….

Funny how your whole world can fall apart in just a few hours.

Last night, still feeling the high from getting rid of the cop and Harry, I'm preparing a delectable meal, when the latest subject texts and says she has to postpone until Thursday. But the time is perfect now! What can I say, except: fine, see you then

After scraping the food into the bin, wasting weeks of labor and skill, I went back to my laptop. Perhaps I could line up another subject, someone a bit easier. Ah. There was the email I had been waiting for from the man I had hired to seek out my past.

Ruth Dell, *it said*. Born in Birmingham, England in 1949. Educated at Oxford University. Became a professor and expert in isolated tribes. Published nine non-fiction books on the subject, widely respected.

Sister died when Ruth was 25. Boy was four when he was adopted by his aunt. He was –

Blah, blah, blah. Yes, I knew this bit, only too well.

Nephew ran away at age 16 (*ran away? That's hardly what happened. Maybe that's the story she liked to give out. It sounds better than: 'I threw him out onto the street without a penny.'*)

A few years later, Ruth had a child of her own, and gave birth at age 42. The child a girl is named Constance Dell. She is now 25 years old.

Of all the futures I imagined for my rotten aunt, the aunt who neglected, abused and abandoned me, this was not it. A child? Why would she want a child when she so hated the one that was thrust upon her? I was a helpless little boy and she despised me from the beginning. This woman, this awful bully, has a child?

Everything has changed. Wherever this child is, whatever she is doing, I will seek her out. She doesn't deserve the love and security that I was denied.

Despite having spent most of the evening at the lab sorting through the evidence from Harry McMurty's disgusting flat, Reilly couldn't relax when she got home in the late hours of the evening. So she went for a run instead.

She waited for herself to settle into the familiar, semi-meditative state that running usually gave her. She wanted that rush of endorphins, followed by the relief and release from tension that came after. But it didn't come. She tried pushing herself harder and harder, her knees pumping like pistons, her breath coming in hard, short gasps. But she couldn't keep it up. She ended up bent over her own knees, wondering what she was pushing herself so hard for. What was she trying to run from?

The following morning, after managing to eventually grab a few hours sleep, she was back at work. Karen Thompson had called her that morning to let her know that she would be able to autopsy McMurty first thing, and Reilly was going down there to oversee.

Like Chris had pointed out yesterday, Inspector O'Brien would no doubt have a fit over the GFU's involvement in a deemed suicide, and she wanted to head the chief's annoyance off at the pass by finding out for sure if her and Chris's suspicions of foul play were correct. The autopsy should determine that.

'So, what have we got?' she asked Karen when she entered the autopsy suite at the city morgue.

'Good morning to you too,' the ME replied.

'Sorry. I've had such a weird week I've forgotten basic manners.'

Karen chuckled softly. 'And here I was thinking it was just an American thing.'

'Nah,' said Reilly. 'Generally, we're a genial bunch.'

'You are looking a little peaked though,' the other woman commented. 'Are you coming down with something?'

Reilly looked at her colleague, so calm, concern showing on her graceful features. For a second she wished she could confide in Karen; about her worries about the Armstrong case, concern about Lucy and her missing sister, about Chris. But she couldn't do that. She couldn't allow her mask of professionalism to slip.

'Oh, I'm still getting over the jet lag is all,' said Reilly. 'Haven't been able to find enough time to catch up on sleep since I got back.'

'Shall we begin then?' said Dr Thompson. 'I heard about Pete Kennedy. I must say, the man gets up my nose sometimes, but I will be glad to see him back on his feet soon.'

Once again, Reilly donned a mask and nose plugs while Karen stood by with a slightly sardonic smile.

'I always say that death is the most natural smell in the world,' the doctor said. 'Like a compost heap.'

In Reilly's experience, it always smelt more like an abattoir, but she didn't say anything.

'This body was delivered as a possible homicide/suicide,' said Karen. 'It didn't take me long to confirm my verdict. This man, 27 years old, appeared to be a mixed bag of health. On the one hand, his body was in good shape. Very little fat, good muscle condition, slight impacting of the fibula, as is common when engaging in high-impact exercise, jogging in particular.'

Reilly's ears plucked up at this, remembering how she and Julius had hypothesized that the unsub had worn latex, possibly as exercise clothing.

'However,' said Karen. 'The corpse shows the kind of deterioration that is endemic to drug users. His teeth are in an advanced state of decay. The capillaries of the nose and the nasal passages are damaged from the abuse of cocaine, and his eyes are bloodshot, the corneas flat. He had two drugs in his system at the time: Benzedrine, a known "upper", meth, or "ice" as it is commonly known, and Lorazepam, a common sleeping agent.'

She paused, and gently turned over Harry McMurty's arms to show the light scarring there. 'He was once a user of heroin,' she said. 'But my guess is that his use of methamphetamine was more recent, as well as more prevalent.' She traced a finger along the finely detailed feathers of the eagle on Harry's arm. 'His last meal was duck,' she said. 'Baguette. Not exactly synonymous with the other symptoms of poverty I have found on his person.'

'What killed him?' Reilly asked.

'Lorazepam,' she said. 'I understand there was a bottle found at the scene?'

'That's right.'

'Interestingly enough, the content of his stomach was clean of any pills. Not a trace. But it was definitely pills that you found?'

'Still half full,' said Reilly. 'I can get them if you want to analyze.'

Karen waved a hand. 'No need. I began to scour his arms, and sure enough, I found a recent puncture from a needle. See here,' she said, holding a microscope over Harry's arm, 'these are all old. The skin has worked its way back over and left the pink worms of scarring. But this one is fresh. Tiny, but unmistakable. I'm running bloods to make sure, but my guess is that he was injected with liquid Lorazepam, which is commonly used for those who are unable to swallow pills.'

'So it was a foul play, then?' asked Lucy.

'I would say so,' said Karen. 'But that's not the strongest piece of evidence. The photos you took of those indentations around the left temple?'

'Yes?'

'Well, those marks were still clear when I examined the body. Someone had pressed something very hard to the victim's temple, for an extended period of time. I analyzed the residue left at the temple, and found it to be microscopic flakes of metal. My guess is that a gun had been held to the victim's head.'

Bingo. It had been what Reilly had suspected when she saw the marks, but she hadn't wanted to give too much away at the time. It was obvious now, that McMurty had been murdered.

But an hour later, in Inspector O'Brien's office, she had a hard time convincing the chief of the same thing.

'It's cut and dried sir,' she argued. 'The ME herself has confirmed that the man was murdered.'

'Maybe he was, Steel. But we've got a written confession for Armstrong and Copper. We've got the narc unit who found the body leaking the note to the press. As far as the world is concerned, this case is over and done with.'

'But it's not.' She dropped her voice to a whisper. 'Armstrong and Cooper's killer is still out there.'

'You don't know that. One of his criminal associates might have cottoned on to what he was doing, forced him to confess and then killed him. Just because he was murdered doesn't mean he was innocent.'

'I know that,' she said. 'But he was innocent of those crimes, I'm sure of it.'

'The murder investigations are closed, Steel,' O'Brien told her. 'Unless something new comes to light, this is over.'

22

THE REPORT HAD THE BARE bones of my aunt's history, but it left out a few salient details.

My mother died when I was four. I had never known my father, but it didn't matter. My mother was everything I needed. She created a world for us both, a world that kept me safe. Each day she would have planned special things for us to do, things that would make me feel loved. We went swimming. We went to the museum, or the park, or the movies. We were poor, but it didn't matter. Had she lived, I would be a different kind of man. Blinder to the evil in the world, but happier.

When she died, I did not know what had happened. I stayed in the house with her for three days, trying to wake her up. I fed her, tried to make her drink. I shouted in her ear, pulled at her eyelids. Eventually the smell, and my crying, alerted the neighbours. Before I even knew what was happening, I was being shipped to Oxford.

My aunt lived in lecturer's accommodation at the university. Not suitable for a child, I felt caged and in the way.

"Don't you touch that," she barked constantly. "Stay away from me while I'm working. Stop making that godawful noise." Sometimes she would place her hands over her ears and scream. She couldn't stand the sound of my voice, couldn't bear to hear me singing the songs my mother had taught me.

It didn't get better when I started school. I was away from my aunt more, and I thought she would be happy to have peace and quiet. But when I got home she would make me stand against the wall and recite what I had learnt that day. I was made to stay there until I got everything completely right. "You can't be as stupid as your mother," *she said.* "I won't have a dummy in my house."

I became withdrawn, scared of the slightest movement. I should have detested her, but I was constantly trying to make her love me, constantly clinging to her leg, begging for her to notice me. Sometimes the power of her hatred for me would surprise us both. One day, when I reached out to stroke her arm, she pushed me so hard that I fell against the window. It cracked. Had it shattered, I would have fallen to my death. She told me: "You must stay out of my way. I can't be trusted around you. You disgust me. You are repulsive."

We carried on in this sickening manner until my teens. I began to fight back then, in small ways. Embarrassing her around visitors by walking around naked, messing up her notes, stealing her money. I thought it was fair game for all the hell she had put me through.

On my sixteenth birthday, I got home from school to find the doors locked. The house was completely shut up.

There was a note for me in the letterbox. "I've done my duty. Never come here again. Never contact me."

I put myself through cooking school. I became the best chef in London. I never contacted her again, but I feel sure she has seen my name. They have profiled me in all the best papers, have complimented my "vision," my "fierce determination". If only they knew what my vision really was.

My aunt was a woman who could not see past her own importance. She thought her career was the only thing that was worth anything. She gave everything she had to her work and gave me nothing. I wonder how she feels when she thinks of me. Guilt? Shame? Regret? But she doesn't have to think of me. She doesn't have to wonder how I am, because she has erased me. She went and gave someone else the life that should have been mine. And now I'm going to take it all away.

Everything else has merely been practice for this.

The day before Kennedy was due to return to work, Chris and Reilly finally made it to Hammer and Tongs.

In his partner's absence, he'd asked her to come along for the interview with the restaurant owner he and Kennedy had missed last time. While it seemed they had their man, Chris wanted to be sure of tying up all loose ends when it came to Jennifer Armstrong's death.

Nico Peroni greeted them both with a warm handshake. He didn't raise his eyebrows at Reilly, the way some people did when greeted by female law enforcement and she warmed to him immediately.

'I'm sorry that we have to meet under such circumstances,' said Nico. 'I hope that you will be able to dine here again, for a more suitable occasion.'

'Thank you,' said Reilly, although the cavernous feeling of Hammer and Tongs wasn't exactly to her taste. 'How long has the restaurant been open?'

'Eighteen months,' said Nico. 'I went into business with Tony Ellis. I'm sure you've heard of him. Not to everyone's taste, but he is doing some ground-breaking things with food.'

'Is he here now?'

'Tony has other restaurants in London and he's not always on site. He designs the menu and cooks for important events, but I am the chef de cuisine. He has the vision.'

'And the restaurant is doing well?'

Nico gave a small but satisfied smile. 'It is doing very well, yes.'

The waitress delivered them three small, steaming coffees, with a shard of biscotti on the side.

'Which of you hired Harry McMurty?' asked Chris.

'It was my mistake, I am sorry to say,' said Nico. 'Tony does not usually take part in hiring staff and the like.'

'Can you tell us what you know about Harry? His personality, anything strange you noticed about him? Basically, everything you remember.'

'Of course,' said Nico. 'I just want to say that I feel very saddened about all this. I feel that in hiring Harry, I may have given him access to connections he might not otherwise have had.'

'We find that these kinds of people are usually very determined,' said Chris. 'He would have found a way, with or without any assistance provided to him. He could be very charming, we've learned.'

'Yes,' said Nico. 'He was very charming, when he wanted to be. But let me start at the beginning.' He took a sip of his coffee, smiled ruefully and began.

'We had just started the restaurant when Harry approached me. He was working somewhere else, but after an incident with a colleague …' here he shook his head slightly, 'he said he felt too traumatized to work there any longer. He said he wanted to be a chef, that he had a passion for fine cuisine, but that he could not afford to put himself through school. He just wanted to be a part of a successful restaurant in any way possible.'

'And so you hired him?'

'I did more than hire him, I'm afraid,' said Nico. 'In a way, I began to mentor him. What I saw was a determined but disadvantaged young man. I knew he could only read and write enough to figure out the menu, but he was very good with clientele. He knew how to make them laugh, how to incite them to be adventurous. He did out here what Tony and I do in the kitchen. He wowed, he impressed.'

'Often common traits in psychopaths,' Reilly commented.

'Yes,' he said. 'I soon began to see that all was not well. I tried to teach him things in the kitchen, and he was a very good cook, but impatient with himself and others. I saw him strike a kitchen hand. I knew that he had problems with the waitresses. I had them quitting left, right and centre. They would fall in love with him and he would treat them badly. I knew that he took drugs, but not to what extent. You must understand,' he looked at them pleadingly, 'it is common for the kids to take drugs in this business. They not only want to do their jobs, they want to do them and then go out dancing until dawn. It is different for an old man like me. Those days are done. I want to do my job and go home and put my feet up.'

'We understand,' Chris told him. 'And that's not why we're here.'

'But it was different with Harry. I realized that he was selling young waitresses hard drugs, and also that he was dealing to some of our customers. He had personal relationships with some of our clientele. If I may speak openly, it was another way to make money for him, to provide companionship to older, rich women.'

He sighed, held his hands out in a gesture of exasperation. 'What can I say? I had been very foolish. I began to see that. Tony wanted him gone, he said he was drawing negative attention to the restaurant and he was right. I was on the cusp of firing him when this happened. I wish I had done it sooner.'

'It wouldn't have made a difference,' said Reilly. 'None of it is your fault. Can you tell us how much access he had to the kitchen?'

'Unlimited, really. The staff are often here earlier than we, and later, cleaning up and doing prep. I trusted him to begin with, simply because he was so driven. Later, when it was clear that he was unhinged, I did not know how to rescind that trust without making him unbalanced.'

'And your use of antimine, or the Joker Fruit?' asked Chris. 'Can you tell us more about that?'

Nico sighed. 'It was something we did when we first opened, to make a splash. Now everyone does it, so we don't do it any longer. But yes, we used it to begin with. Tony prepared it, or I did, under his supervision. I am sorry to say that Harry was present at some of those times. He was intrigued by the fruit, very interested in the method of preparation.'

'Ok,' Chris said, having heard this before from Gemma Collins, the other chef. 'Thank you very much. You've given us some good background.'

They got up and shook hands once more and Reilly noticed Nico wince as he rose. 'Injury?' she asked.

'You could say that,' he answered. 'I cycle—long distance. Just finished a long ride at the weekend.'

Something clicked in her brain. 'All that spandex,' she said. 'Pretty unforgiving uniform.'

He laughed. 'Absolutely. Comfortable though.'

She scanned his left hand. No ring. 'And your girlfriend? She doesn't mind you spending so much time away on weekends?'

Nico laughed again, and reddened slightly. 'No girlfriend,' he said. 'I haven't met the right person. Unsociable hours. I'm sure you know the feeling well.'

'We do,' said Chris. 'Thank you for your time.'

Back in the car, he asked: 'So, what do you think?'

'I think we need to take a very close look at Mr Peroni. Preparation of antimine: check. Knows a lot of women who like fine food: check. Spandex: check. Handsome, youngish, single. And easily able to get close enough to Harry McMurty to kill him.'

23

LUCY HAD HER SECOND HYPNOTHERAPY appointment that afternoon.

'I'm really nervous,' she confided to Gary, over lunch. 'More nervous than last time. Because now I'm pretty certain there's definitely something there. And I'm afraid of it.'

'You're amazing,' said Gary. 'Seriously, you're being so brave.'

'Not as brave as Reilly,' said Lucy. 'My dad tore strips off her the other day. There was something else as well that he was angry about, but she won't tell me what. She doesn't want anything about Grace's case to compromise my therapy. Apparently the mind is really easy to influence. Like, if she tells me she's looking into something, my mind might spontaneously create memories based on that.'

'So no matter what you remember, it probably won't be admissible?'

Lucy took a bite of her sandwich, chewed and swallowed and shook her head. 'No. not in a court. But Reilly wants to see if I know anything that will lead somewhere.'

They were silent for a moment as they ate. Then Lucy said: 'You know, I sort of hope that I don't know anything. Because that means that I've been hiding it all this time, when maybe we could have found Grace. And if she suffered more because of me … then I just won't be able to live with myself.'

'It's not your fault, Luce. Just keep talking about it. And know that I'm here, any time of day or night. You need someone to talk to too.' He blushed. 'I know I'm…a bit full on. But seriously, I come in friendship only. Anything else is your call.'

Lucy nodded. It was a strange declaration to make in the middle of the work cafe with sandwiches and potato salad sitting between them, but she felt its sincerity.

'Thanks,' she said. 'That means something. Really.'

At the therapist's office, the same feeling of weariness and complete surrender overcame Lucy once more. She seemed to float on a sea made entirely of herself, made of her memories. She was carried in the river of her own past. But no matter what, she couldn't take those memories back with her. When she awoke, all her anxieties and thoughts rushed in once again.

'Did something happen?' she asked. 'Did you start yet?'

'We're finished,' said the therapist. 'You were great. How do you feel?'

'I feel fine,' said Lucy. 'A little tired.'

'Yes,' said the therapist. 'Like last time, you must rest. You must not drink or take any drugs, or over-excite yourself.'

'OK,' said Lucy. She blushed. Last time, she had gone out after her session and gone drinking with Gary until the wee hours of the morning. Maybe she should have hypnotherapy to find out how she felt about Gary. Because she didn't seem to be able to tell simply by thinking about him.

As arranged she dropped the audio transcript off to Reilly at her flat. Her boss had told her there was no way she could keep working on Grace's case during work time, not if she wanted to keep her job. Lucy felt bad that she was making her work additional hours, but her desire to find out what happened to Grace was stronger. Anything was worth it now, she knew that.

She hadn't been inside the flat before. Reilly greeted her at the door, dressed in an ankle length green dress. It was unlike anything she ever wore to work and she looked completely stunning. Lucy couldn't help but be envious of Reilly's figure. She was slender, but rounded in all the right places, whereas Lucy was round everywhere. 'You look amazing,' she said. 'Are you going out somewhere?'

'Oh. No,' said Reilly, smiling. 'This is just something I throw on at home. But I was thinking you could stay for dinner if you like. I made fish tacos with salsa verde.'

'Sounds amazing,' said Lucy. 'Hypnotherapy gives me a huge appetite.'

As they sat down to eat the tacos, a wave of nausea washed over Reilly. She pushed her plate away. 'I've been feeling a bit off lately,' she explained. 'Stomach bug or something.'

'Maybe you should go to the doctor?'

Reilly smiled. 'That's what everyone is saying, but I swear I'm fine. Just tired, I think.'

'It's been a rough couple of weeks. What's going to happen with the Armstrong case now?'

Reilly sighed and took a sip of her water. 'Well, Inspector O'Brien thinks we have our man but I'm worried we haven't heard the last from The Chef.'

'The Chef?'

'That's what I've dubbed the unsub. I'm pretty sure the guy is a chef. So much of the evidence points that way. The quality kitchenware, knowledge of food, precision and attention to detail …'

They ate the rest of the meal without talking about work. Lucy confided in Reilly about her confused feelings about Gary.

'I mean, I do like him. I'm just not sure if it's any more than just a friend.'

'Well,' said Reilly. 'It's a tricky situation. But I think that you shouldn't jump into anything if you feel at all ambivalent. There's a lot at stake. It could make your working environment really unpleasant.'

When she left, Lucy felt a little embarrassed at having talked to Reilly about this kind of thing. Reilly herself was so professional, kept her own cards so close to the chest. She would never do a thing like that.

She shouldn't really be blabbering to her boss about her relationship worries. It was enough already that Reilly was listening in on recordings of Lucy's deepest, darkest secrets.

24

WHAT PERFECT SYNCHRONICITY, THAT THE day I plan to kill another victim is the day I should run into the people who have been so awful at catching me.

How wonderful, that they haven't given up completely. I have the woman pegged for exactly what she is. Blindly dedicated to her work, thinking that she makes a difference. I've got news for her: you have made no difference. More will die, and there's nothing you can do.

They would make a nice pair, those two. Beautiful children. But she won't relinquish her clammy grasp on success. Their blindness to me was so complete that it made me feel bold. As though I could go up to them and say: I am the one, and there would be nothing they could do to touch me.

I've been keeping very busy. I have gathered information on Constance Dell. Because of the prevalence of that stupid invention, Facebook, I have found out a lot about my little cousin. Surprise, surprise, a love of long distance running runs in the family. Pun intended. Little Connie has joined a running group.

As a rule, I hate those things. I prefer to run alone, with my thoughts, but in this case I will make an exception. She is very active on the group's page, asking newbie questions and so on. Who better to mentor her than someone who has years of experience? Who better to tell her exactly how she can learn the discipline, the dedication of such a craft? Although, I suspect from her soft upbringing that she doesn't have the same drive that I do, the same capacity for self-punishment. Her profile is full of pictures of her and her witch mother enjoying holidays, Christmas, shopping trips. Sadly, all to soon come to an end.

I prepare for tonight with much anticipation. I imagine that the girl prepares in the same way, moisturizing and scenting her skin, ridding her body of unsightly hair, of any excess.

She will be perfect for the night of her death. Make no mistake, there is something ritualistic in serving people food, even more so in preparing someone's last meal. In the same way, you would prepare a lamb for sacrifice.

I am looking forward to tonight, but it has taken on the feeling of a dress rehearsal. Constance is the main act, now.

After Lucy left, Reilly put the CD of her hypnotherapy session in the player. She would have rather done anything else, but she felt duty bound. She felt exhausted, and Lucy's confessions about Gary had only drained her further. They just served to remind her of her own confused feelings about Chris. She was glad that Kennedy would be back soon to act as a buffer between them.

The session started with the same routine as the time before, the therapist slowly lulling Lucy into a state of openness. Reilly almost felt that she was being pulled into sleep herself. She forced herself to focus.

'Are you afraid, Lucy?' The therapist began.

'Yes.'

'Why?'

Lucy sighed petulantly. 'I told you. Grace says that if I tell, they'll come after me too.'

'Who will come after you?'

'His brother.'

'Why would he come after you?'

'He is bad. Very bad. He did the thing to Grace.'

'What thing did he do to her?'

'You know,' she said. 'You know. Grace came home hurt. She said Darren hated it but he can't stop it. His brother is bad. He makes her do things.'

Oh God … Reilly stopped the recording. Her heart was pounding. The feeling was so strong she put a hand to her chest. She truly thought her heart might leap out. This was the kind of breakthrough everyone investigating the case had been hoping for for almost eighteen years, and it had slipped out of Lucy like a fish from water.

'Is your sister angry?'

'She's upset. She wants to run away with Darren. They love each other. He can't stop it. His brother does it to hurt him. Because he loves Grace. He isn't allowed to love her.'

'What does his brother do to Grace?'

'You know,' said Lucy. 'You know.'

Reilly switched off the recording then. She switched it off and put her head in her hands and cried.

She cried for poor fourteen year old Grace, for having gone through such a thing, Lucy, for having carried it for so many years, and even for Darren himself, who had tried and failed to escape his brother.

She felt, at that moment, that there was truly no end to the misery of the world.

When Chris's mobile rang at 11pm, he almost ignored it. He was halfway through a good book, an excellent glass of red wine by his side. But you can't ignore the call of duty. 'Hello?'

'Chris, it's me.'

'Reilly, what's wrong?'

'Can I come over?' she said. 'I need to see you.'

He didn't ask any questions. 'I'll pick you up, if you like.' he said. 'I'll be there soon.'

Reilly didn't look at him in the car and he didn't ask her what was wrong. But once she was standing in the middle of his living room, seemingly blind to her surroundings, she gave him such a naked look of need that it almost leveled him.

'Reilly…' he began.

'Please,' she said, placing her hands on his chest. 'Don't say anything.'

He took her in his arms and soon all words were forgotten.

It was like returning home after a long absence, Chris thought, like eating when you have been starving.

25

SUCH PERFECTION, THIS TIME. NO annoying phone calls, nothing left undone, or left behind. She was as beautiful as her pictures indicated, as ruthless as her conversations had suggested. Barely was I in the door before she told me what she wanted.

Cook for me, she said, and then feed me.

Gladly, I replied.

I took my time over the food, ensuring that the pork was cooked to perfection; that it would melt in the mouth like cotton candy. I mixed nightshade with the parsnip puree, then garnished the whole thing with those tiny, sweet flowers that are so absolutely deadly.

Why do you wear gloves when you cook, she asked. Don't you want to be close to the food?

I told her that it was an old habit, that it allowed me to work faster.

Will you take the gloves off when you touch me?

Of course, I lied.

And then I kneeled before her and gently placed each forkful in her mouth. It took her slowly, before she even knew it was happening. Her eyes became unfocused, the blood began to recede from her face, leaving it numb. Her tongue and jaw stopped working effectively. I had to scoop the last mouthful from her mouth lest she choked, making her death ugly and violent.

At the last moment she realized that something was wrong, and she looked up at me, pleading for something that I could not give, even if I wanted to.

Please, she tried to say, and I put my gloved hand up to her lips.

No, I said, don't talk.

As she was dying, unable to move, I went into her bedroom. I stood at the foot of the bed, looking down at the brightly pattered bedspread. I lay myself down on it carefully, and began to take in great gulps of her scent. I am searching for the smell of my mother and though I don't find it in the beds of these low women, I come close.

When I got up, I tidied everything away. I left the dish for them to find. I want them to know of my handiwork.

She had closed her eyes. There was nothing else that I could do for her.

I donned my backpack and ran home, running with power, with exhilaration.

When Reilly and Chris woke up together the next morning, there was no shyness or awkwardness between them. She felt completely at home, wrapped in a blanket, drinking the orange juice he had brought her.

'You know, we could just call in sick,' he suggested. 'The Armstrong case is wrapped up for the most part. And we could spend the day just...'

'Two problems,' she interjected lightly. 'We can't abandon Kennedy on his first day back, plus the gossip it would cause just isn't worth it.'

'You're probably right,' he said. 'I wish you weren't, but you are.'

She smiled. 'Aren't I always? Besides, I have a ton of work to do.' She felt a twinge at the thought of talking to Lucy. How would she even begin to impart such terrible news about what had likely happened to Grace? Whatever Lucy had suspected she was hiding from herself, it was nothing as awful as this.

Chris's phone rang and while he talked in the kitchen, Reilly dressed quickly. She would have to get him to drop her home so she could put some work clothes on. She didn't know where all this was headed.

She didn't want to think about it.

They hadn't slept together the night before, but it had been ... intense. Chris, gallant as ever, had put a stop to things before they got too heavy, protesting her vulnerability and state of mind over what she'd learned.

Instead, he had simply held her and listened while she talked, and eventually until she fell asleep.

She checked her phone for messages. A couple of missed calls and a ton of emails. One caught her eye immediately: Todd.

Hey, how are you doing? Just wanted to check in and see how you were since you got back to Dublin. We miss you over here.

Great timing, she thought. Just perfect. As if her life wasn't complicated enough. Of course, the message was completely innocuous, but it didn't do anything to lessen her confusion.

Chris came into the room as she was arranging her hair into a high knot, his mouth set in a firm line. 'You're right. Definitely no rest for us today - or the wicked,' he said jadedly. 'There's been another murder.'

26

NAOMI WORTHINGTON HAD BEEN A homeware designer on the cusp of major success, and her house looked like something straight out of a magazine. Unfortunately, it was now completely overrun by cops and GFU techs.

'Not a great start to my first day back,' said Kennedy. 'It seems as though whoever this guy was, it wasn't Harry McMurty.'

'As I tried, and failed, to convince O'Brien,' said Reilly, grimly. 'He'll listen now, but he'll also have a PR nightmare on his hands.'

Lucy and Gary were already at the scene. If Lucy noticed that Reilly was wearing the same casual dress as the night before, she didn't say anything. Reilly could only hope she would be too distracted by her own concerns to think too deeply about it.

She cleared everyone else from the room where the body was so that it was just herself, Chris, Kennedy and the forensic team. She didn't need a bunch of uniforms fumbling around.

'Gary, has anyone checked the bedroom yet?'

'Yeah, it was the first thing I did.'

'And?'

'Same thing as the others,' said Gary. 'That weird rumpling disturbance of the bedspread.'

'Photos?'

'Of course. I'm going over it for trace now, then we'll get Julius to work his magic on it.'

'Good. Anything else stand out?'

'It's a tidier job than last time,' said Kennedy. 'He did the bloody dishes, the cheeky bugger.'

'All but this one,' said Reilly. Putting on a mask, she knelt down to inspect the leftover meal. She wasn't going to make the same mistake this time.

It was half eaten. The meat was congealing in a white puree, small flowers were limp and drowned in the oily film that had formed since it was cooked. Through her mask, she could still smell the meat, and she thought she could detect a hint of decay, the rottenness that is at the heart of dead things. It took all her strength to hold back her nausea. It was just her imagination, she knew. The meat definitely couldn't be off yet, and there was no way the body had decomposed that fast.

'There's just a fork here,' she commented.

'We noticed some indentations in the carpet,' said Gary. 'It seems like someone was kneeling in front of her maybe?'

'OK, get pressings off the carpet and assess the distribution of weight.'

She took off her mask and tried to get a sense of the room. It was, and had been filled with other people since the murder, so that didn't help. There was the smell of cooking of course, and behind that a certain sharpness. Maybe sweat? It was hard to tell after so much time.

Added to everything else, the victim had favored placing little vanilla soy candles throughout the room and it was that smell, more than anything else, that was getting to Reilly.

'It's still so early,' she said. 'She lives alone. How was she discovered so early?'

'Her masseuse,' said Lucy. 'They keep a regular appointment at this hour. He has a key, and he came in to find her like this.'

'Did he touch the body?'

'Well, yeah. He thought she was just passed out.'

'Dammit. OK, I want you two back to the lab quick as you can to start processing whatever we have. Gary, I want you working overtime on the victim's phone, her laptop. Whatever. My guess is that she used the same dating sites as Jennifer Armstrong.'

'On it,' said Gary.

'Get the bedclothes and the food to Julius before it has time to break down any further.'

'This could be something,' said Kennedy from across the room. He held a small posy of flowers in his gloved hand. 'I'm not going to smell these, I know how lethal this guy's concoctions can be.'

'They're the same flowers that have been used to garnish the food,' said Reilly. 'My bet is that they're highly poisonous.'

'Right,' said Kennedy. 'Another thing for your guys, then.'

The others left, and Chris was outside talking to the masseuse who had been the first on the scene.

Reilly knelt down again to look at the body.

Naomi Worthington was a beautiful girl. According to her ID, she had just turned thirty; her pale skin was flawless and her hair was long and lustrous, untouched by dye. She was slim, but not thin. She wore a low cut red dress and a gold chain hung loosely from her neck. Her feet were bare and her toes were painted a bright green. The color reminded Reilly of the shimmering wings of an insect.

Suddenly she remembered something. The plate, before it had been taken away, had shown the direction of the fork as being away from Naomi. As if someone else had handled it.

It would have been incredibly awkward to feed herself from that angle, sitting where she was. Reilly couldn't be totally sure that her memory was being faithful, but she could check the photos later on if needs be. She was reasonably certain that someone had fed Naomi Worthington her final meal. The thought was a chilling one. To give yourself so trustingly to someone who wanted only to see you dead.

Chris came into the room and stood behind her.

'Did you get anything out of the masseuse?' she asked, without getting up.

'He's traumatized,' said Chris. 'He thought she was sleeping. He said he shook her, but he hasn't moved her from where she is.'

'Did you get a DNA sample for elimination? We need to exclude him from any samples we find here.'

'Of course.' He shrugged as if to say that her question was needless.

'Could he shed any light on the kind of person she was?'

'Like I said, he was traumatized. He just kept saying that she was "full of life", the usual. We can interview him later. You're going at this like a bat out of hell this morning. Slow down, you might miss something.'

'I know,' she said. 'I know I am. But we need to get this guy, Chris. Look at him, leaving little trophies around. I don't care about being careful anymore. I just want to get him.'

'Reilly. Being careful is what we do. You've told me a hundred times or more. Now, let's go over all this again, top to bottom.'

Chris had calmed her down, slightly, and she was able to spend the next few hours going over the scene, taking more samples, checking for foot impressions and fingerprints.

'I've got a couple of clear shoe prints,' she told him, 'but no fingerprints. Just a couple of partials from where he touched the grease from the meat and then one of the surfaces. He was gloved up.'

'No hair from the pillows, either.'

'Julius said before that he thought the unsub was wearing a head covering of some kind,' said Reilly. 'Which makes sense if the guy is a chef. They wear those little caps.'

'True. You're pretty sure that's what the guy does?'

'I'm almost positive,' said Reilly. 'I think you need to go back to Hammer and Tongs today and check out Nico Peroni. Check his alibi for last night.'

'Let's get the results from the ME first,' said Chris. 'Might give us a bit more to go on.' He was running a cotton bud over the surface of the bench. 'I've got something interesting here.'

'What is it?'

'Hard to say. A yellow powder.'

'Don't touch it.'

He chuckled. 'Reilly, I've been doing this job for almost two decades. What do you think I'm going to do, put it in my mouth or something?'

'Sorry,' she said. 'I am on edge today.'

'You want to talk about it?'

'Not now. And I can't. I just don't know what I'm going to say to Lucy though.' She couldn't break Lucy's confidence by telling Chris exactly what she'd heard, all he knew last night was how much it had affected her.

He nodded and looked around, in case they might be overheard. 'And do you want to talk about…last night?'

'No. I don't think I can do that right now either. I'm sorry, Chris. Let's just take each day as it comes.'

'Of course,' he said, but he couldn't hide the faint disappointment in his voice.

'I think we're done here for the moment,' she said, purposefully ignoring it.

She had a uniform drop her at home before going in to the lab, so she could collect herself a little better. Her flat seemed completely alien to her: someone else's house. The dishes from her dinner with Lucy were still stacked in the sink. They would have to wait until later. Everything would have to wait until later. When had her life become such a mess?

She showered, washing the last traces of Chris's woody scent down the drain and put on a sober suit, hoping it would make her feel more in control. She left the house with her hair still slightly damp and the circles round her eyes showing her lack of sleep.

On the way to work, she thought about what she had found out the night before. It seemed no less shocking in the morning light. It never ceased to sicken her the kind of cruelty that was present in the world, and how much of it was aimed at women. It was enough to make anyone feel completely vulnerable. Sometimes she thought that the whole world hated women and there was nothing that could be done about it. She was the ambulance at the bottom of the cliff. She caught the bad guys, but couldn't stop them from appearing in the first place. Get one, three more appear. A game of whack-a-mole.

She remembered rambling on to Chris about much of this last night and wondered now if he thought she was losing it. Lately, *she* felt like she was losing it, out of control and she wondered what on earth was going on with her. Clearly events in Florida were having some after-effects on her. Seeing Todd on the railway tracks like that ...

She pushed the thought away.

Jennifer Armstrong and Naomi Worthington were young, beautiful and successful. The phrase "she had it all" could be applied to them. They knew what they wanted, and it wasn't to be held down to a life of marriage and children. Maybe Reilly needed to stop focusing on the killer and start focusing more on the similarities between these women. Wouldn't that be the best way to lure him out? To predict where he would strike next? She needed to take another look at the dating profiles of these women. It was something she hadn't paid close attention to in the Armstrong case. The lack of similarity to the Cooper girl had confused things. But it was time to go back to basics.

When she got to the office, Inspector O'Brien was pacing the floor beside her desk. It was a wonder he hadn't worn right through the carpet.

'We need to talk,' he said.

'Yes,' she said. 'We do.'

Reilly sat and folded her arms loosely. She watched as the chief put his glasses on, took them off again and fumbled with some papers.

'I suppose you're going to say: "I told you so."'

'I don't think I have to, sir.'

'No, you don't. I'm sorry I didn't listen to you. I know that you're an asset to this team, but you can only be as good as I let you be. And I didn't.'

Reilly was so surprised her mouth almost fell open. She had expected a brusque apology at best, but this was high praise indeed, coming from Inspector O'Brien.

'I don't always agree with your methods,' he continued, 'And God knows, you don't always approve of mine, but I think we respect each other.'

'Of course,' she said. 'Of course I respect you.'

'Good,' he said. 'This case has just got a whole lot harder. I've been talking to the press but they're not going to hold back. One of the first uniforms on the scene has leaked details to one of the big newspapers. It'll be everywhere. You know the kind of thing: "Killer chef strikes again", "Useless gardai pin murders on wrong guy". That kind of thing. My guess is that, by tonight, the death of Harry McMurty will have been turned into a huge tragedy that we could have prevented.'

'A media circus, in other words,' said Reilly. The chief's least favorite thing.

'That's right. I need a solid lead, Steel. I need something to give these guys, to reassure the public that we have some hope of solving this.'

'Well, I *would* be further along if you had listened to me in the first place, sir.'

'I thought we just put all that behind us.'

'A woman is dead, sir. I can't just put that behind me.'

'Yes, and there will be more of them if we don't get this case solved,' he shot back. I need a lead Steel.'

'I've think we've got one,' said Reilly. 'But in order to make this work, I need to know that you won't stand in my way again. I want an absolute guarantee.'

'Fine,' he snapped. 'Do what you need and use what you need. Just bring me results.'

27

'OK,' SAID JULIUS, IN THE GFU debriefing room. 'Even without the results from the Worthington autopsy, the similarities in these cases are piling up. Allow me to elaborate.'

'Go ahead,' said Reilly.

Out of the corner of her eye, she saw Lucy open a packet of biscuits and offer one to Gary. He looked as though she had handed him the moon. She envied them their uncomplicated romance. They might not think it was, but Reilly would give anything for that kind of simplicity. She could see Chris watching her and wondered what he was thinking. Had she disappointed him already? Probably. He couldn't expect too much from her though. She wasn't able to just give herself wholly to someone. Last night … now in the cold light of day she was embarrassed. What would have happened if he hadn't pressed the pause button? What did he think of her, practically throwing herself at him like that? Yes she was upset but they'd been through some upsetting things before and she hadn't felt the need to crawl all over him.

Man, this was a mess…

'So. The DNA found at the Cooper and Armstrong scenes matches the one decent sample we got from the Worthington scene this morning. This guy is good. He barely leaves a trace, but as we all know, a trace is all it takes.' He helped himself to one of Lucy's biscuits and continued. 'The bedcovers had the same kind of disruption Gary pointed out before as well. I haven't been able to test for the same chemical compound that we found on the Armstrong bed yet, but I'll let you know as soon as I do.'

'If I may pick up the story from here …' interjected Gary.

'All yours,' said Julius.

'There is obviously the link with the manner of death: poisoning in both the Cooper and Armstrong cases, and though we haven't got the results from the Worthington scene, it looks like that was our third meal of death. Naomi Worthington had no real cooking utensils of her own. Her fridge was full of condiments. Which indicates that our perp brought his own utensils again. He just didn't leave anything behind this time. Except,' he said, with a dramatic pause, 'I surveyed Naomi's chopping board. It seemed absolutely new, apart from some very recent marks that had been made by a knife moving at speed. With great precision. For your information, I actually tested this myself.' He brought out two chopping boards, identical to the one Naomi Worthington had owned. 'I went and bought these this morning, when we got back.

You can see on this one, I had Lucy chop an onion. You can see that the marks made are from an inexpert and clumsy hand.' He glanced up for Lucy's reaction and was rewarded with an eye roll. 'The second board I took to the café downstairs. Now, the guy in there is only a sous chef, but you can see that the marks on this board are much closer together, much more precise.'

He finished and waited for their response.

'Very impressive,' said Reilly drily.

'You've gone above and beyond the call of duty,' said Chris. 'So. We've got all these similarities. We know beyond a doubt now, that we're dealing with the same guy. We just have to find him.'

The meeting ended with Gary promising to work on Naomi's phone and laptop until "his eyes bled". Julius would analyze the contents of the meal and the flowers and find out what they were dealing with, and Lucy would continue her work in the lab as well, where her sometimes frenetic energy narrowed in on tiny details.

Lucy caught up with Reilly when she was back at her desk.

'Did you hear anything useful on the tapes last night?'

'I did,' said Reilly, cautiously. 'But I don't want to go into it just yet. For now, I think you should take a break from hypnotherapy.'

'Did I do something wrong?' She looked crestfallen.

'No, you've done great. It's just I want to focus on another part of the investigation for now.'

'Ok,' said Lucy. 'Keep me posted.'

Reilly breathed a sigh of relief when she left. She had decided that she wouldn't tell Lucy what she had found until she had a little more information. It was no use upsetting her for no reason. Ethically, it was probably wrong. Lucy had a right to her own memories.

But Reilly didn't want to rip her life apart until she had to.

Karen Thompson was very good at remaining detached from the corpse she was working on. She preferred not to think of the person lying in front of her, but rather as a collection of clues, that when put together, would make a puzzle.

It made her job easier that the bodies put in front of her usually bore very little resemblance to the living. They were merely models of the living. Something for her to take apart and put together again.

The truth was, she was completely obsessed by the body and the way it worked. It was like the sea, sometimes it gave up its secrets, sometimes not. She knew what they said about her. That she dug up corpses in the night, that she carried the stench of death around with her. It was all complete rubbish, of course, but she didn't dissuade the talk. She rose above it.

Death was one of the great experiences of a person's life. It was just as important as one's birth, and just as random, but all too often it was ignored. Simply a by-line. Karen Thompson believed that people should prepare for their deaths, should embrace them almost. It was all well and noble, but she had never had a knife held to her throat, or a gun pointed at her temple.

She was no stranger to violence and its consequences, however. Every day, she saw a different method of killing.

She looked at the corpse in front of her now. Another young, healthy person. There had been a few of those lately. She allowed herself a moment of pure anticipation before she began her autopsy. The incision she made into the body was only the first of many steps.

She removed the organs, checked them for the telltale signs of discoloration. The contents of the stomach must be neatly scooped out and kept for testing. The insides of the body were as neat as a map, but each showed something slightly different. In this one, Karen found something that made her stop. A tiny something. No bigger than a bee. No more than a rumor. A tiny widening, a slight preparation of the body. Goodness, she thought.

The patient's liver was discolored and cirrated, a typical sign of poisoning. Her bowels were blocked also. There had been none of the voiding which is common in death. It lead Karen to suspect a particular type of poison.

She would run the bloods and toxicity tests and then tell the investigators what she had discovered. They would no doubt be impatient.

28

'ATROPA BELLA DONNA,' SHE TOLD the collected faces later that afternoon. 'More commonly known as deadly nightshade. It is quite perfect really, because it is very sweet tasting. Irresistible to young children. All that is needed to kill a grown man is three to five berries and our killer used far more than that. My guess is that they were pureed and used as a marinade for the pork. Very creative.'

Reilly and Chris exchanged a glance. The doc could be a little gruesome sometimes.

'No need to bloody well compliment his cooking skills,' said Kennedy.

'You would be far better qualified to comment on his cooking than I, Detective,' said Karen, tartly. 'Being as it seems that you have actually sampled it.'

Kennedy subsided into a grumpy silence and Reilly suppressed a smile. Things were back to normal.

'But that's not all. He used enough deadly nightshade to kill a horse, but still he garnished the meal with *Letticis*

Moravena, also known as Imp's delight. These are the flowers that were found at the scene. They are also highly poisonous, but sold in selected florists, because of course it is expected that people won't eat flowers. There was no need to include them,' said Karen. 'My guess is that they were used as a kind of flourish, a taunt even. A calling card.'

'Is that it, then?' asked Kennedy.

'If you would have some patience,' said Karen. 'No, that is not "it". My estimate is that the time of death was around 9pm last night. From her body weight and the amount of poison used, she would have taken no more than twenty minutes to die. There is one more thing, of interest, though perhaps not relevance. The victim was pregnant at the time of death. No more than a few weeks, but still detectable to me.'

There was a silence in the room as they all paused to take in this tiny double tragedy.

Things had taken a decidedly macabre turn.

Hi there, I see that you asked a question about preparation for long distance runs? I've done a few of these myself, and I definitely think you need to put lots of work into your prep. If you try to be too ambitious when you're inexperienced, then you might be put off running altogether.

My advice is: Make sure you can go at least one and a half times the distance you need to. If you get lost, you will need to have extra stamina.

Always carry snacks and water. It'll make your load heavier, sure, but it's invaluable. Just practice with that extra weight so that it won't feel too heavy on the big day!

Stretch, stretch, stretch. I can't stress this enough. I know some really good stretches for fast recovery, kind of hard to describe like this, but Private Message me if you want more details.

Run with a partner. Safer and much more fun.

See you at the next run!

My message to the lovely Constance.

I have my first session with the running group in two nights' time. They are bound to be a bunch of amateurs, huffing and puffing their way through a mere 10k, but the boredom is worth it. She will be there and I will see her in the flesh for the first time.

Usually I would be left feeling bored and lacking after a success such as I had the other night. But finding out about Constance has given things an extra flavor. I now have a goal that supersedes all others. I will not rush this. It's tempting to kill her as soon as I can, but it needs to be right.

I will put in all the necessary preparation.

Rory, the GFU's true computer maestro, was back.

Gary was good, but not quite at the savant levels as Rory. In only a few hours, he had managed to get them unrestricted access to Jennifer and Naomi's emails as well as their dating profiles and the private messages therein. He had even dug up a few of Rose Cooper's old emails.

'He's a genius,' said Chris, echoing Reilly's own thoughts. 'But with the amount of stuff he's dug up, we'll be here all night. I'm going to get some food downstairs. Do you want something?'

'Yeah, maybe a pizza slice? Or salad. Yes, get me a salad, please.'

He left the room and Reilly continued scanning emails.

"I just can't commit right now," she read in one of Naomi Worthington's emails to her sister. "I love my job, and it takes up all of my time. I can't seem to manage that AND a serious relationship."

Reilly sighed. The similarities between her and these women were a little too glaring sometimes. Married to their jobs basically. Unable to handle emotional intimacy. Here she was, after practically having thrown herself at Chris, and then backing off completely. It was the right thing to do though. Particularly since she just wasn't sure how she felt about anything at the moment. She kept reading emails. The best thing she could do right now was to keep her mind on the job. Glued to it, in fact.

"...don't know what to do," read another of Naomi's emails. "A baby was never part of the plan. At least, not for a few years. But I keep thinking, maybe this is meant to happen. Maybe I want it to happen. I'm starting to love this thing despite myself."

It was all so sad. Naomi had deserved the chance to see where motherhood took her. It had been snatched away from her cruelly. She was just a woman who like to have a little fun. She liked some pleasure in her life. It didn't mean she was incapable of loving something, or of being a good mother. Reilly could relate to her. Whys should a woman have to go without? Men got to have all of those things: a career, sex, relationships, a family. Why couldn't she have the same?

Naomi's email revealed much the same as Jennifer's. They were mainly about work and the ones that were personal talked about the dates she was going on, or restaurants she had been to. Like Jennifer, she frequented high end restaurants. Reilly noted that she had been to Hammer and Tongs at least twice.

Rose Cooper's emails were a different story. Mainly pleading messages from her mother, begging her to go home. "You sound so unhappy," one read. "I just wish you would come home." If only Rose had listened to her mother, things might be completely different.

Then she saw something that made her heart beat a little faster. An email from Harry McMurty. "I've got a little treat for you…not the kind of treat you can put up your nose. Something almost as good though. I know a guy from a big restaurant and he said he could interview you. Wants your number. I gave it to him but thought I should let you know." Someone must have written it for him, it was far too legible. But this could be the thing they needed. It was too bad he didn't use any names, but they would definitely need to pay Nico Peroni another visit. So what if he said he met Harry McMurty only after Rose's death? People lie.

'Anything interesting?' Chris asked when he came back. He slid a plate of salad and a slice of pepperoni pizza across the table to her.

'A couple of things. Another possible link to Nico Peroni. We've been slack. We have to get him in for questioning.'

'We don't have much to hold him on,' said Chris. 'But we'll get him in. If you think it's something.'

'Apart from that,' said Reilly. 'It's mainly just really sad. These women just trying to make sense of their lives.' She picked up the pizza and the spicy scent of the meat overwhelmed her. There was no escaping it; she was going to be sick.

She flew from the room, with Chris right behind her. She reached the toilet just as she was ill. He stood in the doorway to the bathroom while she was in the stall to give her a little privacy.

'This goddamn stomach bug,' said Reilly. 'It's maddening.'

She saw Chris's serious face in the mirror as she washed her face.

'Reilly,' he said gently. 'Maybe you don't have a stomach bug. All this tiredness, high emotion, nausea. You're the one who's usually first to put all the pieces of a puzzle together.'

When she said nothing, just continued to stare blankly at him, he came up beside her and put a hand on her arm.

'Is it at all possible,' Chris suggested kindly, 'that you might be pregnant.'

29

I ATTENDED MY FIRST RUNNING group tonight. As expected, it was full of idiots. People who have no form, who can't run to save themselves.

But there, in the middle of all this, was Constance Dell, shining like a light. She has long red hair, pale skin and blue eyes. She is nothing like her mother.

We began at a slow jog, and I fell into pace beside her. I made it seem quite effortless, though I had to shorten my stride noticeably.

'You're holding your breath,' I told her. 'Just try to breathe normally.'

She flashed me a smile, too short of breath to talk. She smelt like vanilla and cinnamon, like a cake freshly risen from the oven.

I will enjoy this, I thought. I will enjoy this very much.

After the run, she approached me. Cheeks flushed, décolletage glistening with perspiration.

'You're the guy who gave me the pointers on Facebook, aren't you? Thank you so much.'

'No problem,' I said. 'Any time'.

'I'll definitely be in touch if I need some advice,' she said.

And I hope she will be. She radiates calmness and pleasantness. Again, the complete opposite to her mother.

As she walked away I watched her braid slither down her back like a gold snake.

There is no greater boon than hunting something beautiful.

'Has anyone considered that poison is typically the murder weapon of choice for women?' said Gary. 'Maybe we're barking up the wrong tree completely here.'

'Maybe we would get a break on this case if people would stop coming up with completely idiotic suggestions,' said Reilly bad-naturedly.

Lucy and Gary exchanged a glance, realizing that their boss was not in the mood for joking around that morning.

And Reilly wasn't. She had endured a horrific sleepless night after Chris suggested she might be pregnant. She flat-out refused to entertain the idea, but there it was, niggling at the back of her mind.

She and Todd had indeed neglected to use protection that one night together, but what were the chances? Some enduring jet-lag and an out of whack appetite were *not* enough reasons to make the automatic leap to pregnancy. The up and down emotional stuff was worrying though, because her emotions had been all over the place lately, so much so that she'd wondered if she was going mad, or suffering a particularly severe cause of SAD or something.

There was one way she could find out for sure of course, but Reilly wasn't willing to go down that road. Not yet.

Today was a big day, in any case. Kennedy and Chris were bringing Nico Peroni in for questioning and she wanted to sit in on the interview. She would have to ignore everything else that was going on and try be at her sharpest with Peroni. If he was the killer, it was clear that he was no dummy. She needed her wits about her. She couldn't be distracted by notions of pregnancy or indeed anything else.

I want everyone to keep on with this case today,' she said. 'No distractions. I want you combing through every email, every piece of information we have. Rory, where are we on those private messages?'

'Got them,' he said. 'Not a problem.'

'OK. So everyone has work to do. There are about a thousand trace samples in the lab that still need analysis. I know it's boring work, but it needs to be done.'

'I've got the results back on the Worthington bedcovers,' said Julius. 'Same chemical compound as the other one. Likely spandex, again. And that yellow powder? Pollen.'

Reilly nodded. It was good to hear that the evidence was mounting. It would merely make it easier to put the killer away when they did catch him.

If only it could reveal how they might do just that.

Constance Dell was no fool. She was used to men hitting on her. Every day, someone would find a new and novel way to ask her out. It might be funny or amusing if it wasn't so annoying. What gave men the right, anyway? Did they really think if they followed you around for long enough, or told you how great your legs were, that you would just fall in love with them?

Running was her outlet. Having been a pre-work park jogger for years, she was finally getting more serious about it. It was true what they said about running: it did amazing things for your body, it focused you, it taught you strength and endurance. So the last thing she needed was another guy ruining her buzz as she pursued her passion.

But the guy at the running group didn't seem interested in her like that. Maybe he had a wife, although she didn't see a ring. He just seemed to want to help her get the most out of running. At the second group run, he had shown her some great stretches and had done so without touching her, except to pull her shoulders back a little. It was great.

Not all men are sexually attracted to you. You know that don't you?' said her mother when she told her about it over the telephone. She could almost hear her mother's eye roll from Oxford.

'Of course I know that,' said Constance.

'Great, have fun,' said her mother, and hung up before Constance could reply.

It was a typical farewell from her mother. She was notoriously brusque and not hugely affectionate. The point was that she tried.

Constance had given up trying to explain her relationship with her to others. While other girls she knew spoke of rushing to their mothers for advice about love and jobs, all Ruth would tell her daughter was: "Do what you want, Connie. You have to do what you want."

And forget about going to her for comfort if you had a broken heart. She would pat you on the back for a couple of seconds and say: "That's pretty much my capacity for motherly love, Constance." It was true. Ruth loved her in spades. She just had trouble expressing it.

Instead, Constance and her mother debated politics, sex and religion. Anything under the sun, really. Sometimes Constance took a viewpoint that was completely the opposite to the one she really had, just to see if she could argue her mother under the table. In most cases, she could.

She had studied to be a lawyer, but the hour before she sat the bar, she thought: Is this what I really want? Screw it.

She moved to Dublin and became a music teacher instead. Her mother never expressed disappointment with Constance's whimsical approach to her career and other major life decisions. It was the same old adage: Do what you want.

And I do, Constance thought deliciously, as she ate ice-cream in bed at 9am on a Friday morning. She would spend the day reading *Something From Tiffany's* and lying in the bath until the hot water ran out.

Because who could stop her, after all?

Reilly watched through the one way mirror as Kennedy and Chris questioned Nico Peroni. Even from here she could see the sweat pouring off the restaurant owner. It wasn't necessarily a sign of guilt. He was nervous. Plus, fit people sweated more easily, she knew. The body was accustomed to cooling itself down.

'First off,' said Kennedy, 'we would like you to submit to a DNA test.'

'Do I have to?' asked Nico. 'What are my rights?'

'Legally,' said Kennedy, 'you have the right to refuse. However we can gain a court order that will force you to comply.'

'Then that is what you will have to do,' said Nico.

Kennedy shook his head and made a note.

'We need to ask a few more questions,' said Chris. 'You told us you met Harry McMurty roughly eighteen months before he died, is that correct?'

'Give or take,' said Nico.

'How about you try to narrow it down,' said Chris. 'Be more specific.'

'Maybe a little longer than that,' said Nico.

'Did you know him before Rose Cooper was killed?'

'Yes, I think so.'

'So that's a definite yes?' asked Chris.

'Yes,' said Nico.

At this stage, anyone with a sense of self-preservation would have demanded a lawyer. But it seemed not to have occurred to Nico, despite his assertion of his "rights."

'What was the capacity of your relationship with Mr McMurty before he worked for you?' asked Chris.

On this Nico seemed clear. 'An acquaintance. He worked at the restaurant of a friend of mine.'

'Why did you lie before about the length of time you had known Mr McMurty?' asked Chris. 'It seems like you wouldn't forget that he had worked for a friend of yours.'

'Well, I really began to know him once he worked for me. Before that, I just knew *of* him. Saw him round, so to speak.'

'So to speak.'

'Yes.'

'Can you tell us where you were last night?' asked Kennedy.

'I don't see what that has to do with anything. If I am in trouble for something, you should just arrest me.'

'Answer the question, please,' said Kennedy tiredly.

'I was out on my bike.'

'Where?'

'In the Phoenix Park.'

'Can anyone confirm this?'

'Only if you can track down the hundreds other people who were in the park at the same time. I'm getting a bit tired of this.' Reilly watched as it dawned on the guy at last. 'I want a lawyer, please, if you continue going on in this ridiculous vein.'

'We'll get you your lawyer, Mr Peroni,' said Chris. 'In the meantime I would strongly suggest that you submit to that DNA test. Resisting only makes it harder for everyone.'

The suspect shook his head. They would have to get a court order.

Back at the lab afterwards, having successfully avoided Chris at the station by slipping out before the interview was over, she started to go through the mail on her desk. Lots of correspondence regarding other cases, jiffy bags full of documents that she would have to read sooner, rather than later. It never ended.

There was something else. A thin grey envelope. So cheap and thin you could almost see right through it. She recognized the stamp on the back. It was from the Prison Service.

She almost didn't open it. She received things like this every now and again, sick notes from men the GFU had helped to put away and had seen her when she testified in court. Dirty, badly written things about what they would do to her if they ever got out. Which they wouldn't.

But when she saw it was postmarked as being from Mountjoy, she opened it. It might be abusive, but it might also tell her something.

The script inside was elegant and ornate, so she had a little trouble at first making it out.

"Dear Ms Steel," it read. "I know you will probably want to tear this up when you see who it's from and that's fair enough. I just wanted to say sorry for last week. I lost my temper, and in the process I came close to hurting you and I am sorry for that.

At the time, I wanted to hurt you. I don't deny that. I have these flashes when I want to, or I actually do, these awful things, and afterwards I just can't work out why. I do have a counsellor here. He is helping me with my anger problems, but I still have a long way to go. Obviously.

My rage has been with me for so long that I worry that I would be unrecognizable without it. It shields me. I wonder if you can understand that? Is there anything that you cling to, knowing that without it, you might not know who you are anymore?

My counsellor is also trying to help me to see the truth about my brother. Sometimes I see Brendan as my saviour, the only person who ever truly loved me, and sometimes I know him for a monster. I don't think I will ever be able to feel just one way about him.

I know what you want from me. I know that you want to know what happened to Grace. And part of me wants to help you. But what do I get in return? Here I am, and I know this is as far as my life goes. I don't believe in any redemption for myself. But I could do one last good thing, if I wanted.

I want to know: what will you give me in return? I don't ask for much. I am a lonely man. If you reply this letter in kind, it may be incentive enough.

Darren Keating."

Reilly refolded the letter very deliberately and put it in her handbag. It left her with a cold, creepy feeling. Grace Gorman's old boyfriend was truly a man broken into many pieces. The letter had been sincere in parts, manipulative in others. He was charming, then repulsive. He showed self-awareness, but a total lack of will to do anything with it. Reilly knew that to write back would be a huge mistake. Prisoners like that were con-men. They knew how to play with people.

But what if he did have something to tell her?

30

'OK, JUST ONE LITTLE POINTER,' the guy said to Constance as they ran.

'I'm doing it all wrong, aren't I?' she laughed through her short breaths.

'No, not at all. You're doing great,' He pulled up, and she did too. 'It's just, your strides are a little wide. A lot of short distance runners do the same thing, and it's fine, but if you're going long distance it'll really tire you out. Lean forward a little, so that you're not overextending yourself, and make sure your stride is no bigger than the width of your hips.'

They ran for a few more minutes. 'OK,' she said, 'that does actually feel better.'

The guy at the running group was really helping her out. She had felt her form improve just from the couple of times she had run with him. He was older than her, but definitely fitter, and quite handsome too.

They ran for about 12k, and then she declared herself done in. 'You look like you could go all night, though,' she said.

'Well, I've been running for a long time,' he said.

She laughed, and then asked: 'I noticed you change your pace a lot, from slow to fast. Why? Isn't it better to keep an even pace so that the body can adjust?'

'Not really,' he said. 'Varying your pace helps you build endurance. The bursts of high intensity get your body more accustomed to a higher rate.'

She nodded. 'That makes sense. I have to tell you, I'm grateful for this. I spent the day with my mother.' She rolled her eyes and grinned. 'Almost killed me.'

She noticed a strange look pass over his face, almost like she had stabbed him with a pin, or something. 'Is your mother…not very nice?'

'Oh, no. She's great. She lives in the UK so I don't see her that often but she can just be hard work sometimes. Like, did you ever notice that once your parents get older, it kind of feels as though you're parenting them a little bit?'

'No,' he said. 'I never noticed. My mother died when I was young.'

'I'm so sorry,' she said. 'That must have been very hard.'

Her sympathy came very naturally. One of the best things about Constance was her ability to feel pain for others. Her mother told her it was also a weakness that led her to surround herself with less than deserving people, but sometimes her mother was a crank.

'It was a long time ago,' he said. 'But yeah, it was hard.'

They parted and as Constance walked back to her car, she thought that she had just had a curiously intimate moment with someone whose name she didn't even know.

They had to let Nico Peroni go, but there was the warning that he shouldn't leave town. Reilly had her team working overtime trying to see if there was a DNA match for him with any of the samples they had collected from any of the victim's houses. This stuff could take a long time, but she wanted results.

They'd got a court order to take a sample from Peroni, and she had watched Lucy take a swab from the inside of his mouth. A curiously intimate thing to do to someone.

When Peroni left the station, he looked like he had spent a night in hell. Somehow though, she couldn't bring herself to feel sorry for him.

'What do you think?' she asked Chris.

'I think he's hiding something. We've got the connection between him and the first victim. The others aren't too much of a stretch to make, given that they had eaten at his restaurants. He says he doesn't do online dating, though.'

'Well, that connected the victims, but we don't know for sure that they met the killer online.'

'We're going to need something stronger to hold him in any case.'

'I've got Lucy, Gary and Julius working like robots in the lab. We'll get it as soon as we can, if it's there.'

He nodded. 'He doesn't have an alibi for the Worthington night, but he can't remember where he was the night Jennifer Armstrong was killed.'

'Which, at the moment, means that he could have done it.'

'Yep.'

They were silent for a second, looking through the glass into the interview room, which was now empty. Reilly could faintly see their watery outlines.

'Did you do a test yet?' he asked gently.

She stiffened. 'I don't need to do a test, Chris. I know my own body. It's impossible.'

'Is it? Impossible I mean? Not that it's any of my business but …. if something happened when you were in the States.'

Her silence was enough and she walked out, leaving Chris with his worst suspicions confirmed.

So, something had happened. With who - Forrest? Hardly, although he couldn't be sure. Then he remembered Reilly mentioning something about a son, the one she'd worked an investigation with. Todd. That was more likely. Chris didn't have a right to be angry he knew, but he felt saddened all the same.

It had taken him and Reilly years to get to this point, and now just when they'd reached a major breakthrough, everything had just got a lot more complicated.

On the way home, Reilly's mind was racing. It was ridiculous, she thought, how men thought they knew women so well. So Chris had correctly suspected she'd had a fling. What had happened between them the other night had happened in a moment of desperation.

Yes, Reilly had feelings for him, knew she always had, but she certainly wasn't ready to jump into anything. He had been there for her during so many tough times. She just couldn't imagine being in the kind of place where their relationship was about romantic dinners, movies at the weekends, or spending time together at home after work.

What had happened with Todd had been overwhelming, physical - so overwhelming unfortunately, they hadn't used any protection. She hadn't used birth control for years, not liking how bloated it made her feel. But could it really have happened? In a window that small?

She had become so used to her life alone that the thought of getting pregnant had never occurred to her. It just didn't seem like something that she was destined for. She *still* wasn't destined for it, she told herself and she truly believed she knew her body well enough that she would notice if something major was happening. So she might as well just take the test and nix the possibility. She had enough on her mind without worrying about that, too.

Plus, it would get Chris out of her hair.

She picked up a predictor test at the chemist in Ranelagh village, and perhaps she was imagining it but did the women behind the counter gave her an appraising stare? No, she was just reaching.

Reilly tried to tell herself that she wasn't nervous; wasn't concerned at all, but as she opened her wallet to pay the cashier she realized her hands were clammy.

You might think, that because Constance is so obviously a sweet girl, that I have qualms about killing her. But that's simply not true. Only an amateur would get distracted by a feeling so mild as "like". There is a chance that I might have liked some of the wriggling lobsters I have dropped into boiling pots of water, but I still did it.

The truth is, Constance is means to an end. She is simply the vessel for pain. Her death will not be as easy as the others, but that is simply because I don't want someone to say to her mother: 'She did not suffer." She will suffer, because I want her mother to suffer. It is that simple.

Her running is really coming along, though. Perhaps, if I ever get sick of my day job, I could consider a career in coaching. But my life is so easy right now. Because of my success, I simply have to waltz into the kitchen, make a few tweaks to the menu, shout a few orders, and I am free to pursue my real life.

The inner life is always the real life. So many people concentrate on the exterior. Looks, jobs, education: those are all well and good, but it's the river that runs through us all that we must pay heed to. Ignore it at your peril. I have given up many things to follow my true self, but it has been worth it. He leads me into darkness, and I follow without hesitation.

There last few days have been a little tense. Surprise of surprises, the cop is still alive. My little mushroom ruse failed. He looks no worse for wear. He and the other two, that big handsome brute and that career obsessed American have been hanging around the restaurant. I thought it might be time for me to lie very low, which would be a great pity, just when everything is coming together. Added to this, the papers have begun calling me "The Chef." How very original. Probably every restaurant in Dublin will soon be as empty as a tomb. They have cast Harry McMurty as a kind of much-maligned, completely innocent victim. Nonsense. He deserved his death.

No matter, all I need is time. Time to carry out my most daring, and most fulfilling plan yet. They will not stop me before I have done what I need to do, I will make sure of that.

31

GARY WAS FOCUSING IN ON the Keating brothers, as Reilly had asked him to.

Now that Rory was back, he didn't have to devote so much of his time to playing around with people's computers. He had felt himself getting closer to Lucy, as well, which was another reason to keep going on this case. Something was definitely growing between them, and he just hoped it was more than friendship.

He had asked his buddy in the Justice Department for a list of known aliases on Brendan Keating, but, unlike his brother, it seemed as though the guy didn't use any.

Gary thought about it some more. It seemed to him that the real key to what had happened to Lucy's sister was the house in which they had found Grace's necklace. He shivered. It didn't bear thinking about that place, really, not when you were all by yourself in the GFU lab late in the evening.

He did a search on the O'Toole house, which was currently up for sale and found its listing details and current valuation. It was set at a really low price, maybe because of the location in a rougher part of the city, or maybe because it had had a police cordon around it for weeks. He shot a quick email off to the seller: "Interested in this property. Can you let me have more info? Thanks."

It was a long shot, but maybe it might drag something up from the depths. At least he still felt as though he was doing something. And it wasn't a total lie. He was interested in the property, just not in buying it.

It would be nice to get a result on at least one of these cases. He could see the stress of the murder investigations was getting to Reilly. It was wholly unusual for the boss to show any sign of what she was feeling internally, but the last few days she had seemed stretched tight. As always she had too much going on, and though he and the others on the team tried to take some of her load, she was too dedicated to let them do too much.

Despite being told off by Lucy for speculating about Reilly and Detective Delaney, Gary couldn't help but think that something *had* gone on between them. Delaney, too, seemed even more preoccupied than usual, particularly over the last twenty four hours.

Anyway, no point being here thinking about his colleagues when he should home be in bed getting some shut eye. Reilly set the pace for her team and she was always at work before eight. He often wished for a boss who wasn't such a morning person, but what are you going to do?

Reilly held the stick with a resolutely still hand. She placed it on the vanity in her bathroom, then went out into the living room to wait.

On a whim, she grabbed a piece of paper and pen and wrote:

"Mr Keating, I am not in the habit of being manipulated by criminals, no matter how good their penmanship may be. However, first and foremost, I try to solve crime. So if you can help me with that, then I guess it's worth the correspondence.

You ask if I know what it's like to be overwhelmed by a feeling that you would later not claim to be your own. Of course. This is a very human feeling, one that we are all prey to. It is a human trait to be overwhelmed by rage, passion, grief. But the true mark of being human, I think, is being able to control these behaviors. We are nothing but animals if we do not know how to overcome our baser natures.

You say that you are attempting to rein in your anger, and your letter shows the marks of someone who is coming to self-awareness, perhaps after years of having your mind and thoughts controlled by someone else. So why don't you believe in the possibility of redemption, or at least of improvement?

I send this letter being sure that it will lead to no good, but it's true that I want the information you say you have for me. So, try to give some thought to the position this puts me in. Try to think of Grace's family."

She went outside and posted it in the nearby letterbox before she could change her mind. If she waited until morning, she knew she would rip it up into pieces.

When she came back from the brisk night air, she headed to the bathroom with determination. She was not one to be afraid, or to turn away from knowledge about herself.

But this was the kind of knowledge she could do without.

Reilly inhaled. There they were, two tiny lines, glowing pink.

Such a small thing, to send someone's life completely out of control.

Kennedy and Chris met for breakfast the next morning.

'You know,' said Kennedy, biting into a huge muffin. 'I often wish I had been a cop in New York. The food is just great over there. The delis, especially. You've never tasted anything like it. Josie wanted to go shopping and I said: "Off you go. Meet me here in six hours."'

Chris smiled and shook his head. The mushroom incident may have knocked Kennedy for six, but his appetite remained intact. Perhaps it had even grown.

'Are you all right, mate?' the big man asked. 'You've been a bit quiet the past few days. I mean, even more so than usual. Job's not getting to you, is it? Or are you just upset to see my ugly mug back at work again?'

Chris laughed. 'Nah, nothing like that. Just the flavor seems to have gone out of things lately. I want to get some movement on this case and now it feels like we're back at square one.'

'Maybe you should take a few days off. How long is it since you saw the sun, my friend?'

'About six years,' said Chris, deadpan. 'Yeah. I've been thinking about that too. Maybe I do need a change of scenery.'

Kennedy was surprised. He hadn't actually been serious. For as long as he had known Chris, the job had been his life. When he was forced to take time off, he grumbled about it.

'Not having women troubles, are you?' From Kennedy's experience, the one thing that could bring a man down like this was affairs of the heart. He didn't think Chris had been seeing anyone recently, but you never knew.

'I'm not even going to answer that. You know I lead the life of a monk.'

'Well, maybe that's your problem,' said Kennedy. 'It's just not healthy.'

'I'll be fine,' said Chris. 'I just need to get my head straight. Get something really good on this chef guy.'

'How did it go with Peroni?'

'Still nothing out of him. He doesn't have alibis, but then we don't have anything to tie him to the scene. Reilly's got the GFU working round the clock, trying to match up the samples.'

'Well,' said Kennedy, 'in my experience, a man with nothing to hide doesn't act quite so much like he does.'

'You're right,' said Chris. "Maybe today will be the day when we get the big break.'

'That's the spirit,' Kennedy replied, crumbs all over his mouth.

It hadn't been an easy night for Reilly. In fact, it had probably been one of the worst nights of her life. She found herself identifying even more closely with Naomi Worthington. What were you supposed to do when a bomb like this went off in the middle of your world? A world that you thought you had a pretty good handle on.

She knew that it wasn't a completely ridiculous idea for her to become a mother. She knew that she had a great capacity for love. She knew that she would be capable.

But she definitely hadn't seen it happening this way. How could she possibly handle a baby and a career? She was in an important position at the GFU now, the top of her game. If she took time out now, she might never get back to where she was. She might never climb her way up the ladder. She might be reduced from leading the investigations, to being a lackey on someone's team again, having to suppress her own instinct because she wasn't the boss.

On top of all of her confusion, Reilly felt a sense of shame. How could she have ignored her body like this? She had been pushing the symptoms aside, repressing any doubts or fears that she had. She was a grown thirty-something woman, supposed to be well in tune with her own body, yet Chris had to be the one to tell her what was actually going on with it.

It was embarrassing.

She had no idea what to do. She would have to keep acting as normal. Getting up, going to work, doing what she always did. But at some point she would no longer be able to hide what was going on, which would in turn lead to a whole lot of very awkward conversations.

Apart from the mess of her feelings, there was the practical side of things to consider as well. She had to make a doctor's appointment. That's what you were supposed to do, wasn't it? She was probably supposed to eat lot of iron rich foods, take folic acid, all that stuff. Luckily, she hadn't been drinking much since her return from Florida, on the one hand because there was little opportunity but on the other, because she had thought it might aggravate her "stomach bug." What a joke.

It was times like these that Reilly most yearned to have her mother back, so that she didn't have to be tough, or strong, but could just break down and have someone tell her: "It's going to be all right." Not that Cassie was ever too good in that department but Reilly guessed such a yearning for a motherly love was only natural at a time like this. Should she tell Mike? Her father would be floored at the very idea …but more to the point, Reilly realized, as a fresh anxiety hit her, what on earth was she going to tell Todd?

She didn't even know how he felt about children. The relationship hadn't gone deep enough for that kind of discussion—obviously, or the thought of taking precautions might have occurred to them. But to think that Daniel, her mentor, her long-time father figure, would now in fact be her baby's grandfather … It didn't seem real and Reilly's brain hurt to think about it.

So many implications, worries, decisions….

Well, for the moment all she could do is just take each day as it came. It was early days yet, and by her reckoning she couldn't be more than five weeks into the pregnancy tops. She could only steel herself to get through this as best she could.

She wavered at the thought of Chris, and how to face him, given the breakthrough between the two of them.

Just when she'd wondered if there might be something good happening between them; if they might even have a future, now that possibility was ruined for good.

32

'OK,' SAID JULIUS, THE NEXT morning at the lab. 'Brace yourself. I've got something for you, and I think you're going to be happy.'

'Great,' said Reilly. 'I'm all ears.'

'The DNA we took from Nico Peroni matched some of the trace found in Rose Cooper's flat *and* Harry McMurty's.'

'What about the other two?'

Julius looked disappointed. 'No, nothing from Armstrong and Worthington. No yet, anyway. But this is pretty major, Reilly. Peroni was all over McMurty's place. I mean, everywhere.'

Reilly felt bad for making these findings feel small. The team had been working so hard lately. 'It's great news,' she said. 'Really it is. We finally have something to hold the guy on.'

And it was good news. They were one step closer. Peroni fit the bill in so many ways. And yet … no, she wouldn't go there; she wouldn't go down that route. These days Reilly no longer trusted her instincts.

They just had to bring Peroni in and confront him with the evidence against him.

Nico Peroni was in bed when the detectives came for him, and he looked the worse for wear.

'You're ruining my life,' he cried, as he pulled on some trousers.

Gary and Lucy were waiting in the kitchen. They had a warrant to go through the house and look for any other evidence that would help put Peroni in jail. Gary looked down at his feet as the man was led past them, but Chris noticed that Lucy's eyes bore right into the suspect's face. He knew that she was thinking of her own sister, and the fate that had befallen her, whatever it was. He wondered what Reilly had done with the new information about the Keating brothers, the discovery that had rattled her enough the other night to send her into his arms.

The ride back to the station felt long, made worse by Peroni's muffled sobbing in the back. He looked at Kennedy and saw that the older detective had composed his face into a mask. No wonder people thought cops were emotionless, thought Chris. Look at what they had to face every day. There was so much pain in the world. People did each other so much damage, and they kept doing it. Humans had the power to brand others as monsters, and to become monsters themselves. The infliction of pain begat more pain.

He thought of his ex-girlfriend, Mel with a mixture of regret and pity. She had been the complete opposite of Reilly. She was a lively brunette, and he had fallen in love with her because she was kind, compassionate and had a wicked sense of humor. Until all of that, and his life - their life - was ruined by some random scumbag. Now, Mel was a shell of the person she used to be, and Chris could no longer reach her. He looked out the window, wondering why he was thinking about all of this again. He knew why though. It was because he was fairly certain that such happiness was about to be wrenched from underneath him again. At least this time, he hadn't been in too deep. He wondered if Reilly had taken a test and if his concerns were realized.

If they were, what would happen next? Not with them; Chris knew that ship had no doubt sailed, but how would Reilly cope? He supposed it was none of his business but he knew that something like this would be a major upheaval for a woman like her. Still, again it was none of his business, Reilly had told him as much when he'd made the suggestion.

They pulled up at the station. Chris found he had little appetite for interrogating the falling-to-pieces Nico Peroni yet again, but he would have to do it.

'We've got Peroni in a holding cell, awaiting his lawyer,' he told Reilly over the phone. 'Your crew is at his place already.'

'Good,' she said. 'I'm especially interested in his reaction when you confront him with the DNA evidence that we found at the Cooper and McMurty scenes.'

'You're not coming in?'

'No need. We've got enough on him.'

Her voice was clipped yet he sensed something underneath her tone, something more fragile. 'Reilly, are you OK?'

'I just can't talk about it right now, Chris. I'm sorry.'

And just like that he knew his worst fears were realized. She'd taken the test; she was pregnant.

'I'm here if you need to talk,' he said uselessly.

Somehow, he didn't think she would be seeking him out any time soon.

Lucy and Gary sometimes played a game when they were searching a house, or an area that didn't require the same concentration as a full-on crime scene. It was called "What do I have in my hand?" Of course, they never played it when the boss was around. That would *not* go down well. But sometimes they found really odd things in places and it was a bit of fun to make each other guess.

They had already done it this morning with a tiny bird skull and a lipstick that had been, according to its display case, Katharine Hepburn's.

Gary enjoyed being alone on a job with Lucy. Even if they didn't speak, it just felt good working side by side.

'Any movement on the cold case?' he asked her now.

'I should be asking you that question,' she replied. 'No, nothing that I know of. Reilly's pretty tied up with the Chef investigation of course so I wouldn't expect anything different. I don't know why she's stopped the hypnotherapy sessions, though. I really thought that we were getting somewhere.'

'Maybe she's just worried about you,' said Gary. He surveyed the suspect's bookshelf. He certainly had the library of a killer: *Famous Murders throughout History Grey's Anatomy, Women and Deadly Secrets.* Added to that he had all of the seasons of *Dexter* on DVD. It didn't mean anything, Gary himself watched *Dexter*. Still, it was a bit weird.

'She doesn't need to be worried about me,' said Lucy, carefully going through the contents of Nico Peroni's desk drawers. 'This guy has some really strange stuff. Like this.' She held up a cross on a silver chain. The cross appeared to be made of bones.

'Nice,' said Gary.

'This place gives me the creeps,' said Lucy. 'But anyway, Reilly doesn't need to be worried about me. I'm fine. I can take care of myself.'

'Of course,' said Gary. 'But I think the boss sees you as a kind of protégée. You're definitely her favorite.'

'Don't be silly.' She d blushed a little and Gary could tell that she was really pleased with the thought.

He looked around the room. Lucy was right. This place was creepy. All signs pointed to this being the guy. There were huge black and white posters on the walls of women in 1920's attire, holding weapons.

'I'll be glad when we're finished here,' he said. 'Those posters are enough to give me nightmares. In fact, to ward off that likelihood, maybe you'd like to go out later and take in a movie? Nothing scary of course…'

He looked over at Lucy. She wasn't listening.

'Gary,' she said, but her voice wavered. 'Guess what I've got in my hand?'

He looked at what she was holding and automatically took out the phone to call the boss.

33

MY LITTLE BIRD WAS NOT at group tonight. It is more than frustrating. There is so little time, and everything is ready.

Instead I had to spend an hour running next to an over-excited middle aged woman who kept up a running commentary about her children. Talk slower, run faster I wanted to tell her.

But I have to keep good relationship with these people if I am to see Constance again. What if she never comes back? Young women are like that. They flit from one thing to another, taking what they need from each thing that takes their fancy. Is it too soon simply to ask her out? To offer to cook for her?

This is a harder one than the rest. There were expectations there. This is something far more delicate. Constance has not sought me out. She is not looking for a relationship, or sex. She thinks of me as a helpful acquaintance.

I need to get closer to her, somehow.

Kennedy and Chris were getting nowhere fast. Peroni was steadfastly refusing to tell them how his DNA may have been present in the Cooper and McMurty scenes. Added to that, he had engaged a fancy lawyer who knew his way around the interrogation room.

'Isn't it true that you have already falsely accused one person for these murders?' asked the lawyer. He was a small, skinny man, with a chin like a dagger. 'Harry McMurty's name was dragged through the mud because he was framed as a killer. It caused the victim's families much unnecessary pain. If McMurty was framed, is isn't it possible that my client was also framed? Isn't it possible that you are making yet another terrible mistake?'

Chris was becoming frustrated. 'The samples from Rose Cooper's flat were taken months ago,' he said. 'Why would someone try to frame your client then?'

'Someone with a long game,' said the lawyer. 'You may not know much about fine dining, Detective Delaney, but my client is a successful man. There are many who would only love to see him ruined.'

Kennedy tried again. 'Mr Peroni, any way you help us now will be remembered later on. You are only making this worse for yourself. Now, tell us, can you explain how your DNA may have ended up at those crime scenes?'

Peroni shook his head again and his lawyer held his hands out in exasperation. 'Gentlemen, this is getting ridiculous. My client is clearly as clueless as you are. You must let him go.'

'It's our right to hold him for twenty-four hours,' said Kennedy.

After Kennedy and Chris had a break, they were ready to go in and keep working on Peroni, when suddenly Reilly appeared at the station.

'What are you doing here?' Chris asked, worried by the slightly maniacal look in her eyes. 'What's going on? Are you OK -'

Kennedy entered the room and instantly got a read on the tension. 'Everything all right, folks?'

'Yes,' said Reilly, giving Chris a warning look.

She smiled at the two of them and held up something in her hand 'I've just been to Peroni's house. Look what we found.'

Chris held the little white bag in front of Nico Peroni's face. The suspect's eyes widened, and then closed when he saw it. Reilly watched intently from behind the mirror.

'How did this bag of antimine come into your possession?' asked Chris. Of course, they had no confirmation that the substance was antimine just yet. They needed to get it back to lab first. But Reilly was pretty sure.

Nico Peroni just shook his head. Faced with the truth, he was finished talking.

'We're holding you under suspicion of the murders of Rose Cooper, Jennifer Armstrong, Harry McMurty and Naomi Worthington,' said Chris.

As she heard Chris say it, it was the best that Reilly had felt since her return.

Finally, they had him.

Having delivered the substance to the lab and overseen the preliminary analysis, she was about to leave early in the hope of a well-deserved night's rest when both Rory and Gary approached her at cross angles.

'OK,' she sighed defeatedly. 'You go first Rory.'

'I've managed to find an online profile for a person that both Naomi Worthington and Jennifer Armstrong were communicating with,' said Rory. 'It goes back to a fake email address, but the same address has been used to create a Facebook page for a guy called "Danny Prime". Probably a fake name too. The profile is full of pictures that have been ripped straight from Google images. It's amateur.' He sniffed derisively. 'Anyway, this guy is really active on running pages and things like that.'

Reilly was confused. 'But we've got our guy,' she said. 'Nico Peroni didn't have any dating profiles set up. We've combed his laptop.' She wasn't sure how to feel about this development. It was a bit late in the piece, but she would have to look into it. The fact that the guy was a runner piqued her interest though given the fitness angle running through the evidence all along. Was it possible that Peroni hadn't worked alone?

'And Gary,' she turned to the other tech once Rory had left.

'OK, first of all, don't be mad ...' he began.

'Now that you said that, I already am.'

'I was doing a little more work on the Grace Gorman case.'

'OK...'

'And I just did a search on the house where we found the necklace. I dug up some more information on the ownership history. It's up for sale at the moment and I got in touch with the seller Janey Smith—sister of that OAP Martin O'Toole, pretending to be an interested party.'

'I'm not sure if that'll help, we already know that the brother died years ago and it doesn't look he had anything to do with the more... recent occupant.'

'Maybe but the woman, Smith has agreed to meet, and I thought she might be able to shed some light on a few things about the house and what it was like when her brother was still living there, maybe the story behind the wigs or something?'

'I don't know Gary, that's probably one for the task force.' She sighed. This was the problem with imbuing the team with the same kind of work ethic as your own. Of course Gary wanted to chase this up himself, when it was painfully obvious to everyone that no-one trusted the task force guys. 'When are you meeting the sister?'

'Tomorrow afternoon. Any chance you'd come along?'

She exhaled.

'Ah thanks boss, you're brilliant.'

Reilly didn't feel brilliant when she got home. Yes, it had been a successful day. It was always good to get a killer off the streets. Peroni hadn't confessed as yet, but his complete unwillingness to defend himself or even speak was as good as. They had enough evidence to see him convicted which was the main thing. Pure antimine was hard to come by.

She cooked herself a nutritious meal: spinach, asparagus and quinoa salad with a steak. That seemed like it should have all the vitamins she needed.

She felt so restless. It was as if she should be doing something, every moment, to prepare for what lay ahead. But what? All she could do was wait for the next eight months or so to pass. Isn't that what all women did? At some stage she would have to start making more concrete arrangements, but it was early days now.

In fact, it was so early that she still couldn't be certain of anything. People got false positives all the time, didn't they? She had to book an appointment with a doctor just to be sure. She would do that soon.

After dinner, she took a long bath. She hadn't spoken much to Chris today, though he was obviously curious. She couldn't bear to talk about anything just yet. But to be honest, it was nice to know that he was interested at least. It made her feel as though she hadn't completely wrecked their friendship after all.

She pulled herself out of the bath and looked at her dripping body in the mirror. Had it changed? Was it making its own secret preparations for motherhood? She couldn't see that it had changed. Maybe she looked a little bit … fuller overall, but that could be explained by lack of exercise since she got back from Florida. No, it was impossible to tell. For something like that, she needed the diagnosis of a professional to be sure.

The information that Rory had given her before she left work was still niggling at the back of her mind. It was probably just a coincidence, but it was worth looking into.

She sighed and opened her laptop and typed in the hack link that Rory had given her. Even when something was over, it wasn't really over.

The page was private, but because of the password that Rory had given her, she was able to see it. Pretty innocuous stuff. Just posts about running, really. It was set up so that no one could add him as a friend, but he interacted regularly with the running club in the Phoenix Park, in particular conversing with one young girl who wanted advice.

Unfortunately, there was no way to find out who he really was. Lots of men set up fake profiles for dating, so that wasn't suspect in itself. Probably he was just married. It was weird that he had a bogus Facebook account, but then some people tried really hard to maintain their privacy. After all that heavy thinking—about everything, Reilly thought she deserved to get some rest.

Sleep didn't come easy, though. The events of the past few weeks went running through her head like the wind that was blowing outside. For Reilly, it still didn't feel as though anything was put to rest.

34

WHY DO YOU LOOK SO different from your profile pictures?

Oh, those aren't of me. I only use this thing so that I can keep up to date, I don't like to have my life plastered all over the place.

Fair enough, lots of my friends have pages like that. Maybe I over-share.

No, it's good. Your pictures are really nice. They remind me of family.

That's really sweet.

You keep icing that hamstring, OK? I want to see you back at the track next week. I don't want to have to run with someone else again. Such a pain.

She's beginning to trust me, I can feel it. She didn't come last time because she had an injury. But she actually messaged me to tell me that. She reached out to me. The time is coming closer.

In other good news, Nico Peroni has been arrested. It's mixed news, actually. The heat is off me, for now, but it's not great news for the business. I would prefer for all of this to be taking place far away from me but I have to take my wins where I find them.

I need all my energy for this. My creation for Constance must be the most spectacular yet.

So it seems as though everything is coming together. My only wish is that I could see Ruth when they tell her of her daughter's fate. I want to see the horror and grief rush up on her. I want to see all of her worst nightmares come true.

If there's anyone I'm leaving this legacy for, it's her. Soon she can see the result her selfishness has wrought, so that she can know my pain.

Just in case you forgot about me, Ruth.

Constance sighed and stirred the soup she was making for her mother. She didn't have a hamstring injury. The truth was, her mother had fallen into one of the black depressions that sometimes seized her and Constance had made the journey over to Oxford to look after her. She had just wanted to reach out and talk to someone normal, so she had messaged Danny from the running group. There was something kind of calming about him. Constance wasn't interested in anything more than friendship, but she didn't think he was either.

When her mother got into a place like this, she was hard to deal with. 'You just had to wait it out,' is what the doctors said. She spent the night before telling

Constance: "I've done such awful things, Connie, such terrible things."

It was a common theme of her depression. She would never tell Constance exactly what it was that she had done. Constance didn't think it could be that bad. She was a lecturer, for goodness sakes. It wasn't exactly a life of sin. She had been a good mother, for the most part. Constance knew that her mother had seen a psychologist before she was born, to talk through various issues, but that was her business. She knew that Ruth had mixed feelings about becoming a mother. She wanted it, but feared that she might not be very good at it. Constance had to reassure her a lot on that score.

'Connie? Are you in here?' Her mother appeared at the kitchen door, weak and pale.

'Sure, Mum. I made soup. You have to eat something tonight, ok?'

Ruth nodded. This meekness usually indicated that she was getting back to normal and Constance was relieved. She wasn't sure how much more of this she could handle, to be honest.

'Are you feeling better?'

Ruth nodded again. 'I feel that there are things you should know,' she said. 'About me. Things I've done.'

'Mum, like I said before, I don't want to know. You don't need to tell me anything. This is your business. What happened in the past has nothing to do with me.'

'But it does,' said Ruth. 'I feel that you know me as a better person than I really am.'

'Don't flatter yourself,' said Constance. 'You're flawed. I'm flawed. Everyone is flawed. We just have to do our best to overcome those things and to live with them and move on. You need to stop beating yourself up for something that happened in the past.'

'You really, really don't want to know?' asked Ruth.

Constance shook her head. 'I don't.'

'OK. Then let me just say this: never do something out of a sense of duty, because you will not be good at it. You will disappoint yourself, and everyone around you. Promise me that.'

'I'll try,' said Constance. 'No promises. Making a promise is just another way to let someone down.'

Reilly and Gary pulled up to the industrial block of flats where Janey Smith lived.

'I'm still not sure this is a productive use of our time,' said Reilly.

'Well, look at it this way. The chef case is closed, we've got a little more time on our hands for the moment. So we might as well use it.'

There was rubbish clogging the stairwells, but Reilly refused to take the lifts. 'Those things look like death traps,' she said.

'You know that people get stabbed in stairwells like this one?'

'I'll take my chances,' said Reilly.

After climbing seven floors, Reilly was puffing lightly but Gary was breathing like a wounded wildebeest.

'You really need to get fit,' she commented.

'Do you think it would improve my chances with Lucy?'

'I think it will improve your chances of not having a heart attack in an abandoned stairwell.'

Gary pretended to consider. 'Nah, I don't think it's worth it.'

They knocked on the door of 742. This was a place where dreams came to die. You could feel it in the air. Old people that no one cared about ended up here. Poor families who earned minimum wage and had to feed five kids. And then there were the users, the small time criminals. It wasn't a nice place. Gary and Reilly looked at each other. Why live here if you had a choice? At the last minute, Reilly considered that it might be some kind of set up, but then the door opened to reveal a shrivelled older woman of indeterminate age.

'Come in, come in,' she said, with a great amount of forced cheer. 'I was just tidying up.'

The place was indeed spotless. It had been made as nice as a place like this could be. There was furniture from what were clearly better times, pot plants and pictures on the wall. Less cosy were the creepy knitted dolls that were dotted around the room, but there was no accounting for personal taste.

'We have to be honest with you,' said Reilly, taking an offered seat on a plush couch, 'We haven't come here because we were interested in buying the house.'

'You haven't?' said Janey, sinking into a chair opposite Reilly. It was impossible to tell her age. Her hair, which would have once been black, was stone grey. Her face was crisscrossed with lines, everything about it which would once have been full was now collapsed and sunken. She look at Reilly with resignation in her watery blue eyes. 'What have you come about then?'

'Your brother's house was the site of a crime scene investigation,' said Reilly. 'Has anyone come and talked to you about it?'

'They rang me,' said Janey. 'Wanted to know if I knew who was living in it after my brother died. Sure how would I know that, I said, when I didn't even know my own brother had passed away? Must have been squatters. They're terribly common, all over the place here. An abandoned house wouldn't be abandoned for long.'

'The house was in very neat condition,' said Reilly. 'If it was squatters, then they were very clean squatters.'

'I wouldn't know; I haven't seen the place in years.'

'You never went to see the property you inherited?'

'I didn't see the point,' said Janey.

'We found a number of items in the house. Women's things, like wigs, jewelry and the like. Would any of those be yours or your brother's?'

'No,' said Janey. 'I never wore a wig in my life. And Martin ... I doubt it.'

'When was the last time you were at your brother's house?'

'Donkey's years. When my husband was still alive I think. I'll be honest, my brother and I weren't exactly close.'

'Do you have family yourself, Mrs Smith?' Gary asked, looking around the room which was curiously bare of furniture. 'Children?'

'Yes, my boys,' said Janey.

'Where are your boys now?' Reilly asked. 'Why aren't you leaving the sale of the house to them?' It seemed a lot for such a frail old woman to take on, considering she could barely walk.

Janey's eyes narrowed. 'You know where they are,' she spat. 'Do you think I want to talk about this over and over? I don't. I hate it. I've already tried to help.'

'I'm sorry,' said Reilly. 'I don't understand.'

'I've been asked again and again about that Gorman girl all those years ago,' said Janey, tears forming in the corner of her eyes. 'But I just don't know anything else, other than I know what it's like to lose a child.'

Reilly took a moment to regain some control. She held her breath. 'Wait a second,' she said, realizing suddenly. 'Your boys are Darren and Brendan Keating?'

'Yes, of course,' said Janey. 'I thought that was why you were here.'

Reilly didn't want to come out and say that they hadn't actually made that connection. But now she knew she was close. She could feel that Gary too was rigid with anticipation beside her.

'Can you tell us what you know about Grace Gorman's disappearance?' asked Gary. 'We know that you've been through it all a thousand times now, but I'm new to this case and I really like to hear from people themselves.' He gave her a winning smile, playing up the eager newbie charm.

'Well, all I can tell you is what I remember,' said Janey. 'It was a long time ago. But first let me put the kettle on. I need a cup of tea.'

Chris took a long lunch break and went for a swim. He enjoyed the peace of it, the way his body felt when he was slicing through the water. He knew that Reilly felt the same way about running. That it made you your best, most calm self.

He let the water take him completely, basking in the cool, unchanging blue. He powered up and down the lane, touching the end of the pool and flipping under to start a new length without even thinking about it. It was automatic for him, though at times like these he wished for the endless nature of the sea. How nice it would be to swim for as long as you wanted with no impediments.

It looked as though everything had closed up nicely. They had caught their man, though Nico Peroni was still refusing to speak, and apparently refusing to eat too. They needed more details from him, but they might have to wait until he had undergone a psych test. But for now, they could all concentrate on other work. Sadly, hardly a day went by in this city where there wasn't a serious crime committed, or a body found somewhere. He wished sometimes that his job was unnecessary, but it never would be.

The message from Reilly was loud and clear: give me some space. He could understand that, he really could. It was hard, when they had been getting so close, but he would do his best. He could understand that her world had been tipped upside down. He couldn't even begin to fathom what he would do if he was in her shoes. Would she go back to the States? Surely that would be the wisest decision. She had her father there. And the baby's father of course.

Chris wasn't sure what the nature of that relationship had been. Had she and Todd Forrest been truly close? Had they fallen in love? Or was it just a physical thing? He didn't know why, but knowing would make him feel better. Maybe it would just give him some clarity as to whether something had truly been starting between him and Reilly, or whether she had just been confused and vulnerable.

More than anything, he wished that he knew how she felt about what was happening. Was she in shock? Was she at least a little bit happy? Or did she simply not know how to feel? Chris's heart went out to her. He knew she would dislike the inevitability of it all at least, hate that loss of control that was so important to her.

In truth, it was just one of those days when Chris felt beaten. Beaten by the endless tide of horror that kept washing up on his desk, beaten by his inability to control his feelings in an impossible situation. It would pass, he knew.

He just had to plough on through it.

Something was bugging Pete Kennedy. He was a thoughtful man, but not given to over-analysis. Things went the way they went, that was all, and sometimes it didn't pay to look too closely into them. The Chef murder investigation was closed, and the second after it did, about ten new files were dropped onto his desk, all as urgent and troubling as the last. He kept his head down, getting on with work the best way he knew how: attack it head on.

But something felt a little lacking to him. The end of the latest murder investigation just didn't sit right. It wasn't simply that Peroni must have been the man who'd tried to have him killed. He was more of a professional than that. Pete Kennedy had stared down the barrel of a gun more than once and he had tried very hard to let those incidents go. Carry those around with you, and you would be a dead man walking, waiting for the crack of the next trigger.

Nico Peroni was guilty of something, no question. But the man just seemed more broken to Kennedy than evil. He was no psychologist, obviously. He couldn't look inside a man and see his soul. Kennedy believed unquestionably in the soul, and in good and evil. He believed that some of the criminals they'd dealt with in the past were just born evil. He and Reilly would have agreed on that score.

They had dealt with serial killers before. Men who got a desperate thrill from killing, from making death into a kind of art form. They took pride in their work, and more often as not, once they were caught, they liked to wax lyrical about how clever they had been, how they had gotten away with it for so long. But Nico Peroni wasn't doing that. In fact, he wasn't saying anything, just sitting in his cell, as silent as a bell in an abandoned church tower.

It didn't sit right with Kennedy, but then the evidence was there, wasn't it? Maybe this bloke was different. Not everyone followed the same pattern.

Kennedy would have liked to know one thing, though. It was the same thing he wanted to know in all of his cases: Why? Why would anyone do this?

Of course, the motives never satisfied him. So silly, bordering on petty.

But still, he wanted to know.

Hazy memories were coming back to him from the night he staked out Harry McMurty. He remembered sitting in his car, anticipating his meal. He remembered the knock at the window, the smile of the man who handed him his food. It could have been anyone, of course. Anyone would knock on a window and deliver a meal if you gave them a few quid. But whoever it was, it wasn't Nico Peroni.

Of that, he was sure.

The lab's analysis of the burger had proven that the oil used to cook the mushroom was different from that used to cook the meat. That had been cooked in standard bulk buy canola oil. The fast food restaurant said they used that on all of their food. The mushroom though, had been cooked in virgin olive oil. No surprises there, really. Just confirming a forgone conclusion. But still, that night continued to worm away at him, no matter how he tried to shake it off like he did with his other brushes with death.

He might have to talk things over with Chris, see if he could give him some perspective. That's what having a partner was for.

35

'MY BOY DARREN STARTED SEEING the Gorman girl when he was about fifteen. He was a good boy then, for the most part. He was only getting into some of the mischief that all young boys will. The music, my goodness. All that noise.'

She paused and took a sip of her tea. Reilly knew there was no point trying to hurry her through. Janey Smith had an audience for the first time in years. Besides, Reilly knew you sometimes got the best out of people by just letting them ramble.

'Grace was a good girl. I liked her, but I thought she was a bit young. At fifteen, young boys are looking for things that a younger girl just shouldn't be expected to give, if you catch my drift. But I kept an eye on them and they seemed happy enough. Her parents were very strict so there was no chance of hanky panky around there.'

Janey had put out a packet of custard creams for them. Gary was dunking them, one after another into his tea, transfixed on Janey as though she was telling him a priceless secret.

'They used to do all the usual things kids of that age do, go to the pictures, listen to records, get milkshakes from the chipper. But then,' she paused, looking pained. 'My oldest son, Brendan came back from his dad's place. I want you to understand,' she said, 'I would never have left him with his father if I didn't have to. But he wouldn't let me go without leaving one of the boys behind. Darren was my baby. And Brendan *liked* his father. They were one and the same.'

'Did you have contact with Brendan while he lived with his father?' asked Reilly.

'On and off. As much as I was allowed. I thought, when he came back, that he wanted us to have a relationship. To heal. But he just wanted to use us, to wreck our lives. When I say I lost a child, this is what I mean. Brendan I had lost already, but Darren was mine. He was a good boy and we were a family. Him and me and his stepfather. But Brendan came back and I lost Darren. Watching him change was like watching someone die. I couldn't reach him, no one could.'

'How exactly did he change?' asked Reilly.

'He got mean, like his brother. He began to steal from us, to threaten us. He told us that we had ruined his life. He started getting in trouble. I heard him shouting at young Grace, calling her awful things. I told her to get out and not to come back. I didn't want her mixed up in it all. I knew Brendan was behind it but I couldn't stop it. I couldn't make it stop.'

She struggled to retain her composure. Reilly could see that Janey Smith was a good woman, who had been worn away by the circumstances of her life. It took all the strength she had now, just to get through each day. It was a monumental effort for her even to tell them this story.

'If I could go back in time,' she said, 'I never would have let Brendan back into our lives. I would have shut the door on him. I would have shunned him, if it had stopped all the damage he caused.'

'Do you remember if Brendan and Grace knew each other at all?' asked Reilly.

'Of course they did. Wherever Darren went, his brother followed. Didn't let them have a moment's peace. Brendan called Grace his "little golden girl". He was nicer to her than anyone else. I thought she might have been a good influence on him actually.'

Reilly winced at what she guessed was a completely misguided assessment. No one could have been a good influence on Brendan Keating. Maybe he was obsessed with Grace, and maybe he used her as a way to break down his brother even further, but he didn't care about her. She had no power to change him.

'Do you remember any incidents from around the time of Grace's disappearance? Did Darren and Brendan fight at all?'

Janey thought for a while. 'There was one time,' she said, 'when Darren held a steak knife to his brother's throat. "Leave her alone," he said. Brendan just laughed.'

How could the investigators not have gotten any of this the first time round? Reilly wondered. Darren had put on a good front when Grace went missing, but you didn't have to dig very deep to get to how troubled and unhappy this family had been. 'Do you remember the last time you saw Grace?'

'Very clearly,' said Janey. 'She came over with a carry-all bag and I thought she was going on holidays. She said "I might be", as though she would just make up her mind. It was strange, for a fourteen year old. She looked very thin and sad. I told her again that there was nothing but trouble for her at our house. But she didn't listen to me. Girls are like that, aren't they, when they're young? Always believing that each man is the one for them. The great love. I was the same, with the boys' father. I met him young. My whole life would have been different if I hadn't.'

'Did anything happen that day? Anything out of the ordinary?' Reilly pressed to keep her on topic.

'Grace left crying. I have to tell you, it was a relief. I thought they had broken up. Then three days later the police were knocking on the door asking Darren if he had seen her. He went crazy when he found out she was missing. I thought he had lost his mind. Things got worse after that. He just started acting out.'

'Where was Brendan at this point?'

'He came home a few times, asking for money. Him and Darren were living together somewhere when Darren wasn't in jail, but we never saw Brendan much after that.'

'Do you think it's possible,' asked Reilly, 'that Brendan could have been living in your brother's house?'

Janey stared. 'I have no idea,' she said. 'He certainly knew where it was, but he wasn't close to his uncle. Perhaps. It's not impossible.'

'And did you ever wonder if Darren or Brendan had anything to do with Grace's disappearance?'

'No, I never did. Darren's not a killer and why would Brendan bother? She was just a little girl.'

'Do you know where Brendan is now?'

'Dead,' she said. 'I'm sure of it. And poor Darren is rotting away in Mountjoy.'

On a whim, Reilly asked: 'Did Brendan have any hobbies at all? Anything he particularly liked?'

'Oh I don't know,' said Janey. 'I do remember that from a young age he liked to collect things. Odds and ends. Things he found or stole. Just ordinary, everyday things.'

'Have you ever seen this necklace before?' She brought up a picture of Grace's necklace.

'Yes,' said Janey without hesitation. 'Darren took that from Brendan and gave it to Grace. Brendan was angry when he found out, but Grace loved it so much, she wouldn't give it back.'

When Reilly got home that night her mind was reeling. She was following two strands that would hopefully lead her to the same place. There was her communication with Darren Keating, through which she hoped he would implicate his brother. Now there was their conversation with Janey Smith, nee Keating, which would also hopefully lead to Brendan.

She felt sure of his guilt now. Perhaps Darren had been involved too, but Brendan was the culprit. She just knew it. She just needed some proof. They needed to search the house again, but how could they do that without stepping on the toes of the investigating officers? She would need Jack Gorman's help with this one. It was as simple as that.

Worrying her as well, was the complete helplessness that seemed to come with having children. Janey Smith had loved her children, especially Darren and had tried to protect him as best she could. But he had still been taken as far away from her as a son could be.

How did you stop a thing like that from happening?

36

'MY TIMES ARE REALLY IMPROVING,' Constance told Danny. 'And you get the praise for that.'

'Thanks,' said Danny. 'You were a pretty quick pupil.'

They ran for a while in silence. 'So, how's life?' said Constance. She realized she knew very little about Danny, despite routinely blabbing to him about her own personal life.

He looked a little pained. 'It's OK,' he said. 'Well, it's kind of a weird time of year for me actually.'

'Oh, really? Why's that?'

'My mother died around this time. Usually, next week, I would arrange dinner with a couple of friends, to remember her. Just something quiet. But this year everyone is away. And I'm just not sure how I'll feel facing it alone.'

'Wow,' she said. 'That's tough. I'm sorry.'

'It'll be OK,' he said. 'I'll manage. Just cook up something nice and toast to her memory. She really liked to cook, I got that from her.'

'Look, I know we don't really know each other, but if you want company, I'd be more than happy to come around.'

'Really?' asked Danny. 'That's so nice of you. I just don't really want to be alone. I'd make it worth your while and cook you something special, your favorite if you like.'

'Believe it or not, my favorite is simple old macaroni and cheese,' laughed Constance. 'I feel like that might be a little below your skills.'

'No way,' said Danny. 'One very special mac and cheese, coming up.'

'I need something from you,' said Reilly, sounding braver than she felt.

'And what's that,' asked Jack Gorman.

'I think I've got something… on Grace's case, but I need you to pull some strings.'

'I thought we discussed this. However I might wish otherwise, my hands are tied.'

'It's gone beyond that, Jack. I'm closing in on this, but I can't do it alone.'

Jack Gorman wanted nothing more than to find out what had happened to his eldest daughter. He wanted it so that he and his wife could begin to recover from years of grief and doubt, and he wanted it so that Lucy could stop holding on to the past. He loved his youngest daughter more than anything, but he found that hard to show sometimes. He had been pushing his emotions away for so many years. But now he could see from the determined look on Reilly Steel's face that she really had something. Could it even be possible, after all these years …?

'What do you need?' he asked. 'It doesn't mean you're going to get it, but what do you need?'

'I want to do another sweep of the house where the necklace was found. And I need full access to the current task force files. And,' she added gently. 'I need for you and Lucy to speak openly with each other. Really put your heads together and see what you can remember. You can't avoid this forever, Jack.'

If Jack Gorman was angry that she had spoken so harshly to him, he didn't show it.

Maybe because he knew that she was right.

Things began to move after that. Jack tried to stop himself from hoping for a thing he thought was impossible. But he found, that despite himself, they might find out what had happened to Grace at last.

One night after work, he called his daughter into his office. 'Steel thinks she's close to something,' he told her. 'She's asked me to pull some strings.'

Lucy stared. 'Reilly wouldn't ask for that unless there really was something, Dad' she said. 'She wouldn't get our hopes up for nothing.'

'Well, I still believe that we shouldn't get our hopes up,' he insisted, despite the fact that his were. 'But she wants us to go over some the witness reports one more time and try to remember anything that might help. Together.'

There was a moment's silence. They both remembered what had happened the last time Lucy had tried to talk to him about Grace.

'It's very hard for me,' he admitted. 'For all these years, I've been tortured by thoughts of what happened to my little girl. It's haunted me, Lucy, knowing what I know about this kind of thing. I knew as soon as it happened that we wouldn't see her alive again, and that she had likely died in a terrible way.'

'I know,' said Lucy. 'I understand that. 'And Reilly feels like I might know something, something that I have been pushing away all these years. I want you to help me remember what I was like. What Grace and I were like, together.'

Jack thought for a moment, and his face softened in repose. 'You were close,' he said. 'Two beautiful, happy little girls.' He smiled. 'Of course, I might be slightly biased. You were very protective of each other. Your mother and I didn't stand a chance against the two of you. Grace began to develop her own tastes though. She went through quite a radical stage, influenced one minute by boy bands and the next by all the rock bands of the day, but we didn't worry too much. It was normal. She put safety pins through all her clothes and some of yours, too, though you weren't too impressed.'

'Did we ever fight?'

'My God, yes. You both had such strong opinions. You would scream at each other and half an hour later all would be well again. Grace was a very sensitive person. She wanted to believe the best in people and that they always loved her. We worried that she was too sensitive sometimes. She felt so much for people and animals.'

'I remember that,' said Lucy. She was always bringing home hurt things, like a wounded bird, or a half-dead mouse.

'Of course, we had our troubles with her as well. She began to get very rebellious, resenting us, telling us that we didn't care about her.'

'Did you know she was sneaking out at night?'

He sighed and nodded. 'Of course. We tried to stop it, but short of locking her in, what could we do? Your mother thought that it was natural that she would try to test her boundaries. We had both done the same thing, but it is heart-stopping when it's your own child.'

'I liked Darren,' said Lucy. 'I know that he was older and you thought he might be a bad influence, but I did like him.'

'We liked him too,' said Jack. 'He was a good boy when he first met Grace. We were concerned about the age but it all seemed innocent enough. But it got too serious, too fast.'

'I remember her crying,' said Lucy, eyes shining, 'towards the end. She was so unhappy and I didn't know how to make it better. She didn't want me to tell you.' She bit her lip, on the verge of crying, and Jack put his hand over his daughter's.

'We knew, pet, we knew that she was unhappy. It's not your fault. We thought that it was a teenage thing and that it would blow over.'

'Do you know why? I try to remember but I just can't remember why. I thought she and Darren were fighting.'

He sighed again. 'He had some bad family problems. It was starting to affect him too, and Grace was very upset. She felt like she didn't know him anymore. A few days before she disappeared she came to me and asked if he could come and live with us. She felt, very strongly, that he needed to be out of that house. Of course I said no. It was impossible. I mean, what would his own family have to say about it? She said if I didn't allow it, she would run away with Darren herself. She said she needed to "save" him.'

'He's in jail now, Gary told me.'

'It doesn't surprise me,' said Jack. 'It kept me going for a while, the idea that she might have run away. That we might find her, angry and scared, but alive. But it soon became very clear that Darren didn't know what had happened to her either.'

'How can we be so sure?' said Lucy. 'How do we know that?'

'He was questioned so many times,' said Jack. 'And he never changed his story. I just have to believe that there's another explanation.'

After she left, Jack reflected that he and his daughter hadn't talked so openly in a long time.

Whatever Steel was onto, it might not reveal what had happened to Grace, but it might just save his relationship with Lucy.

37

I DIDN'T EXPECT IT TO be so easy. All I needed to do was tell the truth, really, about the sadness I carry inside me. And whoosh, just like that, she has played into my hands.

Now comes the time for preparation. This one is different. I will take her to restaurant. It's the perfect setting for this one. Something dramatic, something big. And then I will simply disappear, leaving those stupid investigators scratching their heads.

The question is, what to use? I'm sick of mushrooms, of berries. The last of the antimine was planted on Peroni, and of course a good chef never uses the same menu twice. Something that tastes slightly sharp, I think. Something that will ensure the manner of death isn't quite so peaceful as the others.

I have only days to perfect something. It shouldn't be too hard. Without knowing it, I have been preparing for this for a very long time.

It's hard to know where I will go, and what the manner of my life will be once I am finished. Of course, I will continue with my work, but somehow I think the flavor (pardon the pun) will have gone out of it. After you have fulfilled your greatest wish, there can be nothing to really live up to that. I must take as much joy from these last days as I can. The satisfaction from this will last me a long time, if only I can do it right.

It must be executed with merciless precision.

Reilly put her legs up and stared at the ceiling. She had never thought she would be in this position, such a vulnerable, helpless pose.

She didn't know what she hoped for. Part of her wished it was all a terrible mistake: that she wasn't pregnant and could just continue on with her life the way it was before. It would make everything so much less complicated. There wouldn't be the awful tension between her and Chris, the weight of the secret she was keeping from everyone else. She could forge ahead with her career without any distractions. She wouldn't have to have that unbelievably hard conversation with Todd, or Daniel. Again, it was odd to think that her old friend would be her baby's grandfather.

She didn't know if any of them were quite ready for that kind of relationship.

On the other hand, if her early pregnancy indications turned out not to be viable after all, might she be a little disappointed? Apart from all the obvious complications it would bring to her life, didn't a tiny part of her want to know what it was like to present her father with a grandchild? To bring a little bit of family joy back into Mike's life?

Reilly would never get to know how she would feel if she wasn't pregnant though, because the gynecologist moved up to the head of the bed, removing her gloves, and said: 'No doubt about it, you're five weeks pregnant. Congratulations.'

She was numb as they went through preparations for upcoming appointments and scans, talked about her diet and weight and how much sleep she was getting.

The doctor looked at her with concern. 'Are you OK about it all? Bit of a shock, I presume?'

'You could say that.'

'Well, at this early stage, we have to caution people not to get too excited. It's a perilous time. After the first trimester has passed it's usually safer to start planning.'

'OK,' said Reilly. 'Can I still exercise? I'm a runner.'

'Of course. The body is usually fine with exercise it's accustomed to. So I wouldn't recommend taking up tap dancing at this stage. But as long as you don't push yourself too hard, light running should be fine, good in fact.'

'OK ….OK, thanks.' This was surreal. She truly couldn't believe she was sitting in this room, talking to a medical professional about something so utterly unrelated to her job.

'Try to enjoy it, Reilly. Your body has never been through something like this before, and sometimes it will feel like hell, and sometimes it will be euphoric.'

'Euphoric? I haven't had any of that so far. I've been unbearably nauseous actually.'

'Try ginger. Ginger tea, ginger biscuits.' The woman chuckled. 'Just wait until the morning sickness sets in. Then you'll know all about it.'

When Reilly got back to work, she found another letter from Mountjoy Prison on her desk. It was the last thing she felt like dealing with right now, but with the trail on Grace Gorman's investigation heating up, she couldn't afford to ignore it. It could be that she was still wrong about everything, a pile up of coincidences and Darren Keating was toying with her, just for something to do.

She took out the letter and read it.

"Ms Steel, I understand your position, I really do. But I think that you should try harder to understand mine. For almost ten years I have been in and out of jail. I've never really had time to form a relationship with anyone but my brother. I've seen life through his eyes and I'm only now coming around to the idea that he may have been wrong.

You ask why I don't believe in redemption. I believe that in order to be redeemed, you have to have something to change for. You have to want something. I don't want anything, Ms Steel, except peace. That's why I don't mind prison too much, it gives me an opportunity to reflect, to be alone, without the constant pressures of the outside world.

I know you visited my mother recently. She and I are attempting to repair our relationship. I don't want her to spend the rest of her life blaming herself for all that has happened. She sends me the knitted dolls that you doubtless saw in her flat. They are not exactly to my taste, but I keep them anyway. They speak to a kind of innocence that I once had and that perhaps my mother likes to believe I possess still.

She told me that you asked about the necklace that I gave Grace. I remember it well, it was no trinket. It was a real piece of jewelry. I would like to see it again, to be reminded of Grace when she wore it, but I guess that's impossible.

I took that necklace from my brother. He had a collection of things that he had stolen from women he was obsessed with. He started these obsessions young. I suppose, if you wanted to get analytical about it, you could say that Brendan was searching for a replacement mother.

He stole that necklace from one of our dad's women. According to my brother, this woman had long blonde hair and a wide, white smile. She was as nice to him as probably anyone had been in his life. He was enraged when I took the necklace.

My brother didn't start off bad, I don't believe. He started off desperate. He started off looking for someone to love him. I know you will probably laugh at this, but it's the truth. He would fall in love with ten different women a day. He loved hair: black hair, blonde hair, red hair. He would have liked your hair. He loved blondes especially.

I think you know what I'm trying to tell you here, Ms Steel. Do you really need to hear the rest of the story? You and I both know it can't end well.'

There was no doubt in Reilly's mind anymore that Brendan Keating was Grace's killer, and that Darren was involved, but she needed proof. There was the evidence from the house: the wigs, the necklace, the fractured relationship between Brendan and his family, the desperation of Grace to get Darren away from Brendan before she disappeared.

It was all leading to one place. Reilly needed to get back into that house. She was sure that they would find the truth about what happened to Grace there.

Before she went and asked Jack Gorman for an update from the chief, she sent a quick note to Darren Keating.

"You and I know that we are edging on some hideous truth here. It must see the light, no matter how terrible. You know so much of what we have already discovered for this to be wrong. I believe that your brother killed Grace and that you helped him cover it up.

Tell me what you know. I don't believe that you are to blame for this crime, but your culpability in covering it up has caused years of pain for Grace's family. Let's end it now, one way or another."

38

THAT EVENING JACK GORMAN HAD dinner with his daughter at her favorite restaurant.

'I see the city's diners feel safe with high cuisine once more,' he said, eyeing the bustling restaurant warily.

'I don't know if they ever stopped,' said Lucy. 'I think most people were more intrigued with the idea of a murderous chef. It added a little bit of risk to their meal. Brought a little edge to their mundane lives.'

'Do you really think people's lives are mundane?' asked Jack.

'I think people think they are,' said Lucy. 'And then something terrible happens to them and they wish it could all go back to the way it was, boring or not.'

'Is that how you feel?'

'I feel like people should realise how lucky they are,' she said. 'I feel like boring is fine.'

They ordered and toasted Grace's memory quietly, over glasses of merlot.

'I often wonder what kind of woman she would have turned into,' said Jack. 'Sometimes I look at you, and I see her, but that's not fair. You're you, and I'm glad of it. Grace would have been someone else entirely.'

'Sometimes I feel guilty that I've had all the things we talked about when we were young: a career, travel, and maybe one day love and children.'

'I feel sure of it,' said Jack.

'I guess I can't feel guilty forever,' she said. 'I owe it to Grace to live the kind of life that she would be proud of.'

It was nice to spend this time with her father alone. Lucy loved her mother but she spent far more time with her than Jack, despite the fact that they worked in the same unit.

'Did you really hate me getting into this line of work?' she asked now.

Jack smiled. 'I suppose it was inevitable,' he said. 'I probably saw it coming too. You were so interested in my work, and so observant and tenacious. You had all the right qualities. I would have wanted to protect you from the kind of thing that this work involves,' he said. 'But I was too late for that. You wanted to be in the thick of it, and who was I to stop you?'

'Thank you,' she said. 'Thank you for supporting me.'

They talked of lighter things for the rest of the meal, which was delicious. 'We should do this more often,' said Jack.

Afterwards he walked her to her car in the fading light.

'Are you afraid of what we might find?' she asked.

'Of course,' he said. 'And maybe worst of all, I'm afraid that we might find nothing. That all this would have been for naught and we have to go back to that uncertainty and fear once more. I want this to be over, Lucy. It's been so long, and I want us to move on with our lives.'

On the way home Lucy reflected that she wanted that as well. She wanted to be able to fall in love without feeling guilty that her sister never would.

But she supposed that would never happen. Some things you just had to live with, after all.

It was Reilly's first outing with the running group. As a rule, she preferred to train alone, but these people seemed perfectly nice. Very eager and passionate about running. After about ten minutes of standing around talking about technique, she thought: let's just do it already. Talking about it won't get us anywhere.

Finally they started out along the sheltered paths of the Phoenix Park. She stayed at the rear of the pack so that she had a chance to observe everyone. There were a couple of old-timers, her father's age, who still ran with the steady, even pace that they had been using for decades. There were a few women who were returning to running after having children. She supposed that she might soon be one of them. There was a handsome guy, around forty who ran with a younger, attractive woman. This could be the guy from Rory's report she wanted to check on. But there was also another man, around thirty, who ran alone. It could be him either.

The thing was, it could be any of them. She wondered if she was just wasting her time here. They had their guy, didn't they? Nico Peroni was firmly behind bars. Still not talking, but the evidence against him was strong.

Reilly supposed she was doing this because she didn't like to leave anything undone in an investigation. She didn't like loose ends. At the beginning, they had focused very hard on the online dating angle, yet that hadn't panned out. It might still tell them something. She just wanted to be sure.

They ran for about an hour, and Reilly tried to clear her mind of all the distractions of the past couple of months. When Chris's face, or Todd's, floated into her thoughts, she let them go by without concentrating on them. She tried especially not to think of tomorrow, when they would be going over the O'Toole house again, this time surer about who had lived there in the years since Martin O'Toole's death, and that the 'Clive Farrell' who had been signing the pensioner's social welfare cheques was in fact his nephew, Brendan Keating.

She had a feeling it would be a hard, emotional day. For Lucy and Jack Gorman especially of course, but for her as well. The thoughts of her own lost family never got less raw, never went away. She supposed that they never would. It was just something she carried around with her. She did wish that she could protect Lucy from all of it, though. But her colleague too, would have to face the difficulties of her life.

When the run finished they all clustered around and made their farewells. The red-headed girl called: 'See you

Saturday week,' to the handsome older man. He had good form, Reilly had noted. She wondered if he was the guy with the bogus accounts.

'And will you be back next time?' he asked Reilly suddenly.

'Sure,' she said, flashing a smile. 'I'm a little out of shape.'

He didn't answer in the way she expected, just smiled and said: 'You run well.' And then he swung a backpack onto his back and ran off into the dark night.

This cannot be happening. This is unequivocally not happening. I have not come this far to be stopped at the last minute. The dinner with Constance is only days away, and the cop will not get in my way.

Why is she even here? How could she possibly have tracked me here, of all places? I would expect her to turn up to the restaurant, yes, but not at my group. Perhaps it is simply a terrible coincidence. Could that happen? Could we both, by chance, just have stumbled across the same group? It seems too good to be true.

What is certain is that her presence, lurking behind us like a portent of doom, ruined my whole run with Constance this evening. I have come to look forward to our little catch-ups. They are like appetizers before the main course. But I couldn't concentrate with her *there. Couldn't admire the alabaster of Constance's skin, or the glint of her ponytail. I could smell her vanilla scent floating on the breeze and her mint toothpaste on her breath but I couldn't savor any of it.*

Relax, I tell myself. It's fine. She might be here, but she doesn't know who you are yet. She has never met you. But you know who she is. That's my advantage just now, that she has no idea who I am, while I can delve into her life and find out all about her.

There is nothing else for it: I must stay one step ahead.

39

THE NEXT DAY DAWNED BRIGHT and clear, but crisp. Reilly headed straight out to the O'Toole house and Gary met her here.

'Lucy really wants to be here,' he said.

'I know,' said Reilly. 'But I really don't think it's a good idea. Not after last time and especially with those two here.'

She indicated the dark green car which had just pulled up, out of which two plainclothes detectives climbed. They both wore glasses and held coffee cups. The so-called task force.

'Tweedledee and Tweedledum,' Gary mumbled.

Reilly suppressed a smile as she waved to the approaching cops. 'Gentlemen,' she said. 'This is my assisting CSU tech, Gary.'

They shook hands and introduced themselves, but they clearly weren't happy to be there. 'Haven't we been over this before?' said one, Tom Brogan.

'You're overstepping your mark a little here,' said the other. 'Without Gorman's involvement in this, there's no way you would be able to just walk all over it. Anyway, we've been over this a thousand times, that house is a dead end; there's nothing more to find.'

Reilly felt anger building inside her and she had to fight to control. How would these two feel if it was their daughter, their sister, who had been missing for almost two decades, and not just some anonymous girl? Would they show a bit of dedication then?

'I know you've been over it,' said Reilly. 'And so have we. But we've come by some new information recently that makes this property more important to us than ever.'

'Grand,' said one of the detectives. 'Well, don't mind us while we try to do our jobs or anything.'

'Maybe if you actually did them,' Gary said, 'we wouldn't have to.'

And that basically set the mood for the day. Antagonistic and snarky. Reilly sighed. It was going to be a long one.

'I just think that something's off,' said Kennedy.

'The sausages you mean?' asked Chris. They were grabbing a bite at a place near the station which Chris liked because they did good Thai noodles and Kennedy liked because they did sausages and mash. It was a win-win.

'Hilarious,' he deadpanned. 'No this Peroni thing just doesn't feel right to me.'

'We've charged the man with multiple counts of murder, Kennedy. That's a fairly major thing to be having second thoughts about. You wanted to go for the guy, too.'

'I know I did. But it happens a lot doesn't it? You're under pressure to find the right man, so you're quick to arrest the one that fits. People don't understand, but detective work can be like trial and error, just like anything else.'

'I know that,' said Chris. 'I'm not saying we don't make mistakes either, but -'

'But when we do, we're man enough to admit it.'

'Or woman enough.'

'Jeez,' said Kennedy. 'Don't start with that political correctness stuff now. I'm not saying this fella is completely innocent, but I have my doubts. I'd just like to try a few things.'

Chris took a forkful of food, then asked: 'Like what?' He was almost afraid of the answer.

'I want to do a lie detector test,' said Kennedy.

Chris groaned. 'No way. You know those things are unreliable, Kennedy. They're a complete pseudoscience. Half the time people are so nervous they give a false positive, anyway.'

Kennedy grinned and pointed his fork at Chris. 'You know that, and I know that. But the average joe doesn't. And I'll tell you something else as well, for free—half the people who take lie detector tests give in and confess anyway. And do you know why? Because it's more honorable to just tell the truth than to have some machine prove you're a liar. Even if it doesn't really.' His argument was becoming a bit confused. 'Ah feck it, Chris, humor me, will you. Let's just give it a try. I have a feeling, if we set the thing up, just go through the motions even, that Peroni will break.'

'It's O'Brien you need to humor.' Chris pointed out.

But Kennedy was a good cop who only rocked the boat if he really felt strongly about it. If they got an out and out confession, maybe it was worth considering.

Gary and Reilly spent much of the day going over the house, while the task force stood outside talking on their phones, or came in and mocked their efforts.

'Yeah, we did that already,' said one, as Gary tapped on the walls to see if there was anything else hidden behind them.

'Yeah, but of course he can do it better,' said the other one.

Reilly was glad that Gary gritted his teeth, put his head down and just got to work. She didn't know why there was such a treacherous relationship between detectives and forensics, but there so often was. It was detectives who had given her the most crap at the start of her career in the States too. For being a woman, for being blonde, you name it. They either tried to protect her, or rile her, and Reilly didn't appreciate either.

The O'Toole house had been completely cleared of everything by now, but it still retained its creepy atmosphere. She had known that something bad had happened there the first time she came here, and she knew it now. Even without the old blood stains that they had found upstairs the last time, she would have known it.

But being in the house again wasn't giving them anything new. For hours they went over it, top to bottom. They picked up some further trace, hair and fingerprints but there were also beer bottles smashed in the living room. Kids had obviously been here, and they were mucking up any additional evidence related to the house's previous occupants that they might find.

At four P.M., she looked at Gary and said: 'I think we'd better call it a day. There's nothing more here.'

He looked frustrated. 'Just a bit longer. I know something's here. Let me just pull the carpet up.'

She yielded because she knew this meant a lot to him, and also because she didn't want to go back to Jack and Lucy with nothing. But pulling up the carpet gave them nothing but a few grazes. They'd already done that first time round and the floor underneath had no openings. It was just smooth, cold concrete.

But it gave her an idea. 'Wait a second,' she said. 'This place doesn't have a backyard, does it?'

'No, it's standalone.'

'But there's a new development next door.' Relatively new at least. Though eighteen years ago, when Grace Gorman first went missing, the land next to it would have been empty.

A look of understanding swept over Gary's face. 'Reilly. That's a huge job.'

She nodded, and went to look out at the newer development, which stretched as far as the eye could see. 'You're telling me.'

It was one thing for to request a search for a single house, but quite another to look for a warrant to want to poke around in the backyards of other people's houses.

'Reilly, that's impossible,' said Jack. 'If you think you're onto something, and God knows I want this more than anyone, but I just don't see how it can be done. We can't ask O'Brien to get a warrant to go digging up the whole estate.'

'I know,' she said. 'I know that. But maybe just a few nearby? Maybe just to see if there's any sign.'

'If there is … something,' said Jack, 'then it could be anywhere. We're talking about thousands of square meters. If it could be narrowed down…maybe. But as it is, we don't stand a chance. I'm sorry, Reilly,' he said softly. 'But if I can see the impossibility, then surely you can, too.'

He was right, she could. But she was so close, she could feel it. Maybe if she could just be a little more specific…but how?

There was no way of knowing where the body was, if indeed there was one.

40

PART OF THE REASON REILLY was being so single minded about the Gorman case was that it took her mind off her own glaring problems.

The following morning, as she drove across the city, she thought about Chris and how murky and unclear everything between them was. It was so hard to really be honest with herself about how she felt.

Truthfully, she knew she'd had feelings for Chris for a very long time. Feelings that she had pushed down deep, as she was so good at, partly because she was afraid that he didn't feel the same way, and perhaps moreso that it was simply unprofessional. If this … new development hadn't happened, would she have allowed herself to fall for him?

Probably, yes. Despite the awkwardness that it would of course have caused at work, she would have tried to go with the flow and allow it to happen. Because she wanted it to. But now it was impossible and she had to put it out of her mind.

She felt so disassociated from her own body though. She was dismayed that when she thought of pregnancy, she thought of her body being "taken over", "colonised", "invaded" almost. Was it supposed to feel like this?

She wanted badly to ring Mike and pour her heart out, but she didn't want to tell her dad until she knew how she felt, until she knew what she was going to do.

The journey across town took a lot less time on this occasion, faster than she would have liked. She didn't exactly relish the thought of seeing Darren Keating again.

Gary took Lucy for a drink after work.

'I'm really sorry we didn't find anything,' he said. 'I was so sure, Reilly was so sure, that we would. But all we discovered is that it's going to be this huge, maybe impossible job.'

'It's OK,' said Lucy quietly. 'I mean of course I was really hoping that you would find something. But it's not your fault. You can't magic up a result, Gary. I guess I'm coming to terms with the fact that we may never find out what happened to Grace now. That we might have to live our whole lives never knowing.'

'You shouldn't have to,' said Gary. 'I'm still working on it. Reilly's got me going over maps from that area from years ago, trying to see what was there before.'

'Sounds like painstaking work.'

'It's worth it,' said Gary, with the kind of intense look that made her feel a little embarrassed.

'Anyway,' she said. 'One thing I am glad of is that this has brought me way closer to Dad. I've really seen a different side to him these past couple of weeks. A side I kind of remember from when I was younger, but he changed when Grace disappeared. He got so bitter, so over protective. Of course I understand that now, but at the time, I hated it.'

'He's a good man,' said Gary, 'But a scary one.'

Lucy laughed. 'I honestly don't even think he's that scary anymore,' she said. 'I think it's all an act.'

'If it is,' joked Gary, 'it's a really good one.'

Darren Keating didn't look pleased to see Reilly.

'Why are you here?' he asked. 'I wrote to you again.'

'I'm sick of writing, Darren. I'm sick of playing cat and mouse. This isn't a game to me. It's the life of someone I care about, very much.'

'But what about me?'

'What about you?'

'I want to keep writing.' He sounded like a petulant little boy.

'Then keep writing, Darren. Write to anyone you want. But I need answers faster than your style of communicating permits.'

He was silent. Reilly couldn't tell if he was working himself into a rage or not, but if he was she wanted to be right out of the line of fire.

'We've been to your uncle Martin's house,' she said. 'The place we believe your brother was hiding out. And we didn't find what we wanted. But do you want to know what I believe? I believe that Grace's body is buried somewhere, near that house maybe, and that *you* know where it is.' There was nothing from him, not even a flicker of the eyes. 'And do you know what else? I think your brother hurt Grace, hurt her really badly, and I think you've been angry about that all your life.'

She could see him reacting now, his pupils dilating and his hands shaking. He got up swiftly and kicked his chair. It went flying into the opposite wall. The guards were on him in seconds, but when Reilly saw his eyes, she saw that he was in control of the momentary outburst.

'But you can make a difference now Darren,' she continued, realising that this was her last chance, the very last opportunity to find out the truth. 'You couldn't save Grace back then, but you can do something good now, you can finally relieve her family of their burden.' Her voice was almost a whisper. 'Please Darren, please. You know in your heart that it's the right thing to do. Your mother told me you were a good person. Prove it.'

It felt like an age before Darren Keating finally spoke. 'You're wrong.'

Reilly blinked, crushed. She'd been so sure …

'Not Martin's,' Darren continued. 'Our old house … behind the shed' he said, looking like a little boy about to cry.

41

CONSTANCE RAN A BRUSH THROUGH her hair as she talked to her mother over the phone. Ruth was feeling like her old self again, giving guest lectures and advising Constance on how best to plant vegetables in pots on her balcony.

'How's the running?' her mum asked warily. She wasn't really a fan of exertion. There was something so primitive about it, after all.

'It's so good,' said Constance. 'I'm getting really fit and really strong. But did I tell you about the guy I run with? It's so sad. His mum died when he was really little and he has this dinner every year to remember her and this year none of his friends can go. So I'm going to go and keep him company.'

'Sounds a little obsessive if you ask me,' said Ruth.

'Not everyone actually is, mother. I'm just telling you about my life.'

'And you know I'm just a grouchy old woman, my dear. Now go off and have fun.'

Constance would. She had a date tonight with a big, sexy fireman she had met at a fundraiser.

She planned to have lots of fun indeed.

It was the last meet-up before my big night on Saturday with Constance.

I've perfected the menu and I told her. You're going to love it.

I'm really excited, she said. I don't think I've ever had anyone truly cook just for me before.

We ran in perfect anticipation. All these months, all these dead ends, these other, unsatisfactory subjects: it's all just been leading up to this.

The fly in the ointment is the cop. She's definitely looking for something. But I don't think she's found it yet. All I need is a few more days. Then I can go and start a new life somewhere, as someone completely different. I've toyed with the idea that maybe I will feel free then, will just be able to lead a normal life.

But the truth is, these girls are everywhere. Forging paths through the world for their own good, and thinking of no one else. I can't let that go unpunished. I can't let another child suffer as I did. So if you want to point the finger, if you want to name a culprit, you can look past me. I merely carry out the infliction of pain. It's another who has created it. If I had been shown one modicum of love from her in my childhood, then maybe everything would have been different.

But soon I will have a revenge sweeter than I could have dreamed. Not even killing Ruth herself would give me this much pleasure.

I only want to take from her as much as she took from me.

Reilly was stretched so tight, she thought her skin might actually tear as two days later, she stood outside the Keatings' former house and watched the diggers work. Gary was there, and the guys from the task force were sitting in their car with the heater on. She had asked Lucy and Jack not to come.

In case they didn't find anything, and in case they did.

'Do you really think we'll find her?' Gary asked as they waited on the lawn. The house's slightly stunned current occupants had duly complied with the warrant, and had made themselves scarce while the excavation was underway. 'Maybe this guy's just toying with you.'

'There's always that possibility,' she agreed. 'But I just have to trust my instincts. I always believed that Darren Keating knew something about Grace's disappearance, and I also felt he was sincere.' But then the man had also had years of psychological abuse from his psychopathic brother, so there was also every chance that Gary's suspicions were correct.

Either way, they'd find out soon.

It was slow, painstaking work. They had to stop every time something was found, examine and then bag it in case it was important. It was surprising how much junk was in the ground in the area Darren had pinpointed. The shed he'd mentioned was no longer there, and so far they had found an old shoe, the leather disintegrating and moldy, bottles and a plastic bag filled with library books.

'Someone's going to have some overdue fees for those,' Gary joked and she knew this was a sure sign that he was nervous. Her keyed up energy was transferring to him too.

It began to rain lightly. Each drop that hit Reilly's skin seemed to pierce it like a tiny pin. It didn't seem right to go and sit in the car, though. It seemed right to wait out here. Instead she wrapped a GFU wind-breaker around her shoulders and pulled the hood up. Gary did the same, and they looked like the keepers of some ancient grave. Which, she thought, maybe they were.

The rain made the recovery harder. Boots stuck in the mud, items were plucked from its sucking grip only to be lost again. Reilly wasn't going to call it off, though. They had waited too long for this. Lucy and her family had waited too long.

Soon, it started to get dark. They powered up overhead lighting but Reilly knew it was a matter of time before they would have to call it a day. Just a little longer, she prayed, please.

Her legs became stiff and sore from standing in the cold and the run she had gone for the night before. She was out of practice a little and had pushed herself hard. Her reverie was interrupted by one of the diggers leaning down to inspect something and then throwing his hand in the air as a signal.

'He's found something,' said Gary. They made their way over to where the digger was. Both of them could see the white ridges that he had uncovered, white ridges that were being washed clean by the light drizzle.

Bones were white when you set them next to something like dirt, but Reilly knew that under the mortuary lights, they would be yellowish, pitted and flawed.

'Get a tent up,' she said. 'We're not going until we've got everything.'

They waited until the ME arrived, before eventually stepping away to let the recovery team do their work.

Climbing in the GFU van, in such cold and desolate weather, Reilly thought that maybe she was in a slight state of shock. Despite thinking that they were going to find something, and despite the fact that Darren had pointed her here, she still couldn't quite believe it.

'I just can't believe it,' said Gary echoing her thoughts. 'I can't believe that it's over.' His voice cracked a little and she reached for his hand. Sure, they saw dead bodies every day, saw unbelievably tragic things, but this was one of their own.

This was something close to their hearts, sheer proof that none of them was safe from tragedy, all of them marked for death.

Reilly didn't say to Gary what she was really thinking: *It's never really over.*

She called into Jack Gorman's house on her way home. She was covered in mud, and completely exhausted, but the family needed to know and she didn't want them to have to wait any longer. Eighteen years was long enough.

Lucy was there too, sitting with her mother, all frozen in place as they waited for news.

'We found something,' she said. 'Remains exactly where Keating pinpointed. All is subject to analysis of course, but based on Keating's testimony we can only assume that it's Grace.'

She couldn't help but tell them so bluntly. There was nothing else for it. Those were the facts.

As the Gorman family held onto each other in a rush of both relief and sorrow, Reilly thought about the fact she had held back from them.

That Grace's skeleton was not the only one found in that garden.

They would find out soon enough. She wanted them to have this moment for Grace alone.

42

IT HAD BEEN A LONG week, and Reilly was glad for it to be over.

As expected, the examination and DNA analysis of the remains found at the house had very quickly revealed one of the victims to be Grace Gorman. The second skeleton was also female but older, and with no corresponding DNA, identifying that one would be a longer process.

The Gormans had understandably taken time off to grieve for Grace and to prepare for her burial service. So it was once again all remaining hands on deck at the GFU.

Reilly's thinking was interrupted by Chris perching on the edge of her desk.

'Hi,' she said. 'I was just about to leave.'

'Me too. I'll walk you down.'

They took the elevator and once the doors had closed he asked: 'So, how are you feeling?'

She nodded. 'Good. I'm good.'

'I'm sorry for pressuring you into taking the test. It's not my business.'

She shrugged. 'Chris, I'm not really ready to talk about it with you or with …anyone. Not yet at least. I'm waiting for the right moment to tell Todd, but I'm not sure that's ever going to come.'

'But how do *you* feel about …everything?'

'Honestly?' she said. 'I feel angry. Angry with myself for getting into this position. I feel angry that I'm facing something that I'm not sure I want. I'm scared. I'm scared that because I don't really want this, that I'll be bad at it.'

'You won't be—'

'Just don't,' she said putting up a hand up. 'Not right now. I don't need empty comfort or platitudes. I need to be alone.'

Feeling helpless, he watched her disappear into the darkening evening.

On Friday morning, Reilly stood between Chris and Kennedy as the box containing Grace Gorman's remains was lowered into the cold ground.

It was a small service, attended by mostly people who knew the Gormans, rather than Grace herself. Her best friend Georgina was there, though, grown into a beautiful young woman, a reminder of what Grace could have been, had she had the chance.

Reilly watched Lucy stand strong and brave as she farewelled her sister. They were the kind of women who faced tragedy and then got up and faced day after day head on. There was some comfort in that, really. They couldn't be kept down.

Afterwards, most people went for a drink, because the day had been hard and long, but Reilly grabbed a quick bite and then headed home in the cold.

She felt numb, both physically and emotionally. She didn't want to think about anything, although she knew that was an immature path to take. Even though the murder investigation had been wrapped up, and Grace Gorman had finally been found, everything felt lacking and flat. She just couldn't see ahead to the coming months and what they would bring.

Was Dublin really right for her—especially now? More and more the same question played on her mind. It had seemed like a great fit at first. She was always refreshed by change. But since coming back, she just wasn't sure. The last couple of weeks had left her feeling sucked dry. Maybe it was just the pressure she was under from all sides.

When she got home, there was a message from her father on her machine.

'Hi hon,' Mike said. 'I just wanted to check in and see how you're doing. Hope you're not too stressed out. Give your old man a call when you get a chance, OK.'

How she wished she could call him right now and pour her heart out. But it would have to wait.

The next day when she arrived at work, Kennedy had set up the GFU's lie detection machinery in the interview room. Apparently Nico Peroni was to be interviewed again but he didn't know about any test. The lie detector was merely a prop, he told Reilly, to be used in the hope that Peroni would break.

Her doubts about the investigation had dimmed over the last few days. She had too much on her mind to be obsessive about a case that had already been closed. But out of respect for Kennedy, she would go with along with it and oversee.

'Everyone ready?' she asked, when all was in place.

'All set,' said Chris.

'I'll have to ask you to observe only, Kennedy,' said Reilly. 'You're with me.'

He sighed but took his place behind the window of the interview room. 'I just know something's going to happen today,' he said.

Reilly hoped not. She'd had enough of things "happening". She could really do with some time to sort out her own problems. She snorted to herself. Time: what a luxury.

'OK, bring him in.'

When Peroni was led in, he looked nothing like the handsome, cheerful man at the helm of Hammer and Tongs a week before. His pallor was grey and loose skin hung from his cheeks in folds. He looked at Chris with complete resignation.

After he was seated in front of him, Chris said: 'Mr Peroni, we would like you to submit to a lie detector test. You have been consistent in your claim that you are innocent, and as such, we would like to give you an opportunity to clear some things up for us.'

There was a spark in Peroni's eyes. 'I'll do it,' he said, his voice croaky with misuse.

'Why are you agreeing to do this now?' asked Chris. 'Why not just talk to us before?'

'Because I've got no choice,' said Peroni. 'I've lost my restaurant, my reputation, everything. I've got nothing left to lose.'

Chris attached the wires to his chest, which was waxed, he noticed. This was a ruse, anyway. All they wanted from Peroni was some answers. A confession, preferably.

'When did your acquaintance with Harry McMurty begin?' he asked.

'About two years ago. He came looking for a job, but I didn't have anything at that time. We struck up a friendship.'

'Why didn't you tell us this before?'

'Because the nature of our friendship was not…we were romantically involved.'

'I see,' said Chris. 'And why not be honest about that? There's no crime in homosexuality. No crime in a consensual relationship. Why would you lie to us about it?'

'He was blackmailing me,' said Peroni. 'I had some bad habits. Some debts. Harry threatened to expose me if I didn't employ him and if I ended our relationship.'

Kennedy turned and raised his eyebrows at Reilly. 'I knew that fella was a bad one,' he said.

'Why didn't you go to the police?'

'I was ashamed,' said Nico. 'But I was also in love. I really believed that underneath it all, he was a good person and that eventually he would see the error of his ways.'

'Did he introduce you to Rose Cooper?'

'Yes, he tried to make me jealous. But she was sad, and sick with drugs. It didn't work. But I went to her flat when he was selling to her. And then she died.'

'And you had nothing to do with her death?'

'Nothing.'

Reilly was starting to get a very, very bad feeling as she watched the conversation between Chris and Nico unfold.

'Did Harry introduce you to Jennifer Armstrong and Naomi Worthington?'

'I never met either of those girls,' said Nico. 'Never.'

Reilly needed Chris to plough through. They needed to get answers to all of her questions, even if, hearing the answers, she was beginning to come over faint.

'Did you kill Harry McMurty? And try to make his murder out to be a suicide?'

'No,' said Nico. 'I didn't. I loved him. For all I knew that he was bad, I still loved him.'

'How did the antimine come into your possession?'

'I took it from his flat,' said Nico. 'I went round to his house and discovered him dead. I panicked and shoved it in my pocket, because I didn't want it to be worse for him. He was many things, but he wasn't a killer.' Nico's sobs began to reverberate through the room. He was both hysterical and relieved to tell someone of what he had suffered. 'I loved him,' he cried, 'but he just used me again and again. Promised to make me a laughing stock. Promised to ruin Hammer and Tongs. And now he's dead.'

As Nico continued to sob, Reilly saw that the machinery was printing the results of someone clearly telling the truth.

But it didn't matter. She already knew he was telling the truth. But what she didn't know was what on earth she would do next.

'I knew it,' said Kennedy. 'I knew he wasn't our guy.'

'Don't pat yourself on the back too soon,' said Chris. 'We've still got a murderer on the loose.'

'This is terrible,' said Reilly. 'How could we let this happen?'

'It's not your fault, Reilly,' said Chris. 'We all thought it was him.'

But deep down, she knew that she had ignored her gut. She had wanted so badly to catch the killer that she had told herself it was Peroni. She had let herself believe it, even when there were pieces of the puzzle that didn't fit.

'This means we have to go right back to the beginning,' she said. 'Everything. We can't leave a single thing undone. O'Brien is going to have my head.'

'We've made mistakes, too,' said Kennedy. 'None of us is perfect.'

'But I should never have gotten so distracted,' she said, placing her head in her hands.

'It's been a long day,' said Chris. 'Let's just go home, relax and sleep on it and start again tomorrow morning.'

'I agree,' said Kennedy.

'We imprisoned an innocent man,' said Reilly. 'How are we supposed to sleep on that?'

43

ON THE WAY HOME SHE couldn't stop thinking about Nico Peroni. She was horrified that he had suffered so much when his biggest crime was to be fallible, to be in love. How much love could blind us, she thought. It blinded Peroni to the fact that Harry would never change, it blinded Grace to the true danger of her situation, and Darren to the monster that his brother really was.

She wondered if she would ever find herself blinded by love. Up until now, she had seen her lovers clearly, almost too clearly. Like Todd. Passionate, physical, but reserved. Unwilling to give himself up, just like her. At least she saw herself clearly too.

Peroni could have saved them so much trouble if he had just told the truth in the first place. But he had been so ashamed of his failings, he had been willing to stay silent.

Why are we so afraid to be human, thought Reilly. Every day, they saw the worst of human nature, she thought. But to be ashamed of loving someone, even to the point of weakness…. She didn't know. It was all too hard for her to fathom right now.

She would go home and take a long hot bath and get an early night, she thought. Tomorrow they would have to begin again. And face O'Brien. She looked at her watch: 6 P.M on a Saturday night. She wouldn't even look at her caseload, she thought. Her mind needed to recharge.

At home, she poached herself an egg and had it on toast with some wilted spinach. She would have liked something else, but she truly could not be bothered cooking.

In the bath, she thought some more about the past week. It had been a very emotional time. Lucy had emailed Reilly and told her that she was dealing with some "delayed grief."

Reilly thought that this would probably be a healthy thing, in the end. She had passed on all the information she'd learned to the cops on the task force. They would go and question Darren Keating further. She almost wished she could have spared him more pain, but there was no chance of that. But it may help his case that his brother was clearly a manipulator and an abuser. He had set Darren on a path of crime from which he had never returned.

She immersed herself in the hot water, relishing the slight sting on her skin. There was nothing left to do there at least. The Gorman family would try to move on, and in a few weeks a case just like it would probably turn up on somebody's desk. That's just how things went.

She wondered if perhaps now that this was behind her, Lucy might give Gary a chance. He had supported her throughout the investigation and given up his personal time to help solve it. He was a good guy, Reilly knew. He had heart, and that was important. Strength, brains and bravery meant nothing without heart.

Chris had all of those qualities, too, she thought. But what did that have to do with anything? She quickly pushed the thought from her mind.

She thought again about Peroni's assertion that he had "lost his restaurant" due to the investigation. But was that really true? Surely his partner - his co-owner, had been keeping things afloat, no matter what was going on with Peroni. What was the other guy's name again, Tony Ellis …

Suddenly she sat bolt upright.

How could they have been so blind? If Peroni was innocent, but so much of the evidence gathered centered round the restaurant, then surely they should have looked into the other partner also. Why hadn't they? Probably because McMurty and Peroni had distracted them, and Ellis was so shadowy and indistinct, painted as if he wasn't actually involved at all, but had merely put his name and reputation to the place. Which is exactly *why* they should have looked into it further. She pulled herself out of the bath in a hurry, water sloshing all over the floor. With a towel wrapped around her she went and booted up her laptop.

Before she could sit down, her cell phone rang and she answered without thinking or first checking the display.

'Hey, Reilly, it's me.'

She flushed despite herself, almost as if he would know by just talking to her. 'Hi …how are you?'

'Great,' Todd said. 'I've just been thinking about you. Thought it would be nice to hear your voice. And it is.'

'How is everyone?' she asked. She tried to ignore the fact that her heart was beating harder. Whether from delight or nervousness, she didn't know.

'Everyone's good,' he said. 'Dad's great, we miss you lots.'

'I miss you guys too.'

There were a few seconds of silence during which she could hear the crackle and jump of the line from across the Atlantic.

'So,' he said. 'I was thinking of swinging by your neck of the woods sometime soon. Just for a few days. I've always wanted to spend some time in Ireland. I thought if you had time, maybe we could catch up?'

She had a few seconds of shock before she was able to speak. 'Sure,' she said. 'I'd like that.'

'Great. Nothing's set in concrete just yet, but it'll probably be July or August. I just wanted to run it by you.'

'Of course.' It was on the tip of her tongue to tell him, but she just couldn't get the words out. It wasn't the right time.

'Great. I'd better shoot, I've got to be at the lab soon. But don't be a stranger OK? I'll keep you updated about my plans.'

'I won't,' she said. 'I'll be in touch.'

After they had hung up she leaned her head against the cool counter, completely forgetting for a second what she had been in the middle of doing.

The hour approaches. Despite all my fears, everything has gone to plan. That woman, the cop, has not been on my case again.

I've since found out a little bit about her life. She's a woman with a tragic past and has turned that tragedy into a nice little career for herself. You would think that it would make her value the important things in life, but it's just made her completely obsessed with her profession and a rise to the top. She's one of those women who will ignore everything if it means success. It's a wonder I didn't come across her on the dating sights, trawling for a casual fling to fill her lonely nights. I would have taken great joy in ending her. There would have been some irony in that.

But really, all other joys are petty compared to what will happen tonight.

I considered a range of ingredients for Constance. I wanted something traditional, something with a little dramatic flair. I considered Tetradotoxin, that substance found in the blue ringed octopus and the puffer fish. But it simply works too quickly.

Then I thought about arsenic. It's an illustrious poison, used to kill Napoleon, George 3rd and Simon Bolivar. Undetectable too until someone found an ingenious way to test for it. Also in its favor is that was once used as a cosmetic. It made women's complexions lustrous and pale. How tempting to kill a woman using a mark of woman's vanity. But again, too quick, too chemical.

Aconite was next, but the leaves of this are so toxic that one can die after just touching one. I didn't want to leave room for any nasty accidents. But the fact that it causes asphyxiation was tempting. How nice for Ruth to know that her baby died in a terror of feeling the breath being sucked from her lungs, her eyes bulging and her tongue swelling from the pressure. But it was simply too dangerous. I didn't want a Romeo and Juliet scenario.

Hemlock it was then. That famous poison, used to kill Socrates. Just 100 milligrams, or about eight leaves will kill a person. It's a terrible death. Paralysis comes over the body slowly, but the mind is left wide awake to experience every second of the death. I plan to tell Constance exactly why she is dying as the hemlock does its work. I will tell her that her mother is a monster, and that it is by Ruth's own hand that she dies. I want her to die knowing that the world isn't the perfect place she has been brought up to believe in. I want her pain, but I also want her understanding. Is that so hard? That someone should finally understand me?

All these years I have been laboring to become the best version of myself. I have tried to overcome the darkness of my upbringing. I am successful, I am smart, I am strong.

No one knows the real me. It would be nice to tell just one person. I have thought about whispering it in the ears of the dying, but they've never been right. Those women are exactly the ones who would see me abandoned and mistreated again, if they could. They see me as weak, as vengeful, when really I am trying to do something good for the world. No child should have to be lonely. No child should have to be blamed for the failings of another.

But Constance is different. She believes in family, in kindness. If she knew me, I think she would understand me. I think she would forgive me.

I have made great sacrifices to live this life. Do you think that I didn't wish for a good woman of my own, a family of my own? But I have dedicated myself to teaching the world its errors. To teaching women, one by one, that they can't have everything.

After tonight, Tony Ellis and Danny Prime are no more. It will be a new country, a new name. The man remains the same though. The man and his passions.

I have decided to enjoy my time with Constance. There are two mac and cheese portions bubbling softly in the oven, one laced with hemlock, one not. A glass of merlot breathes on a table specially set for us both. We will eat an entrée of the lightest, fluffiest duck parfait that you can imagine. Constance deserves the undiluted pleasure of my cooking before she dies.

I am not expecting anything to go wrong, for there to be any mistakes. But just in case, I have prepared a syringe filled with the liquid I used on McMurty. It would be a great shame to use it, as it would ruin the purity of my plan, but if the need arises, I will.

There will be nothing to get in the way of my ultimate goal. Ruth Dell will feel my hand reach for her, as she felt it a thousand times when I was a child, when I wanted her comfort.

But this time, I will be the one ignoring her pain, her need. She will know what it is to feel true pain.

Reilly had regained her composure a few minutes after Todd's call. No way could he come here, to Dublin, anytime soon. Although wouldn't it be best to tell him the news in person? Why? So that he could see her own doubt written all over her face? Yeah, sure, what a great idea.

But she had been about to do something, had wanted to find out more information about Hammer and Tong's elusive co-owner.

She had forgotten his name, so she just searched "Hammer and Tongs". A few clicks later she hit on a profile of renowned chef Tony Ellis carried out by the *Irish Times* Food and Wine Review.

He grew up in London it read, with less than illustrious beginnings. Tony Ellis had been on the street at sixteen. 'I probably ate from the rubbish bins of restaurants I later worked at,' he joked. He didn't elaborate further on his childhood, except to say that he was proud to have made something of himself. He became a premier chef in London, it said, able to whip up all the classics, but more than capable of wowing. About eighteen months ago he'd come to Dublin to oversee the opening of a new restaurant by Nico Peroni. 'I believe food is like art,' he said. 'It has to evolve. It has to keep changing and it has to shock people. If people find it unpleasant at first, then that's only because their minds haven't caught up with the times.' Reilly made a face. How arrogant. This guy had no right to be telling other people what they should like and dislike, or that there was something wrong with them if they didn't like his food.

At the end of the piece the interviewer asked if there was anyone special on the scene. He said he was too busy, that his various restaurants kept him working such grueling hours that it was impossible to date.

But who would be your ideal woman, pressed the interviewer, if you could date. 'Someone traditional,' said Ellis. 'Someone with understated taste, who would raise our children with undivided attention and love.' Reilly almost threw up. Who was this guy, anyway?

She scrolled to the bottom of the piece to see a picture of a man who wasn't looking at the camera, but was studying something to the left. It wasn't a good photo, but there was no mistaking it.

She was looking at the guy from the running group; Danny Prime.

44

CONSTANCE GOT READY FOR HER evening out with her usual irreverence. She knew it was supposed to be a solemn occasion, but it was also a celebration, yes? Of life. So a bright orange dress was completely appropriate, as were the little cat earrings she donned. Maybe Danny's mother had liked cats.

The more she thought about it, the more it seemed a little weird that she was having this remembrance dinner with a guy she barely knew, for a woman she definitely hadn't known. But life was like that, wasn't it? At least, hers was. Strange things happened to her all the time. She jumped from one thing to the next, trying to learn as much about life as possible. Her mother told her to slow down, to savor things, but she didn't want to savor things, she wanted to gobble them right up.

So anyway, this wasn't a completely out of the blue situation to find herself in. Someone was going to cook her dinner, and they would have a nice time. She probably wouldn't see much of Danny after this. She had started to date the firefighter and boy, was that an experience. There's nothing quite like a man who can lift you with one arm. And she had taken up yoga, which she felt was better for her mind and body. So she just wouldn't be running as much. It would be a nice way to say goodbye to someone who had helped her.

She checked the address he'd given her one more time. Baggot Street was in an upmarket area of town. Maybe Danny was rich. Well, it would be nice to get a decent meal. Ruth hadn't taught Constance to cook so much as to throw things together. She lived on salads, soups and hot chips.

She threw her coat and headed out. She would be a couple of minutes late but she was sure Danny would understand.

Reilly cursed as she threw on some clothes. Anything that came to hand. What day was it? Saturday. What was the time? Just before 7 PM. And why did that mean something to her. *Think,* she told herself as she pulled on a pair of boots.

And then it struck her like someone had poured cold ice water into her veins. The girl, the pretty red head from the running group. 'See you Saturday week?' she had yelled. 'Eight sharp,' Danny Prime had replied. 'You know the place on Baggot Street, yes?'

Reilly knew there wasn't a second to spare.

The traffic was murder. There was a storm forecast, so of course everyone had figured this was a good time to get on the road. Reilly inched forward, her windscreen wipers going like crazy.

It was imperative that she get to the restaurant in time. She picked up her phone and dialed Chris. Voicemail. She left a message that she knew she wouldn't remember later, just garbled explanations and instructions. When she hung up, she tried to dial the nearest garda station, for back up, but her phone died. Low battery. It seemed that these days she just kept on letting herself down.

Well, it's just you now, she thought. No time for anything else.

Chris was at the gym, trying to put some miles between him and his day. If it wasn't for Kennedy, an innocent man would still be in prison.

Well, this was why his partner was a top ranking detective: he was good at his job. He might hide behind his bluster a lot of the time, but he was sharp as a tack. Part of being a cop was learning when to trust your instinct and when to know that you were being paranoid.

The truth was Chris himself had been too distracted by the burgeoning connection between himself and Reilly to look too closely at what was happening. And Reilly had probably been distracted by her own problems. Thoughts of Todd Forrest, perhaps. No, that was unfair. Reilly was the best investigator he had ever worked with. She just had too much on her plate, that was all.

And he hadn't helped her, really. He had confused the issue further. It would have been better for them both if he'd just kept his feelings to himself. It had just made the ensuing revelation of her pregnancy even harder. Now she didn't want to talk about it, didn't want to acknowledge that it was happening.

He supposed that if Reilly had a flaw, it was her belief that she could control things, just by wanting them to be a certain way. He knew it wasn't true, that you expended precious energy trying to bend your life into a particular shape. He had learnt to let things go a little, to let life wash over him. People might say that it was the attitude of someone who had given up, but the truth was that Chris didn't want to fight his life anymore. He just wanted for things to be a little bit better in the lives of everyone he knew. Another impossible dream.

At least there was the rest of the weekend to look forward to. Tomorrow was little Rachel's birthday and there would be the party at Matt and Emma's house. Though looking after a room full of shrieking four year olds was not for the faint hearted.

So, yes, Chris told himself, there were still things in life that were good, things to look forward to. He had let himself hope for something, to imagine that he wouldn't be spending all his nights at home alone. But he had learnt his lesson. He just needed to live his life the best he could and not worry about love and its confusions. He and Reilly could just continue working together and he would support her in any way that she would let him. If he couldn't be in her life in quite the way he wanted, then he would be a friend. It would have to be good enough.

In the meantime, maybe it was time to think about a holiday. He had travelled when he was younger, but he hadn't gone anywhere, apart from a weekend down the country, for a very long time. Maybe he should try somewhere completely different like Vietnam, or Australia even. It would be good for him to get a complete change of scene. It would probably be beneficial for his work as well. The change would revive him and refresh him, focus him a little bit.

He stopped the treadmill, feeling satisfied with the thinking he had done. It was good to clear up your thoughts, to sort out the swirling mess and put everything in its proper place.

If Chris noticed the women who gave him a few sidelong looks as he made his way to the changing rooms, he didn't let on. He was used to attention from women, but most of it just slid off him.

He showered and dressed and made his way out into a bleak summer's night. A light rain had begun to fall. He got in his car and slid an Etta James CD into the stereo. He needed something light hearted and cheering. Just then he noticed that the message light on his phone was flashing. Kennedy, maybe, or Matt? He checked. No, it was Reilly. He dialed through to his messages straight away.

It was so rushed as to be almost incoherent. She knew who it was she said, and he was doing it again. Right now. She was going to Baggot Street and she needed him to come too, and bring back up. Fast.

He sat in the car for a few more seconds, taking deep breaths and trying to figure out exactly what Reilly was talking about. She knew who the killer was? And she was going there now to stop him? Where? Baggot Street.... did she mean Hammer and Tongs?

A surge of pure fear ran through his body, and even in the warmth of the car a cold sweat broke on his brow. Had he stopped and considered for a second what he was feeling, he would have known that all his thinking in the gym earlier had been for nothing.

He loved Reilly Steel. Nothing else really mattered. Life was full of twists and turns. But he did love her.

But Chris didn't stop to consider his feelings. He only knew that he had to get there as soon as he could. Reilly was in danger.

The message had been left half an hour ago.

45

WHEN CONSTANCE TURNED UP AT the address on Baggot Street that Danny had given her, she wondered if she had misunderstood his invitation. Was he actually taking her out for dinner? She hoped not, that would seem too much like a date. But the restaurant looked closed. She pushed against the partly open door, and called: 'Hello?'

The dining room was empty of people. The tables were all still set up, hung with ghostly white cloths. The cutlery was glinted like ice and reflected the dim light from the candles that had been lit and placed around the walls. One table, in front of the fireplace, was set with a twisted bunch of flowers. A picture of a woman was propped up in the centre of the table, too. Constance went closer and picked it up.

It showed a woman, smiling shyly at the camera, her hair twisted into a knot, a scarf tied stylishly around her neck. A small boy hugged her knee, beaming up at her.

'My mother.'

Constance was so startled when Danny spoke that she almost dropped the picture. 'She's beautiful,' she said, gulping a little.

'Yes, she was,' said Danny. 'It's the only picture I have of her.' He clapped his hands together. 'Now. I hope you are hungry.'

'I'm starving,' admitted Constance. 'I've been fasting in anticipation. But, Danny, what are we doing here? This place is one of the best restaurants in town.'

'Why, thank you,' he said, with a slight bow.

'What do you mean?'

'Didn't you know? I own this place,' he said.

'Are you serious? That's amazing. Everyone wants to eat here.'

'Yes, it's been fun,' he said. 'But in light of recent events, I think it's time for a fresh start. An exciting, new venture.'

'Oh, yes,' she said with a slight shudder. 'I heard about the chef here. That he was arrested on suspicion of murder. It's terrible. You must feel strange, having known him and had him work for you.'

Danny shook his head. 'I didn't know him all that well actually. I think people like that are always slightly unknowable, don't you think?'

'Yes, I suppose so,' she said. 'I can't imagine what makes people do things like that. Though they should also be pitied, I suppose. Clearly they're not in their right minds.'

His smile faltered a little. She supposed it must be hard for him. The actions of his chef had cost him his business. 'Nico was a very frustrated man,' he said. 'A lot of anger. But let's talk of more pleasant things, shall we? Wine?'

She readily agreed. It wasn't every day that you got to drink from the cellar of a place like this. She found that she got tipsy quite quickly, probably because she hadn't eaten all day.

'Goodness,' she said. 'I'm all over the place. But this wine is amazing.'

He laughed. 'Don't worry about it. It's nice to have such festive company. My mother, from the little that I remember of her, was a lively person.'

'Did your father raise you after she died?'

He shook his head. 'I never knew my father. I suspect he took off when he discovered that my mother was pregnant. And she wasn't around long enough for me to get old enough to ask. So I'll never know. I was raised by my aunt after she died,' he said.

'And that wasn't a happy experience?' she ventured, seeing the way his face had changed.

'God, no. It was awful. I would rather live through anything than face that again. No child should have to go through that.'

'I'm sorry,' she said. 'It sounds hard. Some people aren't equipped to deal with children.'

'No,' he said, with an odd look on his face. 'They're not. Let me go and get the first course and we can continue this discussion.'

'Sounds good.'

She looked around after he had left. It was a little spooky, eating in a completely empty restaurant, especially one as large as Hammer and Tongs, but it would make a good story for her friends later on.

She looked at the picture. It was so sad. Danny was a nice guy, if a little odd. She guessed that he spent a lot of time alone. But who knew what he would have been like if his mother had lived.

He set the parfait in front of her, with delicate croutons next to it.

'Bon appetit.'

After the first bite, she had to hold herself back from eating the rest in a single bite. 'This is amazing,' she said. 'I've truly never eaten anything so good.'

'Well,' he said. 'After you told me you wanted mac and cheese, I thought I had better do something slightly flashier to start. But tell me, what was your childhood like? You seem to be the kind of person who radiates with the happiness of a great childhood.'

She laughed. 'Well, I'm glad I give off that vibe. But it's not exactly true.' She paused. 'It feels weird to complain at all, actually, knowing that what you went through was a million times worse.'

'No,' he said. 'Don't feel like that. Pain is all relative, isn't it? Especially to a child. The smallest thing can seem like a devastation.'

She nodded. 'You're very balanced and perceptive. Sometimes people with such awful backgrounds wallow in self pity for the rest of their lives.' She took another bite of the parfait and smiled. 'My mother wasn't a bad person, but she was very conflicted. She would love me with all of her heart one day, ignore me the next. A lot of the time, I had to reassure her that she wasn't a bad person and that I loved her. When she did something horrible to me, she would just feel flayed with guilt the next day. It was just weird. I mean, I know she went through some stuff before I was born. Sometimes I feel like she had me just to prove that she could.'

'I'm sure she loves you, though.'

'Yeah, she does. I love her, too, but it's definitely better now that I'm older. We're on more even ground, and I get more distance.'

He nodded. 'It sounds…complicated.'

'Well, nothing's ever simple. At least I'll have something to tell my therapist about in ten years.'

When Reilly finally arrived at the restaurant, she was so tense that every particle in her body was screaming with the need to act. She swung her car onto the curb in front of the building. She didn't have a plan beyond exposing this guy and saving this poor girl. However she had to do it, she must stop Tony Ellis, the Chef. She only hoped that she wasn't too late.

When she entered the restaurant, her eyes took a moment to adjust to the dim light inside. Two people were sharing an intimate dinner at a table by the fire. They turned to look at her, surprised by her intrusion.

'Don't eat another bite!' she yelled to the girl. 'He's a killer.'

The girl half stood, looking confused. Who was this crazy woman? 'What are you talking about,' she said, uncertainly, as though unsure of whether it was possible to reason with someone as unbalanced as this one clearly was. Then she frowned. 'Wait, aren't you from the running group?'

'I'm with the police,' said Reilly. 'You need to get out of here. This guy is dangerous.'

In the seconds that it had taken them to have this conversation, Tony Ellis had begun to move towards her, his hands outstretched in a placating manner, an apologetic half-smile on his face. 'I'm sure we can sort this out,' he said. 'This terrible mix-up. You poor thing, you're in a terrible state.'

If he had reacted with less concern, Constance might have run. But she was rooted to the spot. She saw Danny approach the woman, as if to comfort her. She saw the woman put her hands up to protect herself, but it was too late. Then, at the last moment, he sunk something into her neck and she slumped to the floor. Before they closed, her eyes flashed a last plea to Constance: get out of here.

But when Danny turned to her, a terrible smile on his face, Constance knew that it was too late. She had made a terrible mistake.

'No use running,' he said. 'I saved some of this for you, too.' He held up the syringe and she saw the clear liquid slosh in the tiny glass tube. 'But I wanted us to have a civilized conversation. Things were going so well, and now they're ruined. But even best laid plans sometimes need to be adapted. You learn that early on, working in a kitchen.'

He sounded so normal, spoke so reasonably. But Constance had just seen him kill someone. Hadn't she? Certainly, the woman on the floor showed no sign of life.

Her body was loose, her skin pale. She watched for the rise and fall of the woman's chest, but couldn't see it.

'Who are you?' she asked.

'The Chef of course,' he replied. The simplicity of his answer chilled her to the bone.

Chris was, as Reilly had been, stuck in traffic. He rang her phone a hundred times, but he kept getting her voicemail.

He rang Kennedy instead. 'It's me. Something's gone very, very wrong. I need you to get down to Hammer and Tongs straight away, with back up. Reilly thinks she's got the killer, but I can't get through to her.'

'I'll be there as soon as I can,' shouted the older man, as if he was yelling through a storm. Chris looked outside and saw that the weather had gotten worse. He could barely see the car in front. The rain swirled white and then yellow, illuminated by the headlights.

He knew he could count on Kennedy. His partner would do everything in his power. But would it be too late? Why, oh why, had Reilly done this? If she had just waited half an hour, they could have gone together. It was the kind of typical behavior she always engaged in, this belief that she could control everything. They'd been down this road more than once and while he'd always admired her tenacity there was no doubt it was dangerous. Especially now.

When he got to Hammer and Tongs he saw her car parked at a wild angle on the street outside. Chris fought the urge to burst through the doors of the restaurant. Instead, he holstered his gun and headed for the back.

It never hurt to make a surprise entrance.

46

REILLY HAD FELT THE COLD metal slide beneath her skin and then felt a quick descent into heat, then cold, then numbness. She tried to move her mouth, her limbs, but it was of no use. It was like being drowned in mud. She was powerless.

As she had sunk to the floor, her last coherent thought was: 'Please don't hurt the baby.'

Now she seemed to exist in a kind of fantasy world, a soundless place of images and faces. There was Chris, smiling ruefully at her, as though he was both pleased and disappointed. Todd with his usual implacable and unreadable stare.

Then her father, reaching out for her. Pete Kennedy, Daniel Forrest. All of them were looking at her like she was in bad trouble, and they couldn't help.

Finally her mother watching and smiling at her from a place she couldn't reach. She wanted to get to her, wanted to ask Cassie something, desperately. What was it? She couldn't remember. She felt herself reaching out, trying to touch them. Her mother got up, shook her head and smiled at Reilly. Then Jess appeared, shutting a door between them that Reilly hadn't even known was there.

That was the last thing. Then a long slow slide into darkness, which felt endless and irreversible.

She was nowhere. She was gone.

'But I don't understand. My mother is your aunt? So we're…cousins?'

'That's right,' he said, 'I must say, you're taking the news that your mother was a heartless torturer of a young boy quite well.'

Constance shook her head. It didn't make any sense. Or did it? Hadn't her mother tried to tell her something like this? Hadn't she told her that she had done unforgivable things?

'I don't understand,' she said again. 'Ruth was the one who did all this to you. I wasn't even born. Why are trying to hurt me? I haven't done anything.' She wasn't trying to be cruel to her mother, but Constance was nothing if not practical. She needed to understand Tony's motives.

Tony shook his head. Really, she was deliciously innocent. 'What good would killing Ruth do?' he asked. 'She might have a couple of minutes of fear. But if I kill you, she gets a lifetime of grief and regret.'

Constance saw, for the first time, that he really meant to do this. Until now, she had thought if she kept him talking long enough, that she might be able to talk him out of it.

'It wasn't supposed to be this way,' he was saying. 'But that stupid woman ruined the moment really. It was supposed to be a far more intimate affair. When the poison took hold, I was going to tell you why you were dying, as your body seized up and you could feel the life draining from it. But it's going to have to be a little less theatrical now, I'm afraid. I don't suppose I could persuade you to voluntarily eat your last meal?'

She looked at him with disgust.

'No? That's a pity. Luckily I have a little pure sample. Once you're asleep, it will make little difference to you.'

As he moved towards her, she clutched the knife that she had slid off the table in her hand. It was just an innocuous butter knife, smeared with the remains of their parfait.

'Just stay still will you?'

But she didn't, she lunged at him and felt the needle prick her skin roughly as she thrust the knife wildly at his face.

She was unconscious before she knew if she had made contact or not.

Tony Ellis, his eye streaming blood, went calmly into his kitchen to fetch the hemlock.

No, it hadn't gone to plan, not at all. But there was a silver lining. He would now have two victims, not just the one. Did it really matter how Constance died? Wasn't the main thing that she did die, and that Ruth knew why? That was the main thing. It's what he had wanted all these years. It didn't matter how it happened as long as nothing stopped him.

In the kitchen, he prepared the syringe with the liquid hemlock. It would have to be half for each woman, but it wouldn't affect the efficacy. Hemlock was deadly. There was no antidote.

Because of his concentration, and the extreme care he was taking with the hemlock, he didn't see the big man lurking behind the door. In fact, Tony had no idea that his deadly banquet was over until he found himself face down on the shiny bench.

Someone roughly cuffed him, and though he struggled wildly, he was thrown into his own freezer. 'Hope it's not too chilly in there,' said the voice. 'But I can't have you sampling your own concoction.'

47

IT HAD TAKEN ALL OF Chris's strength not to kill Tony Ellis with his bare hands there and then. But he had more important things to deal with, and the main thing was that the guy didn't get away.

When he got to Reilly, his heart was in his mouth. It seemed to be an eternity before he found her pulse, faint through her cold skin and fading with every second. He placed his warm mouth over her cold one and breathed into it, until Pete Kennedy burst through the door like a white knight, a small tribe of guards behind him.

Reilly had no idea of the chaos caused by her adventure at Hammer and Tongs. The scene was madness as ambulances arrived like angels of mercy and cops swarmed the place. Tony Ellis was found in the restaurant freezer in a state of trauma. Being locked in there had brought back the hours of his childhood spent locked in dark places. His confession was swift but garbled. They would re-interview him again once he had undergone a psychiatric assessment.

Constance Dell was revived quickly at the hospital, having spent less time under the influence of the drug. Reilly was a trickier case. She was deep under, and her pregnancy complicated things.

Chris had to ring and break the news to Mike. He would be on the next flight, he said, panicked. Chris hoped that the urgency wouldn't panic her dad too much and the long flight back over the Atlantic might tip him off the wagon. That was the last thing Reilly needed.

He sat in the waiting room outside emergency all night long. He fielded calls from Jack and Lucy Gorman, Gary, everyone who knew and loved the fearless Reilly.

Lucy was especially upset. 'She's done so much for me,' she sobbed down the phone. 'Please tell me she's going to be OK.'

But Chris couldn't tell her that. To everyone, he had to repeat the same thing, over and over: 'I don't know. I don't know what will happen.'

Kennedy sat with him through the long night. He was grim faced, but stoic. 'We won't lose her,' he told Chris. 'She's tough as old steak, that one.'

Reilly would appreciate the sentiment, if not the comparison, thought Chris.

Near dawn, the doctor came and gave them the welcome news that Reilly would be OK.

'She's very sleepy,' he told them. 'It was an extremely close call, but you can see her for a minute or two.'

'And the baby?' asked Chris, completely forgetting about Kennedy's presence.

'Yes, the baby will be fine as well,' he said. 'But Ms Steel will need to rest and stay off her feet for the next few weeks.'

Chris was so relieved he didn't even notice his partner's jaw almost drop to the floor.

Reilly opened her eyes when Chris entered her room. 'Did we get him?' she asked.

'We got him, Reilly. You got him.'

'And is everything…?'

'The baby's going to be fine,' he told her, his eyes shining a little.

She smiled and drifted back to sleep. Chris shook his head in wonderment. She truly was as tough as "old steak."

48

WITHIN TEN DAYS, REILLY WAS back at her desk, though with vastly reduced hours.

Her father had stayed with her for a week and it had been wonderful to spend the extended time with him. They had some very tough conversations where Reilly had to figure out her plans for the future. Mike was adamant that she talk to Todd Forrest, and soon.

She knew the time ahead would be hard, but she also knew that it would be worth it. She would have help, too, one way or another.

'Welcome back, Reilly,' said Jack Gorman on her return. 'It's very good to see you here again.'

'Thanks,' she said. 'I hope that you're feeling better, too.'

'It's been a hard time,' admitted Jack. 'Lots of joy, lots of grieving. But it's given me some perspective that perhaps I didn't have before.'

'That's good,' said Reilly. 'I know that Lucy is happy that the two of you have become closer.'

Jack smiled. It made him very happy as well, to have gotten to know his youngest daughter better over the past few weeks. He wasn't going to let that slip away from him.

'Also, while you were in the hospital, the chief sent over a request from Tony Ellis' last almost-victim, Constance Dell. She wants to meet you personally and say thank you. Here are her details. It's your choice whether you follow it up of course.'

Reilly took the piece of paper. As a rule, she didn't normally engage with victims. But she was breaking just about every rule in the book these days. Baby brain, wasn't that what they called it? That was her excuse anyway.

So why not one more?

Reilly met Constance Dell on a bright summer's day at a cafe in the city centre.

'Thanks for seeing me,' said Constance. 'I just feel like I needed a little bit of closure. It's been a really tough couple of weeks. And I want to thank you,' she said sincerely. 'For saving my life that night. You almost lost your own and I would have felt responsible.'

'T's my job,' said Reilly.

Constance raised her eyebrows. 'Your job is to go rushing in on serial killers as they go about their work, completely unprotected? Forgive me if I say that I don't envy you.'

Reilly laughed. 'Sometimes my methods aren't entirely orthodox. You're not having flashbacks or anything are you?'

'I'm getting some help to deal with it all,' Constance admitted. 'But the hardest thing is learning about my mother's role in all of this. I mean, I know her to be a difficult woman, but I never dreamed that this was in her past.'

'It's a hard thing to deal with,' said Reilly.

'I think she's only just coming to terms with how bad her treatment of Tony Ellis actually was. She's felt guilty about it for years, but she's blocked out so much else. And it's so hard to see her as that cruel woman. I mean, it's hard not to feel sorry for him. He was just a helpless child.'

'It's easy to feel sorry for the child,' said Reilly. 'But the man had a choice too. He didn't have to prey on helpless women.'

'I know,' said Constance. 'It's hard to think that the nice guy I met was actually a killer.'

'Serial killers are very good at hiding their true natures,' said Reilly. 'Many of them are charming. None of this is your fault. He manipulated your emotions so that you would feel sorry for him. If you're guilty of anything, it's being too kind.'

'I just wonder if I should start taking things a bit more seriously. I'm always out and about, trying to suck the most fun out of life. Maybe I should try to settle down a bit, be a bit more level headed.'

Reilly smiled and shook her head. 'That's exactly what you shouldn't do,' she said. 'Or, you should do what you want, but I'll tell you something: the world needs joy. It need people like you, just like it needs more serious people like me. Just follow your instincts, and you'll be fine. If I've learnt one thing, it's that you have to trust in yourself.'

'I'll drink to that,' said Constance, raising her coffee to Reilly's cranberry juice.

Now that the investigation that had sucked up so much of their time was over, Reilly didn't see much of Chris.

She tried not to think too much about him either, and how good it felt waking up to see his face while she was in the hospital. Whatever was between them would have to remain unspoken. Things were just too complicated just now.

When she had thought she was going to die, her thoughts had been about the baby. For the first time, she had thought of it as a real thing. She had been afraid for it. But now that things were back to normal, Reilly felt the familiar fears for her career and the life she knew, and whether or not she would make a good mother.

Chris sought her out at the lab one day and asked her to go for a coffee. 'Or a banana smoothie or something,' he joked. 'Whatever you're allowed.'

She found she couldn't say no. He had saved her life after all. And whatever else, he was her friend.

'Did I ever thank you for that, by the way?' she asked.

'Thank me for what?'

'Saving my life - again.'

Chris smiled. 'Well, not in so many words, not exactly. But you've been busy. And I, you know, *sensed* your gratitude.'

She laughed. 'Well, I'm glad. Because I am very grateful, Chris. I know it was stupid of me to go rushing in like that. But I couldn't help myself. I had made too many mistakes and I needed to save that girl. I just couldn't have another one on my conscience.'

'I know,' he said. 'I felt the same.'

'Does it ever keep you up at night? Thinking of all the ones you couldn't save?'

He grimaced. 'Sometimes, yeah it does. I think back through the years to all these cases. Young women, young men. Old women and men. And I think if only I could have stayed one step ahead, or just have gotten there a little sooner, then everything could be different.'

'If we were superheroes.'

'Exactly. But you can only do what you can do. You can't be perfect.'

'I guess,' said Reilly, 'that I should take that advice. Just focus on taking each day as it comes, doing what I can do.'

'I think that's a good idea,' he said. Then he exhaled, as if unsure whether or not to continue. 'And I know you'll be a good mum, Reilly. You don't need to worry.'

'Ah, but I do. I do worry. I worry that my whole life will change and I won't be able to keep up.'

'You know,' he said. 'I do have some experience with children. I can help you, if you're still staying around here that is. I make a pretty good babysitter.'

She smiled, feeling unbelievably sad for some reason. 'That's good to know. Thank you. And if I am still here, I'll definitely take you up on it.'

'So you are thinking of going back to the States then?'

'It depends, really. On whether…' she trailed off.

Of course, thought Chris. It depends on whether Todd Forrest was going to be involved or not. Well, he would be a fool not to.

'OK,' he said. 'Just as long as you know that I'm here. For whatever.'

She nodded. It was comforting to know that she could count on someone.

But deep down, she knew that she would be alone, really. It was her life and her future, and it was up to her to keep it afloat.

Later when she got home she thought about her earlier question to Chris: Do you think about all the ones you couldn't save?

She knew that she did. It was something that took up a lot of her mental space, that kept her going and kept her focused on her job. All those faceless women that she hadn't saved. Sometimes the feeling of responsibility got so strong that Reilly felt like she should have been able to reach back through the years and save her own mother, her own sister too. Keep them close and safe and out of harm's way. She had tried with Jess, but she had failed. Badly.

But Chris was right, she thought, staring out of her window at the leaves on the trees, her phone in hand.

You could only do what you could do. And she would, she realized, as she brought up Todd's number. She knew she was strong enough.

As the world kept going, and tragedy kept knocking at her door, Reilly would be there to meet it, in all its guises.

It was just what she did.

THE END

ABOUT THE AUTHOR

Casey Hill is the pseudonym of husband and wife writing team, Kevin and Melissa Hill. They live in Dublin, Ireland.

TABOO, the first title in a series of forensic thrillers featuring Californian-born CSI Reilly Steel was an international bestseller upon release. It was swiftly followed by subsequent books, INFERNO (aka TORN) HIDDEN, THE WATCHED, TRACE and CRIME SCENE, the series prequel.

Translation rights to the series have been sold in multiple languages including Russian, Turkish and Japanese.

For book updates, news and competitions, check out the Casey Hill Facebook Page at **www.facebook.com/caseyhillbooks** or follow on Twitter **@caseyhillbooks**.

Official author website **www.caseyhillbooks.com**

Printed in Great Britain
by Amazon